THE GIRL WHO SWAM BETWEEN WORLDS

Paperback ISBN: 978-1-7640997-1-4

Editing, Typesetting, and Formatting by Chloe Higgins @booklystediting on Instagram

Editing by Sarah Sudol @writewayedits on Instagram

Proofreading by Blake Curran @nouncertaintomes on Instagram

Cover art by Ciara Hartford @dark_zephi_art on Instagram

Map design by Saumya Singh/Inkarnate @saumyasvision on Instagram

Internal designs by @mgsdesiigns on Instagram

Internal character sketches by @starturnart on Instagram

Author's Note

I have dreamed of being an author for as long as I can remember—probably from when I first read *Harry Potter* or *The Spook's Apprentice*. And to finally be able to hold my very own story in my hands is the most surreal moment and something I never thought could be possible until this year.

There are no specific content warnings for this book. This is a young adult (YA) story, written for children and teens between the ages of 13 and 17. Adults who read this should be aware that this is not in line with the current trend of YA books. The only swearing you'll read is the word 'shit' roughly two times throughout the entire 80,000-word story, and while there is a romantic subplot, it is just that: a *subplot*, with no graphic sexual scenes in sight.

The only content warnings I feel could be relevant are **implications of captivity**, **purposeful harm to oneself** (not specific self-harm, but purposefully doing something despite the potential for it to cause harm), and **being forcefully taken from parents**. Whether people believe these are content warnings or not is irrelevant. No one truly knows the experiences other people have gone through, so it is safer to label what could potentially be triggering.

With that in mind, please read forth and (hopefully) enjoy *The Girl Who Swam Between Worlds*.

SPIRIT GARDEN
MILITIA BASE
LADY EIRA'S HOME
ALVARO'S HOME
ABANDONED HARBOR
THIDIN KINGDOM
ONE OF THREE KINGDOMS OF HARUKAI

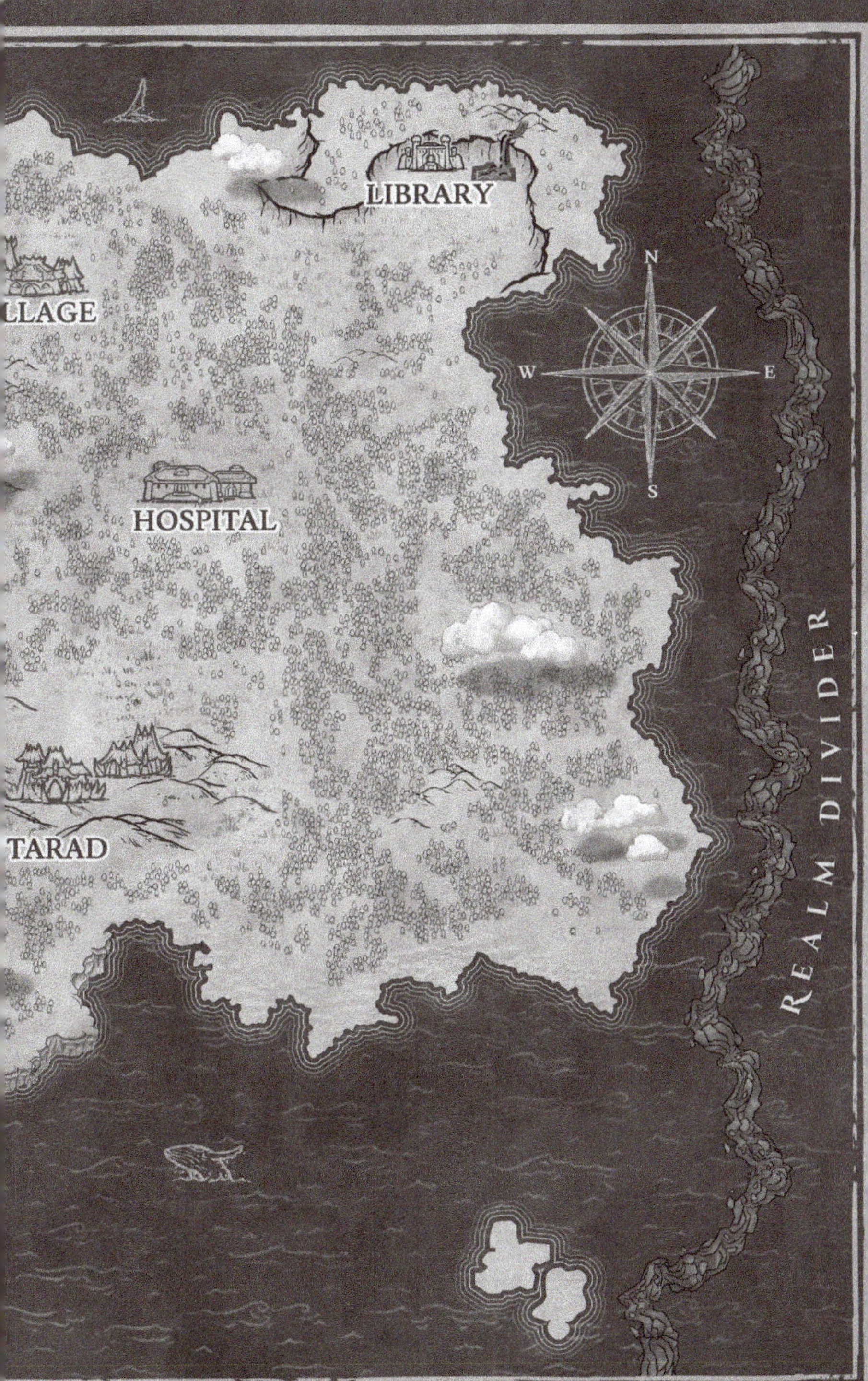

LIBRARY
LLAGE
HOSPITAL
TARAD
N
W
E
S
REALM DIVIDER

The Folk of the Thidin Kingdom

Mixed Genetics of the Folk

A Note on Mixed Breeds

These are just some examples of the types of mixed breeding of folk in Harukai. In rare cases, some folk are born with genetic abnormalities. For example, a centaur can be born with fairy wings, which is considered an abnormality because the wings are too light and fragile to carry a centaur.

Another abnormality may be any folk who are born with fairy-like wings in place of their arms. Harpy wings work in this way because they are made from feathers that grow from the arms. Fairy wings, on the other hand, are too delicate to be attached to arms and can easily tear if used in such a way.

Some folk may also be born with one single fairy wing and one single harpy wing to make up their pair of wings. This can make it extremely difficult to fly, and even more so if their harpy wing is in place of their arm.

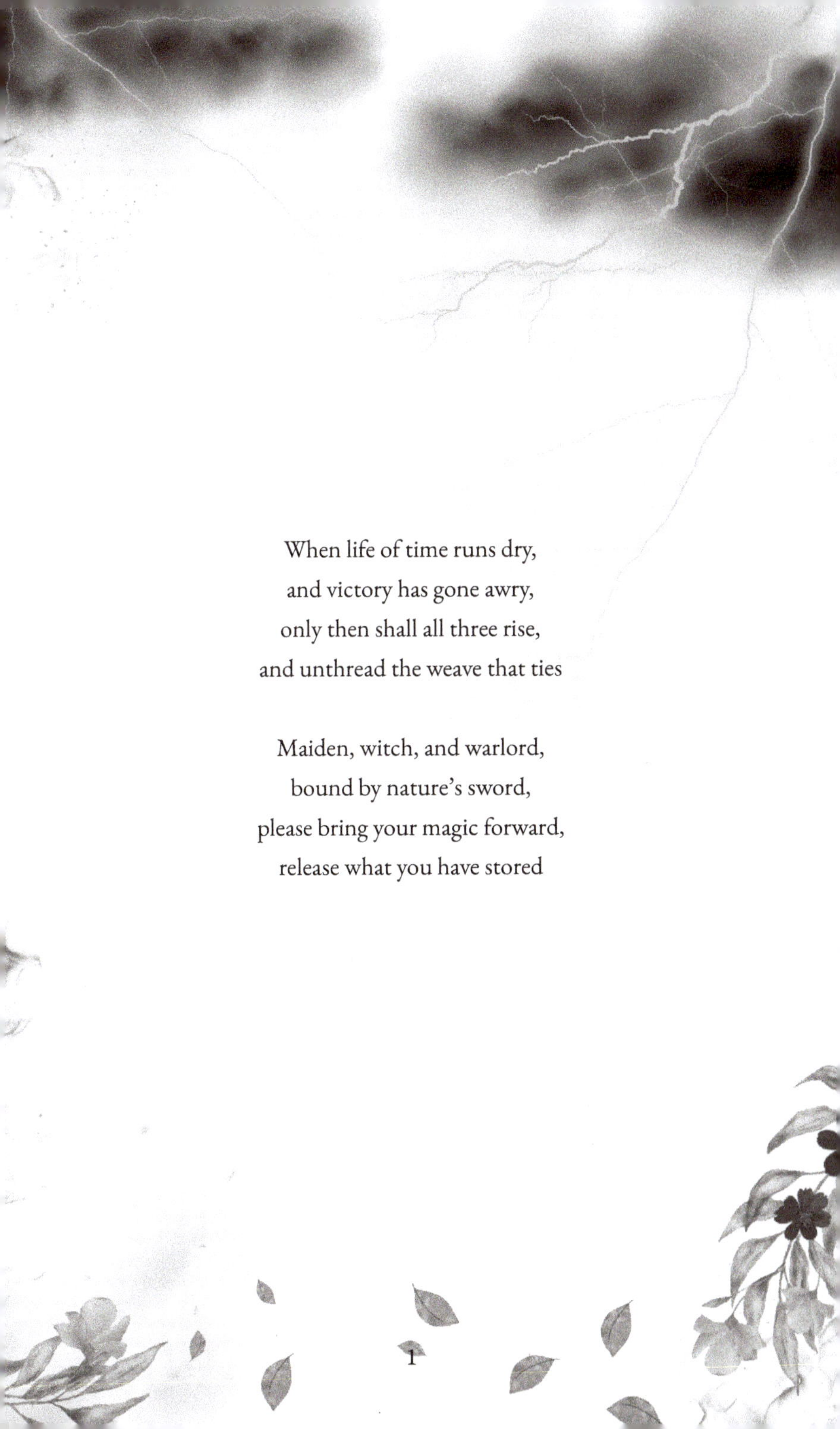

When life of time runs dry,
and victory has gone awry,
only then shall all three rise,
and unthread the weave that ties

Maiden, witch, and warlord,
bound by nature's sword,
please bring your magic forward,
release what you have stored

Prelude

Some stories are meant to be told. Others are meant to unfold. But Ivy's story ... Well, hers is more than just some mere *story*. Yes, this is a story of self-discovery, of romance, of strength—both internal and external. But Ivy's journey is one that faces centuries of fear and answers centuries of questions. The tale of Ivy spans realms and encompasses more than herself—me being one of the *more* in this context, because this is a legend that I unintentionally stumbled into. Although, if you are of the belief that fate's strings are plucked whenever needed, then perhaps my appearance was not so unintentional.

However, all of this will be learnt in time. Your questions will be answered; your quench for more will be satisfied. But for now, all you shall know is that there is much more to this young girl than even she can comprehend.

And now, her story must be told—or rather, *unfold*—and I must be the one to tell it. So, sit back, try to relax, and watch as the legend of Ivy Medina is woven into the fabric of time.

PART ONE

THE GIRL WHO DREAMT

*Sometimes I wonder if all of this is
a dream. If my soul is still imprisoned as it once
was, and I have merely conjured up
something so grand to drown me of my
eternal misery. But even I could not
have imagined the emotional turmoil that holds the pieces of
this legend together.*

One

Most people who spend the better part of their life living on a beach eventually grow tired of the scenery—but not Ivy Medina. At six months old, she refused to leave the water, and at sixteen, she was just the same. Every weekend she would head for the beach in her swimmers and scuba diving gear—which encompassed goggles, flippers, and scuba tank as long as her back—and explore the ocean. And while every weekend's activities occurred as expected, today was rather peculiar to begin with.

Her parents had been arguing, and while that wasn't particularly unusual, that morning Ivy had managed to overhear the topic they fought over. Her name had been thrown about in the midst of their whispered conversation about some tremor they had felt during the night. Ivy was a heavy sleeper and hadn't felt any such tremor, so she had absolutely no idea what they were talking about, but that didn't matter. What mattered was how in the world that tremor and Ivy were related to the same argument.

In complete honesty, her parents had argued over her plenty of times throughout her life—it was one of the only things they ever did together. However, she never could quite understand what else they spoke about—that unexplainable phenomenon where you only hear your name being said and nothing else—and every time she tried to ask, both her parents told her not to worry. After a few attempts, she figured it wasn't worth her breath.

After that morning's usual yet unusual argument, when Ivy was preparing for her weekly ocean exploration, her mother practically shooed her out the door and into the water, muttering, 'Don't forget those stories I used to tell you,' and, 'Are you wearing your ring?' When Ivy had questioned why any of that mattered, her mother, rather than answering, stopped them at the water's edge and held Ivy's face in her hands, then said, 'Remember everything I told you. I love you, Ivy. In this world and the next.'

'I love you too, Mum,' Ivy replied, confusion lacing her tone. 'I'll see you later.'

Now, Ivy climbed up the monstrous rock wall cutting through the ocean of Divided Beach (which was quite impressive while wearing flippers and carrying a scuba tank), and about halfway up, she stopped on a rocky ledge and faced the ocean.

Her mum was nowhere to be seen—presumably having returned to the house—but further along the shore, an abandoned boat lingered at an old harbour. The boat had always lived there for as long as Ivy had lived there, never being used. Similarly, the harbour itself had also never been graced with the presence of people.

Ivy adjusted her goggles and secured her mouthpiece, before proceeding to jump into the water backwards. The splash caused a school of puffer fish to disperse—but don't worry, they all found each other and continued on their way.

Once she was back where she belonged, water coursing around her like the air she breathed, she began searching for new areas of the ocean to explore. Ivy had been exploring the same beach all her life, yet there was always something new to be discovered. She found new anemones and waved hello to the fish surrounding them. Although the fish were unable to wave back, Ivy liked to believe they understood the meaning (they didn't).

The sea floor was a canvas of sand, crabs and clams scattered like paint thrown sporadically. Ivy dusted her hand across the sand in search of seashells and collected a few in her palm, admiring the way they sparkled under the rippling sunlight. She kept them in her hand as she watched crustaceans weave between seaweed and rocks, waving to them as she did the fish. To her utter satisfaction, one of the crabs raised a claw to her.

Not long after that crabby interaction (pun entirely intended), Ivy arrived at one of her favourite places in this part of the ocean: an underwater stone forest.

Pillars of stone sprouted from the sea floor like magnificent trees. Each pillar was painted in a layer of slimy green algae, some of it creeping into cracks along the eroded stone columns. Most of the pillars were broken, some even looking like tree stumps. This place reminded Ivy of a lost kingdom in a fairytale, the souls of mythical underwater beings weaving between the pillars, reminiscent of the bedtime stories her mother used to tell her. Stories about merfolk and sirens, and other wondrous sea folk living and laughing and loving. Perhaps this was where her mother drew inspiration for those stories.

As she swam through the desolate kingdom, her finger grazed the band of twigs that made up the ring she wore on the middle finger of her right hand—the ring her mother had asked about earlier. There was no rhyme or reason to this action; it was merely as though a hidden part of her needed the comfort the ring provided.

She left the forest of stone pillars and swam towards the rock wall she had jumped from, making her way back to the surface for a breath of fresh air and to quickly add her shells to her collection, when she came across something rather peculiar: a hole.

It wasn't the hole, however, that was entirely peculiar—although it was strange enough considering it had never been there before today—it was what she saw swimming *in* the hole that was most peculiar.

Ivy wholeheartedly believed she saw a human man covered in scales. A head of red hair entered the hole, followed by an entire torso, arms, and legs with *scales*.

Clearly, her mind was playing tricks on her, because why on earth would there be a human covered in scales swimming in a hole in a rock wall? She must have conjured his presence from the depths of her mind after being reminded of her mother's bedtime stories. But even more strange was the fact the scaly human didn't have a tail. Merfolk in her bedtime stories always had tails.

So, just as any curious young person would, Ivy followed her imagination.

Now, the hole in question was carved into the side of the rock wall, and as she tried to look in, she noticed her entire head and shoulders could fit comfortably inside the hole's jagged edges. As for what was inside the hole, Ivy could not see a thing—other than those shimmering blue scales in the distance.

At this point, any logical human would turn around and leave the hole alone for fear of getting lost or ending up trapped. Or perhaps those people would even take their shells to their home first, then return to the hole. However, all logical humans seemed to be adults, and Ivy was quite clearly not one of those. So, off she went, diving into the dark and seemingly dangerous abyss, seashells clutched in her hand, in a hurry to not lose the scaly person.

The hole became wider the further she swam. So wide, in fact, that she was able to successfully perform breaststroke without hitting the sides. Schools of fish tickled her underarms and tangled in the strands of hair that had come loose from her braid. She shook her head to release them and felt their fins tickle her legs as they escaped. When she readjusted herself after the small moment of distraction, she found the scaled human was gone.

In her desperate attempt to satiate her curiosity, she continued her path through the tunnel of midnight sky. The tunnel was so dark that Ivy was unaware of the fact that she started to swim down, further into undiscovered territory. You would think that soon she would feel the water shifting around her, encasing her in a tight, pressurised bubble, but you must remember this: Ivy was not consciously thinking about travelling down, and at the ripe old age of sixteen, she was still quite naive.

This naivety did not last long, however. With no guiding light of scales, Ivy decided she'd much rather turn back. She attempted to spin around effortlessly, but just as the tunnel had grown wider, it had now grown smaller. She twisted her body and tangled her limbs in the hope that she would find some manoeuvre to turn herself around, but she was unsuccessful.

Ivy was trapped.

Her heart rate rose; her breathing quickened. Now, Ivy realised, she had made a horrible mistake (as if excitedly swimming into a dark underwater tunnel was *ever* a good idea). She tried twisting herself again but to no avail. Her limbs scraped the rocky edges of the tunnel, and her clunky scuba tank was getting in the way, but she couldn't very well abandon it. The tank would last her four hours; she at least had enough sense to decide that her best course of action would be to continue swimming rather than wasting her oxygen on panicking. After all, this tunnel *must* lead somewhere.

She took some slow, agonisingly deep breaths, then continued on her way.

After what felt like hours but was only fifteen minutes (young people can be quite dramatic at times), scattered dots of light appeared ahead of her. Without a second thought, Ivy hurried towards the light source, the presumed end of the tunnel, her breaststroke hands scraping against the rocks.

Her heart eased at the sight of a hole signalling the tunnel's exit. Once out, she took a brief moment to search for the scaled boy, who was nowhere to be seen, then swam straight to the surface for the breath of fresh air she had been aching for. She ignored the fish on her way up (they didn't think too much of it) and broke through the water, instantly removing her mouthpiece and moving her goggles to her head. Air rushed into her lungs; her shoulders released the tension she didn't realise they were holding. Her fingers instantly searched for the ring on the second finger of her right hand, making sure she hadn't lost it, before she rubbed her eyes free from water. Vast open ocean greeted her with two dark lumps marking what she could only assume were islands. She spun around, expecting to find the continuation of the beach that her home lived on.

That wasn't the case.

In the distance lay an island with shimmering sand leading towards brown trunks topped with glistening leaves; coloured flowers dotted the ground where the trees grew from. Utterly beautiful, yet the beach was completely void of people. How could that be?

'Hello?' Ivy called. But alas, there was no response.

Desperate to be on land after her treacherous journey through that dreaded tunnel, Ivy swam to shore, panting heavily as she fell onto the sand of the unknown land. After she caught her breath, she stripped herself completely of her goggles, scuba tank, and flippers, placing them against one of the nearby trees. Tilting her head back as far as it would go, she gazed upon trees of deep brown with tangles of vines raining down from the treetops. Emerald leaves grew from those vines and shimmered under the sparkling sun. A warmth spread through her, beating like a song in time to her heart. Ivy had thought this place was beautiful from a distance, but now? Mesmerising was an understatement.

The trees stood in a pool—no, a sea—of purple and red and blue and green and orange and violet and pink flowers more vibrant than any colours back home. And just to the left of where she was standing was a footpath of fallen autumn leaves. She thought it strange that the leaves would be yellow and orange and red when they were green in the trees. If they were old, should they not be brown and shrivelled? If they were new, should they not be green and fresh? She didn't allow herself much time to think on the matter and instead followed the path of fallen leaves through the forest.

Her hand shuffled the shells she held, leaves crunching beneath her feet as her eyes wandered, admiring the whimsical forest. Tree-tops shrouded the sky, only allowing a shred of sunlight to guide her path. But it wasn't long until her travelling was interrupted.

'I would not come any further if I were you.'

She froze at the deep, menacing voice and snapped her head in the direction it came from, which was directly in front of her. It was too easy to be distracted in a place as wondrous as this, and if the owner of the voice hadn't spoken, Ivy would've walked straight into them.

Except, they did speak. And now, Ivy was face to face with a … She rubbed her eyes and blinked away the stars that appeared, refocusing on the foreign being before her. Surely her mind wasn't playing tricks on her anymore. This must be some sort of fairytale or a dream—and a vivid one at that. Because there, with hooves planted in the soil beneath the fallen leaves, and human eyes watching her, was a faun. A *faun* with dark skin dotted in beautiful white freckles, what looked to be a human torso beneath his white shirt, black ruffled hair with ears slightly above where human ears would be, their pointed tips dusted in brown fur the same as his legs, branch-looking antlers growing from his hair, and hairy goat legs poking out below his sapphire kilt.

Without a second thought, Ivy slapped herself across the face, hoping to wake herself from this dream. When that didn't work, she pinched herself.

The faun remained.

I'm definitely dreaming, Ivy thought. *Mum also told me stories about beautiful lands with fauns and fairies and other creatures. Perhaps my mind has conjured up an extremely vivid dream.* She looked around at the forest and flowers again, then back to the faun. She wasn't entirely certain a dream could look and feel this real, but nevertheless, she decided it was the only possible explanation. Because what else could this place be?

Since this was absolutely and most certainly a dream, she chose to ignore his menacing tone. She couldn't be in any danger in her own mind. However, her next two steps were slow and trembly. And then, the faun spoke again.

'I told you not to come any further.'

Ivy froze, then quickly adjusted her demeanour into a more casual stance. With her arms crossed, she stared the faun down and said with feigned confidence, 'Why not? This is *my* dream.' She wasn't entirely certain about that statement. 'You don't get to tell me what to do.'

'Because,' the faun explained, seemingly ignoring her comments, 'as far as I can tell, you do not belong here.'

Her feigned confidence quickly transformed into slight, yet real, stubbornness. 'Well, my mind created this place, so I must belong here.' But did she belong here? If this really were some strange, vivid dream conjured by her mother's bedtime stories—which it most certainly was—then why would she be told she didn't belong?

The faun scrunched his brows at that, crinkling the white freckles along his brow line, and folded his arms across his chest, mimicking Ivy. 'I am merely being cautious.'

Ivy had spent her entire life being homeschooled, her only experience with people other than her parents being on small outings to the shops or markets and wandering among strangers. She had never truly had the opportunity to make friends and to learn how to appropriately communicate with new people. In fact, her parents were the only people she truly knew, her mother being her only friend. So, she supposed it was perfectly natural to ignore his statement and change the subject.

In an effort to feel more comfortable, she shrugged and said, 'I'm Ivy. What's your name?'

The faun's eyes widened, and Ivy could have sworn she heard a slight gasp. 'Alvaro,' he answered, before quickly collecting himself and taking a bow. 'It is a pleasure to meet you, Miss Ivy.'

'Oh, no, just call me Ivy. And please, don't bow.' Definitely a dream; no one ever worshipped her in reality. She took another good look at her surroundings and asked, 'What is this place?'

Alvaro stammered, 'W-why, this is the Thidin Kingdom. One of the three kingdoms of Harukai.'

'It's beautiful,' she whispered.

Alvaro twiddled his fingers in a nervous fashion and asked, 'I-I do not mean to be rude, but uh, how did you get here, Miss Ivy?'

Her head snapped back to the faun. 'How did I get here?' *But this is a dream.* 'That shouldn't matter. This place is just part of my imagination,' she told him, except the small tremor in her voice betrayed her confidence.

'Yes, you mentioned that. But humour me, will you?'

Was this a dream? *Of course it is,* she told herself. 'I ... I swam through that tunnel in the wall,' she explained, gesturing behind her to the rock wall in the ocean barely visible from this far into the forest. She'd *swum* into this land, an impossible feat; *surely* this was a dream.

'Ah, yes, I thought that might have been the case.' The human girl and the faun stood in silence for a moment before Alvaro asked, 'Would you like some tea? I trust you have nowhere else to be at the moment?'

The only place she needed to be was home, but if she were dreaming—which she absolutely was—then she was already home. And a cup of tea would certainly calm her nerves.

'I'd love some tea.' She took a step closer, then realised she shouldn't leave her belongings lying around in foreign places, even if this were a dream. 'I left my stuff at the beach. Can I bring it with me?' she asked.

'Absolutely.' Alvaro followed her to where she had left her scuba gear. 'You certainly should not be leaving your belongings in unknown lands.' Ivy smiled at the unusual similarity of their thoughts—something that could only happen in a dream. He carried her scuba tank, remarking, 'What a strange contraption,' and she held her goggles and flippers in one hand while keeping her seashells in the other. It was only when she stood next to him did Ivy realise how tall he really was. She would have to say he was at least seven feet tall, but she was never too good with numbers.

Alvaro gave a close-lipped smile that Ivy returned, and together, a human and a faun walked side-by-side through a whimsical forest.

Two

The leafy footpath forked to the left. It was a peaceful walk, a calm silence between the two. There was still a discomfort circling Ivy, but she rolled her shoulders and pushed it aside.

This was a dream.

That beating warmth she'd felt when looking at the trees on the beach quietly coursed through her with each step. Leaves rustled and birds tweeted. Ocean waves crashed against a rocky shore. Not that Ivy could see the rocky shore, but she'd lived sixteen years on a beach with a rock wall—she knew the sound of waves hitting rocks like it was her own voice. She knew the sound of water, no matter what it was doing or what it was hitting, like it was her own soul.

Her thumb grazed her ring, rubbing against the ridges of twigs that made the band. It wasn't long until Alvaro led them out of the forest and into a clearing where a large tree lived in the centre; surely one of the largest trees Ivy had ever seen, with a trunk as wide as her small home and leaves overhanging like rainfall. She followed

Alvaro around the side to a door made from bark, decorated in leaves and more of those colourful flowers from the beach. From the door was a path of stepping stones, with flowers and mushrooms of various sizes on either side, leading towards a tunnel at the edge of the clearing framed by tree branches and vines.

'Miss Ivy?' came Alvaro's voice from behind her. He waited inside the open front door, and next to that doorway was an arched hole through which Ivy caught a glimpse of furniture.

She stood motionless, staring at the faun who stood inside a tree. Trees didn't have doors. People couldn't walk inside a tree—at least, not in reality. Yet the grass beneath her feet was just as real as the swimmers that clung to her skin.

Her mind was playing a cruel trick on her.

Ivy stepped through the open doorway and into a circular room. Lavender, bamboo, and cedarwood greeted her. Leaves of all shades of green travelled along the walls of the trunk, a warm yellow light speckled among them. The furthest part of the curved trunk wall was carved to create a kitchenette—a bench ran along the wall with open shelving above for produce, crockery, and herbs. A square bamboo table lived in the centre of the room. To Ivy's left, two cushioned chairs facing the kitchen sat below the hole she had seen from outside, which she now realised was a window with two tree bark shutters open wide. The entire place reminded Ivy of a cosy cottage.

'Let me get you that tea,' said Alvaro.

Ivy wandered through the small room, cautious yet mesmerised. 'Is this where you live?'

'Why, yes it is.' Alvaro hesitated, then looked over his shoulder from where he stood at the kitchenette and asked, 'Do you like it?'

'It's ... It's beautiful. The most beautiful home I've ever seen. Which isn't saying much since I've only ever seen my home, but this ...' Alvaro sat on one of the lounge chairs and placed two cups of tea on a side table between them. Ivy sat beside him and said, 'This is incredible.' She lifted the cup of tea to her nose, a delightful eucalyptus scent wafting from the steamy beverage, before taking a sip. A citrusy-pine warmth trailed down her throat. Ivy hummed at the warm, tasty liquid. 'This is delicious.' Another sip: a honey-like sweetness mixed with the eucalyptus, and something else she couldn't quite make out. 'Thank you. You're being very nice to me.'

'Oh, it is quite all right.' Alvaro also took a sip of tea and hummed, just as Ivy had. 'I do apologise for my earlier caution. We, ah ... Well, we do not tend to get visitors here in Harukai. Especially not humans,' he explained, before mumbling, 'Not as guests, anyway.'

Ivy considered apologising for her own caution, but she knew she would only be doing so out of politeness, not because she was truly sorry. She had every reason to be cautious of a strange, mythical being telling her she didn't belong in a place that was most certainly a dream.

And yet, the tea was too warm to be a dream, too sweet to be fantasy. But she was sitting inside a tree next to a faun. And visitors not being common surely meant this was a dream ... right?

Instead of saying anything, she sat with Alvaro, a *faun*, in silence, drinking tea, her eyes travelling around the space. She couldn't help but wonder what it would be like to live here, in a tree, with leaves as lights on the walls. She looked out the window and saw herself walking through the garden-like tunnel, or down the path of fallen leaves and onto the beach, diving into the ocean. She saw herself having fun. But then again, wouldn't anyone give up their life to live with the trees and the flowers and the mushrooms, in a dream-like world crafted from a bedtime story, never realising what they would be leaving behind?

'So,' Alvaro said in a slightly trembling tone, interrupting her imagination. 'I presume you have a family back in the human realm?'

'Human realm ... Do you mean Earth?' Alvaro merely nodded his reply. 'Ah, yeah, only my parents.' Why would he care about her family?

'And what are they like?' he asked cautiously, taking a sip of tea with a trembling hand.

Ivy scrunched her brows, but answered, 'Um, well, my mum's name is Dorothea—'

'*Ockh!*' Alvaro choked, hot liquid spurting from his mouth onto his shirt, lap, and the ground. 'Oh, I am so sorry, Miss Ivy. Did I get any on you?' Ivy just shook her head. He went to the kitchen and wiped himself and the floor with a cloth.

'Ah, did you still want to hear about my parents?' Ivy slowly asked.

'Oh, no, there is no need for that,' Alvaro replied quickly. 'Let me get you some clean clothes.' He made his way to the right of the room and began climbing a ladder.

Actually, would you call it a ladder if it's only made from cut out notches in the tree wall? Ivy supposed so, because what else would you call it? As Alvaro climbed, Ivy's gaze trailed up with him, and she noticed the room she was sitting in had a ceiling of heartwood (for anyone reading this who is unaware of what heartwood is, it is the term used to describe the ringed centre of a tree—I thought using the proper term sounded nicer than 'centre of a tree,' yet here I am, describing it anyway).

She followed the heartwood rings out towards the window behind her. Everything about this land—from the bright, colourful flowers to the tunnel of trees she could see through the window—was eerily similar to her mother's bedtime stories, of seemingly never-ending forests and sprawling oceans. Far too similar for this place to be real.

'Miss Ivy,' Alvaro called from the top. 'Are you coming?'

Oh, she supposed she was. At the base of the ladder, she looked up. It wasn't too far of a drop if she needed to run. But this was a dream—why would she need to run?

She climbed the ladder, passing one bedroom and entering another at the top—the most beautifully decorated bedroom she had ever seen. A single bed sat in the centre with fresh sheets covered in the design of those exotic flowers. More light leaves coated the walls, and pots with flowers were scattered throughout. Next to the entrance was a built-in dresser with a mirror, carved the same as the kitchen, and a closet next to it in the corner. Opposite the dresser was a window the same as downstairs.

'There is some clothing in the dresser and closet you can wear. They should fit you nicely,' Alvaro explained. Then he gave an awkward smile and half-bow before making his way down the ladder.

The first thing Ivy did was shut the window. Then, she placed her shells on the dresser and searched the drawers, which were home to a variety of pants, shirts, and undergarments. If this were a dream, why should she need to get changed? But if this were real, how could she be standing inside the top level of a tree?

Clopping and whistling sounded from downstairs, right before a door opened and closed. The window had already been open—perhaps it was the front door. Was Alvaro leaving? She leant over the opening in the floor of the bedroom where the ladder started and listened, not entirely certain what she was listening for. But a stale silence lingered. She moved to climb downstairs but stopped. Even though she was somewhat certain this was possibly a dream, she felt rather vulnerable remaining in her swimwear, especially if she were to spend more time with Alvaro.

She found some undergarments in one of the drawers and quickly changed into them, then found a pair of light brown pants that felt like leather and slipped them on; they fit her legs easily but were a bit of a struggle to buckle around her lower belly and derriere.

The closet housed an array of skirts and dresses. She flicked through the hanging garments and chose a long green skirt with a brown belt looped over the hanger. An orange shirt in one of the open drawers caught her eye. She peeled off the tight pants and replaced them with the skirt and belt, followed by the shirt, and looked at her new ensemble in the mirror.

The orange shirt was quarter-sleeved and had an overlapping cross-over section across her chest, slightly accentuating her breasts, with green and gold embroidery mimicking the light leaves sprinkled throughout Alvaro's home. The skirt was a deep sage green that hugged her waist and billowed down below her knees.

She found a pair of brown boots sitting in the bottom of the cupboard and socks in one of the dresser drawers. Once the boots were laced, she opened the window and checked herself in the mirror one last time. Sunlight streamed through and hit the embroidery on her shirt, causing it to shimmer as though the light leaves were actually shining. The outfit was ... magical. Enchanting. Something she couldn't possibly imagine.

Her braid was dry and crispy with salt, but some curls had fallen free and now framed her face. She unravelled the hair tie holding her braid and pulled apart each crispy strand, combing her fingers through the curls, until her hair fell stiffly over her shoulders and down her back.

When she was done, she sat on the bed for a moment and admired the room. A comforting presence was in the air, like the feeling you get when you meet someone, and it feels like you've known them all your life. But a shiver ran down her spine.

She could *feel* the cotton shirt on her skin.

She could *feel* the cushioned mattress she sat on.

She could *feel* the warmth of the sun from behind.

If this wasn't a dream, then where was she?

Harukai, Alvaro had told her. Yes, the *faun* had told her. But the memory of that conversation was real. Could dream versions of oneself have memories?

'Ugh!' Ivy grunted, throwing her head in her hands. 'What is wrong with you? This place is beautiful! Just experience it, and I can either wake up or swim home when I'm ready.' She took a deep breath and sat up, noticing the flowers in their potted homes had bloomed towards her, like they were watching her—but obviously they weren't, because flowers can't see.

Ivy made to climb downstairs but spotted her pile of shells on the dresser. Should she take them? She certainly didn't want to leave them behind, but if this were a dream, they would be lost anyway. If this were a dream, she probably would have forgotten about the shells, or maybe they wouldn't even be there.

But she was standing inside a *tree* of all things.

Ivy breathed a frustrated sigh and snatched the shells before climbing down the ladder, landing on the ground with a soft *thump*. She looked around the small room, but Alvaro was nowhere in sight. As expected, he must have left. She stepped outside and walked around the tree to the back of the clearing, finding a beautiful garden of various vegetables, herbs, and fruits—but no faun.

She tossed up her options: sit on a lounge chair inside a tree and wait for Alvaro—who was, by no other definition, a complete stranger—or explore the vast, foreign, whimsical land.

Well, that was certainly an easy decision.

She could follow the path of fallen autumn leaves through the trees and back to the beach, but she was ever curious about the tunnel of trees at the edge of the clearing. So, without another thought, she followed the stepping stones and made her way into the tunnel.

THREE

Tree trunks grew in curving angles, outward at first, then meeting at the top to create the walls of the tunnel. Purple and green leaves draped down like curtains, with flowers woven through. Petals and leaves fell into her hair and clung to her curls as Ivy brushed the vines aside. Around the tree roots sprouted mushrooms and flowers in their own little jumbled groups, and as Ivy passed, the flowers turned their pistils to her just as they had in the bedroom, but she was as oblivious as anyone ought to be, considering the landscape she traversed. As she inched closer to the end of the tunnel, chattering and clattering emerged, and that strange warmth flooding her became stronger.

Soon, the overhanging trees of the tunnel gave way to grassy mounds, the trail of vibrant flowers always nearby. Ivy wondered how those flowers would look at night. Would they still shine so bright, or would they lay shadowed in darkness?

Over the grassy mounds, a line of trees was clustered together, the quiet chattering from earlier now louder. Through the gaps between tree trunks, movement and colours could be seen. Trees formed a wall to Ivy's left, no entrance or walkway to be seen, and the right revealed even more trees but with another path of those magnificent fallen leaves bending around the mounds.

Ivy made her way to the right, through the trees and along the autumn-coloured path towards the sounds of life. Once she rounded the corner and found the end of the path, there in all of its glory was what Ivy could only assume was the main sector of this land. The forest trees thinned to reveal a hilly clearing of smaller grassy mounds covered in those rainbow flowers and colourful mushrooms of all sizes jumbled together. Deep green leaves dangled from the treetops, like curtains along the edge of the clearing. Ivy's gaze followed the dark brown tree trunks up to the open patch of clear blue sky, sunlight streaming down on the bustling people of the ... What did Alvaro say this place was called? It was definitely a kingdom. Ivy rattled her brain. *Th ... Tharin? Thida? Thidin? Thidin!*

Sunlight rained down on the Thidin Kingdom, bathing everyone in a bright yellow light. And those people, those creatures, fairytale beings, were just as her mum had described in her bedtime stories. Wide, magnificent, glittering fairy wings, faun and centaur hooves, and harpies with their rustling feathered wings and clawed feet. *Folk,* Ivy remembered her mother calling them.

Except, her mother had never named the kingdom, nor the land. That was a strange addition indeed. But surely something so reminiscent of those bedtime stories couldn't very well be real. Surely ...

Ivy cautiously stepped out of the trees and into the vast open space. So far, no one had noticed her presence. She watched as folk bustled about, noticing the variety of clothing styles among them. Some folk—both male and female presenting—wore skirts and dresses made from leaves and flower petals, while others were draped in loose-fitting shawls with slits at the back for winged-folk. Some even wore kilts, skirts, pants, or shirts, not unlike the clothing Alvaro and herself wore. Centaurs, however, were donned in a type of tunic-shawl designed specifically for their unique bodies, which clothed their torso like a shirt and draped over the bottom part of their body.

Slowly, Ivy walked through the clearing. Stalls were sprawled throughout the wide space, some squished between small hilly planes of grass, others built into large colourful mushrooms, and some scattered like random paint splatters across the clearing. Any that weren't part of a mushroom or tree were built from tree bark, and somehow flowers bloomed directly from the small structures. It was a kaleidoscope of colours with autumn-coloured leaves pebbling the grass, creating a footpath through the area that most folk seemingly ignored anyway.

As she got a closer look at the folk, Ivy noticed the mixed genetics among them. Some harpies, who traditionally had wings in place of their arms, had their feathered wings sprouting from their back as fairy wings did, while other harpies simply had fairy wings instead. Fauns were also spotted with either set of wings, and even some centaurs clopped along with harpy wings folded back, reminding Ivy of the mythical Pegasus.

Like Alvaro, fauns had antlers in all sizes, with those white freckles circling their eyes and eyebrows and dotting the rest of their skin. Glittering marks could be spotted on fairies, but she couldn't tell what the designs were. Some harpies had extra feathers along the humanoid parts of their bodies, while most centaurs had two different skin colours in patches along their bodies.

Eyes followed Ivy as she wandered, and she tried to ignore the way they seared into her spine, tried to ignore the way that now-uncomfortable sensation heightened, feeling like a light rhythmic beat. She followed the path of crinkly leaves, and as she wove through the market, she noticed each stall was decorated in such a way that displayed whatever products they sold. A clothing stall named Woven Designs was draped in swatches of woven cloth; Pointed Precision, which looked to be an armoury of some sort, had daggers and shields attached to the front; clusters of fruit dangled down the front of a fruit stall called Finest Fresh Fruits.

More folk turned their heads as she passed, too obvious to ignore. The air was coated in whispers, some only mumblings, others just loud enough for her to hear.

'Is that who I think ...'

'She looks like ...'

'It must be true ...'

The folk drew closer to Ivy, forming a circle around her, some reaching out to touch her arms, her hair, her face. A tendril of claustrophobia began to grow inside her, twisting spindly vines around her lungs.

'It's really you ...'

Who did they think she was? Why were they reaching for her like she was some God-like figure?

'We've waited years ...'

For what? For her? The claustrophobia vine cradled her lungs, expanding its limbs to other surrounding organs.

'I didn't think it was true ...'

The circle was smaller now, constricting, the folk jostling Ivy amongst them, some taller than her, everyone touching and murmuring and praising, all kinds of wings crowding her vision. This fantastical, fairytale-like dream world was now a nightmare.

Ivy pushed through the crowd, shoving fairies and fauns and centaurs and harpies out of her way. Once she'd broken through, she made a break for the trees, not turning back.

Four

Ivy weaved through spindly trees and over hills of grass, dodging mushrooms and flowers. Unbeknownst to her, the rainbow flowers once again turned towards her as she passed, following her as they had in the tunnel. She kept running, not daring to look back, afraid a stampede of folk would be chasing her. A tree slightly larger than the others came into view and Ivy ducked behind it, taking this small moment of reprieve to catch her breath and listen. No footsteps could be heard, no mumblings. No more touching like she was their long-awaited saviour. Only wind tickling her cheeks and rustling the leaves, birds tweeting and water rushing.

Ivy peeked her head out from behind the tree just to be sure no one was following. Nothing but trees and mushrooms and flowers and overhanging leaves greeted her. She breathed a deep sigh and leant back against the tree, released from the claws of claustrophobia.

'This is just a dream,' she reminded herself between trembling breaths. 'It makes sense for me to be favoured in a dream.'

But she was unconvinced.

And now, she was in the middle of an unknown forest, all alone. Ivy could easily go back the way she came and find her way to Alvaro's home, a somewhat safe place, but she didn't particularly want to be caressed by a bunch of strangers—no matter if this was a dream or not.

There was no footpath in this part of the forest, just soil and grass and flowers and mushrooms, everything painted in sunlight speckled from the tiny gaps between leaves on the treetops. She took a deep breath to calm her nerves, then decided to wander through the forest.

The way her boots pressed into the ground felt so real. The sharp edges of the shells scraping her palm was too real. Her thumb mindlessly flicked the band of her ring while the knuckles of her other hand grazed the petals of some nearby flowers, their softness tickling her fingers in a way that couldn't happen in a dream. She continued to follow that speckled sunlight until the forest abruptly ended.

Before her, a towering structure of marble pillars and textured ivory columns was built into a cavernous cliff face, jutting out towards the forest. The front columns were replaced with four female statues all in different poses, their palms facing the sky with more stone protruding from their open hands to hold the entablature. (I once again find myself educating you common folk on terminology I use. The entablature is the overhanging top of the building).

Ivy stepped out of the trees, her eyes wide. The sound of rushing water from earlier was louder now, resonating from the right of the menacing structure, where water fell from the top of the cliff, splashing into a pond surrounded by rainbow flowers and speckled mushrooms. She quietly moved through the space, not wanting to disturb the natural sounds of life with an unnatural crunch of a stick, and admired the imposing goddesses acting as columns to the building. As she got closer, she noticed that what she originally thought was merely extra stone in the statue's hands was actually the elements of nature.

The first one, on the far left, held both hands to the ceiling with her palms facing up and fingers meeting in the centre. Wavy stone splashed from her hands to the entablature, with more cascading down her body. Water.

Next to her stood a goddess dressed in rippling, flame-like stone with only one arm facing up, fire emanating from her hand. After the flame statue, on the other side of a grand stone staircase, was one in a similar yet more graceful pose, her body dotted with textured stone resembling soil that she pushed more of towards the top of the building.

The fourth and final of the goddess-like statues had both hands up in an outward arch formation, her fingers pushing out and the heels of her hands touching. Swirled stone poured from her hands, helping hold the entablature in place. And just like the others, her body was encased in that same swirling stone. The element of air.

Ivy followed the wide, jagged stairs towards the arched entrance between the flame and earth statues. Looking up at their magnificent forms, she felt miniscule, like an insect. One wrong move and one of those deadly, element-wielding beings would come to life and squish her with their toe. And if this were a dream, Ivy feared they may just do that. She ran her hand along the staircase railing, the cold stone stinging her hand. How could something so real be a dream? But how could something so unreal be, well, *real*?

At the top of the stairs, a rustic mahogany door greeted her, resplendent against the ivory stone. It reached all the way to the top of the stone structure, much taller than the goddess-like statues since the roof arched above the pillars. There were no door handles, no door knockers, no locks. Only gold embossing and a single line down the centre indicating it was two doors. Ivy placed a hand on either side of the thin line and pushed, the doors swinging open with force.

Splatters of coloured spines graced bookshelves along the walls, sunlight shining through a glass domed ceiling, painting the marble floor in yellow streaks. Thin trees grew sporadically throughout the space, with tables and chairs placed precariously around their roots. The natural habitat of the written word. Folk lingered in some of those seating areas, but none looked her way, all too engrossed in their books. Considering how many flowers and mushrooms Ivy had seen in this land already—and the fact that there were actual *trees inside*—she was somewhat surprised to find the library void of any of those vibrant colours, despite this being an indoor place.

Knock knock.

To her right, a young woman with golden brown skin and matching antlers poking above her caramel-coloured hair stood behind a curved desk. Flower petals danced across her torso and over her breasts, some resting in her long, straight hair. White freckles lined her eyes and the sides of her face, some mixing with the petals covering her body. The desk was low enough where the division between torso and faun legs could be seen, with fur the same colour as her hair sneaking up her stomach. The faun's eyes widened at the sight of Ivy, the corners of her slightly open mouth turning upward.

Ivy turned to check if anyone had followed in after her, but alas, she was the only one in the faun's line of sight. 'Ah, hi,' she greeted.

The faun scrambled for paper and a pen—only it wasn't paper and a pen. It was, in actual fact, parchment and a quill. The quill was dipped in a pot of ink before the faun scribbled across the parchment. Ivy's uncertainty about the reality of this world increased tenfold, because something so real yet so ... medieval made her question, well, everything. When the faun was done writing, she slid the note across the desk.

Ivy looked around again, making sure there was no one else the faun could possibly be handing a note to. Then, when she confirmed she was in fact still the only person standing in the entrance, she approached the desk, the faun watching her every step.

The note read: *Are you who I think you are?*

Ivy stared at the parchment, unsure on how to answer, because how on earth would she know who this faun thought she was? One of those mumblings from the folk in the main sector of the kingdom flew into her mind. *'Is that who I think ...'*

Ivy swallowed, glanced up at the faun, and asked, 'Who do you think I am?'

The faun scrawled a new message on the same parchment. *You must be. My name is Leyrah. You'll need some books.*

Then, before Ivy had a chance to reply, the faun—Leyrah—was rummaging under the counter. Barely a moment later, she returned with two of the largest books Ivy had ever seen in her entire life. The stack landed on the countertop with a loud *thunk*, and Leyrah pointed to her last message on the parchment: *You'll need some books.*

When Ivy didn't move or respond or do anything other than stare dumbfounded, Leyrah pushed the stack of tomes across the counter to her. And when Ivy again didn't react, Leyrah frowned and furrowed her brows. *I was told you would need these,* she wrote on her scrap of parchment.

'I ...' What did that mean? 'Sorry,' was all Ivy could think to say. That tendril of claustrophobia snuck its way back into her body, slowly creeping around her organs. 'I don't know what you're talking about. You're thinking of someone else. I'm not even from here.' Ivy started backing away towards the door, the grip of claustrophobia tightening. 'This is just a dream.' She wasn't sure if that last statement was for Leyrah or herself. The door came into view in Ivy's periphery. She turned and found two handles, one on either side of the seam, and she grabbed one of them with her free hand without hesitation. Her muscles strained with the effort of pulling an enormous door made from wood, but she managed to open it wide enough for her to fit through. Her organs were suffocating under the grasp of that single tendril inside her. She looked back and saw the faun reaching her hand out, her mouth forming the word *wait,* but Ivy said barely above a whisper, 'This is just a dream,' and left the library.

FIVE

Down the stairs, past the majestic statues, across the small clearing, and into the forest once more. 'This is just a dream,' Ivy told herself again and again, but uncertainty clung to her like her salty, sticky swimmers had earlier that very day.

Her thumb instinctively found her ring, twirling the band until the sapphire gemstone was underneath her finger. A nervous habit, but there were certainly worse ones to be had: nail biting, nose picking, teeth grinding. No, instead Ivy fiddled with her mother's ring that she now wore for a reason she didn't quite know. Her mother was still alive, yet she had gifted Ivy her treasured ring on her sixteenth birthday—an heirloom despite Ivy's lack of heirdom. Ivy treasured it like her mother treasured the love that forged it. The love she knew was from someone other than her father—but from who, she wasn't privy to knowing. The love that would follow her mother across time and space, as she had told Ivy upon gifting the ring.

Ivy swerved through the whimsical forest, not knowing and not entirely caring where she was going, just as long as it was away from the library and the main area of the kingdom. She'd made sure she walked in a different direction to how she'd arrived at the clearing, so she prayed she was nowhere near the mob of people prying at her. The thought of their hands grasping at her, pulling her and passing her around the circle, sent a shiver down her spine. Perhaps she should try and leave, but her swimmers and scuba diving equipment were at Alvaro's home, and again, she wasn't particularly keen on facing those folk just yet. Hiding was a much better, albeit temporary, solution.

Sunlight continued dotting the grass of the otherwise dimly lit forest, the trees only allowing the rays to shine through tiny gaps between leaves. Ivy gave herself a moment to admire the mushrooms speckled sporadically along the forest floor, some smaller than the palm of her hand, others reaching past her hips. (And a rare few, hidden deep in the depths of this kingdom's forests, were taller than her. *Mushrooms* taller than a human girl.) Colours not unlike the flowers blooming at every turn splashed the mushroom tops, as though a child were given paint and a brush and told to go absolutely wild. A truly remarkable sight.

But not as remarkable as the sight ahead, trees thinning and light blossoming at the end of the forest. Ivy stepped off the soft grass and onto even softer sand. Sand of the same beach Ivy had stumbled upon when she first arrived in this place. Sand that shimmered like crystals under the sun, sending a sense of familiarity through Ivy—a reminder of home, of what waited beyond that marvellous rock wall dividing the ocean once she had her gear and could swim back through. The fact she had swum here should have been enough to convince her entirely that this place was real—and perhaps it was, but the thought of entering a world all too similar to her mother's bedtime stories by *swimming* into it was unfathomable.

Ivy unzipped her boots and slipped off her socks, stashing them and the shells in the shoes. She buried her feet in the sand, smiling as the white crystals found their way between her wriggling toes. Her feet guided her to the clear blue water rolling up the shore, until the white frothy tips of the waves encased her feet and fell back into the ocean. Whatever tension and fear she held was washed away; that creeping tendril of claustrophobia she hadn't realised still held her captive slowly untangled itself. Not caring for the clothes she wore, she waded through the small waves until she was submerged up to her knees, the hem of the green skirt resting atop the water.

Her eyes scanned the ocean, the silhouette of those two islands in the distance barely visible from here. Then, she found the rock wall to the left of those islands, and as she trailed her gaze along the length of it, a flash of red caught her eye. Her eyes flicked back to find the source. There, a hand gripping the rocks and hoisting up the torso of someone with red hair. Or was it orange? A copper of sorts, hard to pinpoint from this distance. Their arms were painted with a sparkling blue and green design, almost like ... scales.

A flash of a memory struck Ivy's mind of a boy covered in scales with red hair entering the tunnel in the rock wall, causing her to follow him. Could this be the same person?

'Hello,' Ivy called without thinking.

The scaly boy dove beneath the surface, leaving rippling water in his wake. A few moments later, his head and shoulders appeared above the water not too far from where she stood. 'Hi.'

Up close, Ivy could make out the contours of his face. His wet copper hair—yes, it was definitely copper—framed a sharp jawline and sparkling blue eyes. A splattering of blue scales marred the sides of his face, stark and mesmerising against his pale skin. And poking through those damp strands, right where his ears should be, were blue webbed fins. Or, perhaps, where his ears *were*. He was ... The only word she could think to describe him in this moment was beautiful.

'Uh, hi,' she greeted again. 'I'm Ivy. What's your name?'

One corner of his lips turned up. 'Theon.'

She tested the name on her tongue, 'Theon.' His smile widened, as though he enjoyed hearing her say his name. 'Were you on the other side of the wall?' she asked.

'I was.'

'Hmm.' Ivy crossed her arms and assessed him, a smirk forming on her face. Confidence shone through now that she was back in the ocean and not weighed down by uncertainty and fear. 'You're not much for words, are you?'

Theon chuckled, a warm sound that caressed her ears and enveloped her body. 'Sorry, Ivy.' She quite liked the sound of her name coming from his lips. 'I'm usually a lot for words, but I haven't had much experience with anyone from the human realm. You ... fascinate me.'

Ivy's smirk transformed into a smile—probably the first true smile she'd held since being in this land. If all of this was revealed to be a dream, she quite liked this part of it. But at the possibility of this being nothing more than something from her mind, her heart dropped barely a centimetre. Before she could respond, however, another voice interrupted them.

'Miss Ivy.'

Her head snapped behind her and homed in on the tall faun with dark skin and even darker fur exiting the forest from the path of fallen leaves.

'I have been looking for you,' Alvaro said. Ivy turned back to Theon, but he was gone, no rippling water indicating he had dived away, as though he was never there. 'Why did you leave?'

'Sorry,' Ivy said, although she didn't particularly know why she was apologising. Alvaro was a stranger—yes, he'd given her tea and clothes and had so far shown nothing but kindness towards her, but she didn't think she needed to apologise to him for leaving. 'I couldn't find you, so I went for a walk.'

'There is no need to apologise. Did you, by chance, go into the kingdom?'

'I think so. I went through that tunnel in front of your house and found a bunch of stalls and people. I ...' She was about to tell him about the folk, how they had spoken to her—or rather, spoken *about* her—and touched her and encircled her, but she didn't want to speak about the experience. 'It was nice.'

Alvaro watched her, as though he sensed her hesitation, but thankfully didn't question her further. 'Would you like to come back to my home? I picked some fresh fruit.'

Ivy considered that for a moment. Before Theon had shown up, she had been planning on leaving—whether by waking herself up or swimming through the tunnel—but now, she quite liked the idea of staying here a little while longer. So long as she didn't meet any strange folk again. After all, this truly was the most beautiful place she had ever seen, and if this were to be the first and last time she was ever here, she didn't particularly want to leave just yet. She also silently hoped she would see Theon again.

'I'd like that,' Ivy answered.

She waded out of the water and grabbed her boots before following Alvaro back into the forest and to his home.

Six

Thankfully, Alvaro didn't take Ivy through the kingdom—she wasn't ready to be practically bowed down to. They walked along the same path in the same calm silence they had earlier that day, with the same faint beating inside her, until they exited into the clearing of Alvaro's home.

Eucalyptus and forest fruits welcomed Ivy as she stepped inside his home—she still couldn't fathom the fact he lived inside a *tree*—and sat in the same chair as before, only this time a bowl of fruit joined the two teacups on the side table. She wondered for a moment that if this truly were a dream, then why would her mind bring her back here? The subconscious was a strange and incomprehensible thing, certainly not something anyone should be questioning. Yet it also wasn't something that could conjure a world and people and conversations that felt so realistic and didn't distort in her mind like most dreams did.

'You must be starving,' Alvaro said, interrupting her thoughts.

Ivy hadn't felt hungry, hadn't even thought about food, but now her stomach grumbled at the sight of the fruits. She didn't recognise any of the colourful fruits from home, but they looked delectable, and her stomach grumbled even louder. She reached for one but paused. She didn't know who Alvaro was, other than a faun who had given her tea and clothes. Despite the fact she never had the opportunity to wander the world back home alone, her parents always told her never to accept anything from strangers. These fruits could be poisonous. The tea could've been poisonous, and yet she'd drunk that without hesitation.

'There is nothing wrong with the fruits, I assure you,' Alvaro said, as though reading her thoughts. Then he took one himself and ate it, proving the fruits were edible. She still wasn't entirely certain, but her stomach grumbled, and she felt strangely comfortable around Alvaro. So, she took a piece of purple fruit the size of her palm and bit into it.

An explosion of sweetness sprayed her tongue and the inside of her cheeks, unlike any fruit she had ever eaten. The next was the colour of wine and gave a soft crunch, attacking her mouth with a delightful citrus flavour.

'These are amazing,' Ivy said between the chunks of fruit still in her mouth.

Alvaro merely smiled. 'So, Miss Ivy—'

'Please,' Ivy interrupted, swallowing the fruit, 'just call me Ivy.'

'Oh, of course. A force of habit, perhaps ...' Alvaro gulped, his gaze trailing to the ground for a moment, before returning to Ivy. 'So, *Ivy*, how did you like the Thidin Kingdom?'

'It was ...' She was brought back to her brief time in the kingdom, the mesmerising sunlight drenching everyone and everything in golden light, while the folk reached for her like she was their last mouthful of water. 'Well ... it was beautiful,' she finished.

'Is it much different to the human realm?'

'Oh, uh, yeah. There's nothing really like it back home. This place is like a fairytale, awfully similar to the stories my mum used to tell me.' Ivy took a bite of another piece of fruit.

Alvaro furrowed his brows and asked, 'Stories? What stories?'

'Mum used to tell me bedtime stories'—She paused, swallowed the fruit, then continued—'about a land kind of like this one. My favourite is the one about a mermaid who falls in love with a faun. It reminds me of *Romeo and Juliet*, except without all the death.'

'Oh. How wonderful.' Except, Alvaro didn't sound enthralled. In fact, he sounded concerned, but Ivy didn't dwell on it. Talking about her mum had caused her mood to flatten; she supposed it was time for her to leave.

'Look, this has been great,' Ivy started. 'The fruits are delicious, and your tea was amazing. Oh, and your home is ... wow. But I should really get going.'

'Get going? Do you mean you wish to leave?'

'Yeah. You've been so nice, Alvaro. But ... I've never been away from my mum for this long. I mean, usually I'm just swimming, so it's not a big deal, but it feels different, being in a different place, whether it's a dream or not.' Ivy was rambling, but she couldn't quite help herself.

'A dream?' Alvaro asked quietly.

But before Ivy could comprehend what he'd said, she closed her eyes and tried to jolt her brain awake. She opened them, hoping to see her bedroom wall or ceiling depending on which way she slept, but instead, all she found was the inside of a tree and a faun sitting next to her. Her lips parted and her heart began a rapid beat.

'This isn't a dream,' she whispered, except, she knew that already, she just hadn't wanted to believe it. 'Where am I?' But she knew where she was. She was in a foreign land, one that was too similar to her mother's fairytale stories yet *existed*. 'I need to go home.'

The only time she had ever been away from her mother was while she was swimming, and perhaps she hadn't been gone longer than usual, but this was a completely different world. Alvaro may not have said it specifically, but he'd asked about the human *realm*. That was proof enough this place—Harukai—was a separate world.

Waves roiled inside her, searching for an escape. *She* needed an escape. This land was spectacular, but it was foreign. Ivy was without her mother, her only friend, her source of comfort, and was sitting in a stranger's house.

Her heart pounded, waves of emotion splashing against her bones, seeping through her flesh. 'How do I get home?' she cried. But she knew the answer to that, as well.

Swimming.

Without another word, another tear, Ivy bolted from the house and ran straight to the forest, bare feet crumpling the leaves of the footpath as she fumbled through the trees. She veered off the path slightly, hoping to trip over protruding tree roots in a futile attempt to jolt awake like she usually did in dreams, despite knowing full well this was not, in fact, a dream. She almost fell but instinctively caught herself.

Alvaro's hooves could be heard following her, along with, 'Miss Ivy, wait,' being called.

But she didn't stop.

It was only when she wasn't trying to trip that she did. And each time she did, no matter whether it was over tree roots, rocks, or her own two feet, she tumbled through jumbles of mushrooms and bumbles of flowers and crumbles of leaves.

But she never woke.

Finally, the path veered right towards the beach. The fallen leaves soon gave way to sand and as the shore became steeper, Ivy stumbled and rolled to the water, adding sand to the mix of leaves and soil and bark and twigs that gripped tightly to her now constrictive clothing. It all weighed her down, the world itself keeping her prisoner. She gave a loud grunt, frustration finally revealing herself.

'Miss Ivy!' Alvaro had caught up to her, his hooves coming to a halt beside her. 'Are you all right?'

Ivy ignored him, and instead dove into the water, heading straight towards the rock wall. She wasn't sure why she bothered—her scuba gear was still at Alvaro's, and she wasn't even wearing swimmers—but she continued her efforts.

A muffled splash sounded behind her, presumably Alvaro, but she kept swimming, deeper and deeper. Her chest tightened. Water squeezed her limbs, her organs.

She opened her mouth—

A pair of strong arms wrapped around her waist from below and pushed. Bubbles rushed past as whoever held her raced to the surface. Water flew into her mouth, only to be coughed back out as she emerged. Ivy could have sworn she had swum deeper than that short distance. She was flung over the shoulder of her saviour, coughing up more water, and as she assessed their back, it was quite clear Alvaro wasn't the one carrying her. Someone with pale skin, blue scales, and two webbed fins in the centre of their back carried her towards the shore, past Alvaro who stood in the low waves, and out of the water. A flash of copper hair caught her eye as she was placed on the sand before being instantly rolled over.

'You're insane,' a faintly familiar male voice said.

Ivy coughed her lungs up, water splattering the sand, a comforting hand rubbing her back as she did so.

'Miss Ivy.' Alvaro knelt beside her, both his hands in view while the unknown one remained on her back. 'What do you think you are doing?'

Once she finished spitting salty water from her lungs, she took a deep breath of salty sea air. 'I don't know,' Ivy admitted. Water streaked down her face, and whether it was from her eyes or the ocean, no one would ever know. 'I just want to go home.'

Seven

Sand crept between Ivy's toes, the softness tickling her skin in an all-too-familiar way. Her scuba tank hugged her from behind, a comforting reminder of home. Alvaro stood by the lapping waves, waiting.

After her earlier panic, Alvaro had taken her to his home so she could change back into her swimmers and scuba gear. He'd explained that she could easily return home the way she came, through the underwater tunnel, but he wanted to give her an escort. Although she was perfectly capable of making the trip herself—especially considering that's exactly what she'd done when arriving here—the truth was, she was slightly afraid. The tunnel was dark and long and small, and her friendly vine of claustrophobia had come to say hello just at the thought of swimming through, so she hadn't said anything when Alvaro mentioned the escort.

The escort, Alvaro had explained, would be from the Noa Kingdom.

'The Noa Kingdom? What's that?' she'd asked.

'Why, that is the kingdom under the sea.'

'Under the sea? An entire *kingdom*?' The stone pillars in the ocean back home, her mother's stories, the scaled boy she'd met earlier—Theon. What a strange coincidence ... 'So, there are like, actual merfolk down there?'

'Precisely.'

Now, Ivy and Alvaro waited on the beach where Ivy had first arrived and coincidentally where she had almost drowned. Alvaro had sent a Scarla to the Noa Kingdom—a messenger bird that could fly and swim, capable of travelling and delivering messages between all three kingdoms.

'What's the third kingdom?' Ivy asked as they waited for the escort.

Alvaro flinched at the sudden sound of her voice cutting through the silence and turned to her. 'Oh, the third kingdom of Harukai. That would be the Savan Kingdom.' She nodded as though that were all the information she needed, not wanting to further interrupt whatever thoughts he had. Then, Alvaro smiled and explained, 'It is the kingdom in the sky.'

A *kingdom* in the *sky?* If Ivy had yet to realise whether Harukai was real or not, a kingdom in the sky would confirm her assumption that it was a dream. So, that begged the question: How was that possible?

Before she had a chance to ask, a familiar head of copper hair appeared a few metres from the shore, only this time his shoulders were also visible.

'General Alvaro,' Theon started. 'You sent for me?'

General?

'I did. Thank you for meeting with me on such short notice, Theon.'

Theon's eyes slid to Ivy, a smile forming on his face.

'Theon, this is Miss—'

'Ivy,' Theon finished. 'It's good to see you again.'

Ivy returned his smile and said to Alvaro, 'We met earlier, when you found me on the beach.'

'Ah,' was all he managed to say, but the corner of his lip curled up slightly.

'So,' Theon said. 'Why did you call on me, Alvaro?'

'I need your assistance. Miss Ivy requires safe passage back to the human realm. I trust you can see this through.'

Theon's face scrunched. 'Why not ask my mother? Or, better yet, why not go straight to Lord Tullius?'

'You know very well why I have not asked your mother. And as for Lord Tullius, he does not need to know of this meeting,' Alvaro stated quickly. 'Since you witnessed Miss Ivy's earlier ... display, I presumed you would be the best folk to ask.'

A back of pale skin with blue scales and fins. A flash of copper hair. Had Theon been the one to rescue her earlier?

'You presume correct.' Theon stood and made his way closer to shore. Scales the colour of the ocean coated his legs entirely, partially travelling up his torso, across the left side of his chest, and over his shoulder. More scales lived along his arms, all of them shimmering under the setting sun. A trail of fins line the outside of his arms from shoulder to wrist. He wore a brown belt with a shortsword tucked into a sheath on one side, a larger sword on his back, and a dagger strapped to his thigh. Ivy wondered how the belt and weapons didn't ruin in the saltwater, but the thought vanished when her eyes met his hair. Damp copper strands stopped just below his shoulders, water dripping from the ends onto his chest and down his torso. Ivy's gaze followed the droplets as they made a path down his scaled legs and into the water. A warmth bloomed in her stomach.

'You want to touch them?' Ivy blinked back to reality and found Theon staring at her, a boyish grin spread across his face. Her breath caught in her throat. When she didn't answer, his smile grew wider, slight crinkles forming in the outer corners of his clear-blue eyes. He continued, 'My scales. Do you want to touch them?'

Ivy nodded a bit too quickly for her liking. She shrugged off her scuba tank, then removed her goggles and flippers—gosh, how ridiculous must she look? The warmth in her stomach turned to butterflies fluttering about at this boy who looked like pure perfection and clearly *lived* and *breathed* underwater, yet she stood there with her scuba gear like some awkward girl who clearly could not breathe underwater. It was truly embarrassing.

Ivy rolled her shoulders back and strode forward, feigning confidence she definitely didn't have. Her toes touched the water, a comforting presence that soothed most of her nerves. Theon's eyes sparkled like his scales as she made her way closer to him. The fluttering in her stomach increased, an uncontrollable swarm inside her.

'Hi,' he said, quiet enough so only she could hear.

'Hi,' she whispered back. Her breathing surprisingly eased in his presence, like he was both the tide and the anchor for those unfamiliar feelings. 'Sorry for staring.'

He released a breathy chuckle. 'Don't apologise.'

They watched each other for a moment, like they were the only two people on the beach, in this world, this universe. And according to Ivy, they were. Her heart would cherish this moment for eternity, and she prayed she could visit this place again, if only to see him, if only to experience these newfound feelings once more.

'Here.' Theon looked down and grabbed her hand, bringing it to his chest and laying it just below his heart.

Ivy trailed her fingers across the smooth surface and slight ridges. She smiled, mesmerised by the scales. She felt Theon's eyes burning into her, tugging her gaze up, up, up, until she was swimming in the ocean of his eyes. Strands of his pale orange hair fell in front of those eyes, like strings of firelight.

He was utterly beautiful.

Her eyes found their way through his clumped hair to one of the blue webbed fins poking through the strands. From there, her gaze travelled down to his neck; four blue slits marred his skin. Without thinking, she moved her hand from his chest and through his hair to his neck, but before she could touch the slits, he pulled back. Her lips downturned and she pulled away.

'Sensitive,' he quickly added. 'It's a sensitive spot, that's all.' He gave her a reassuring smile, and she smiled too.

Alvaro cleared his throat, interrupting their moment, and both Ivy and Theon quickly stepped away. 'She said she arrived here through the tunnel,' Alvaro started. 'Is it safe to assume it is still open?'

'It is.'

Ivy's head snapped to Alvaro. He hadn't known if the tunnel was still open? There was a chance it could have been closed and she wouldn't have been able to return home?

'Very well.' Alvaro nodded, wringing out his hands, ignoring the way Ivy stared at him. 'And I trust you will get her home safely.'

'I promise.'

'Well, Miss Ivy,' Alvaro started. Ivy took a step towards him, turning fully so her neck wasn't twisting back. 'It was a pleasure to see you.' He leant forward, bowing to Ivy.

'Oh, you don't need to bow,' Ivy said.

Alvaro stood and continued, 'I hope we can see each other again soon.'

Her heart swelled. Alvaro had let her into his home, taken care of her without reason, and now she had to say goodbye. Yes, he was a stranger and could have been something other than kind, but he wasn't. Without thinking, and without truly knowing why, she walked over to him and wrapped her arms around his waist, her head pressing just below his chest.

He jolted slightly. 'Oh.'

'Thank you for taking care of me. I'll never forget you and your kindness.'

Alvaro's arm tightened around her shoulders, his other holding the back of her head. 'Goodbye, Miss Ivy.'

'Bye, Alvaro.'

Ivy walked back to where she dropped her scuba gear and set herself up for the swim home. Theon gave Alvaro a nod before making his way deeper into the ocean. Ivy followed, and when she was chest deep, she turned back. Alvaro had followed her a few steps, his hooves now submerged. She waved. He hesitated, his chest rising and falling in quick breaths. Then his shoulders relaxed and he waved back.

55

EIGHT

Theon's scales shimmered underwater, guiding Ivy towards the tunnel imbedded in the rock wall. From this angle, she had a better view of the two fins on his back. A large one sat between his shoulder blades, while a smaller one was directly below it. The flutter of his legs—he didn't have a tail like the merfolk her mother told her about—kept him afloat as he looked inside the gaping maw that would take Ivy back to her home. His hair floated around his head, revealing those slits in his neck and how they contracted, something they certainly weren't doing earlier. *Gills*, Ivy realised. How else could he breathe underwater?

He turned to Ivy and asked, his voice muffled by the water, 'Can you hear me?' She nodded her response, unable to speak due to her mouthpiece, and he smiled. She tried not to think about how she looked swimming in her scuba diving gear. How utterly ridiculous. 'I'll go through first,' Theon said, 'and you follow me. Just like you did earlier today,' he added with a wink. Ivy's eyes widened, and his smile deepened, a chuckle escaping his lips. 'Let's go.' He swam inside the tunnel opening, and she followed.

The tunnel would have been just as dark as the first time she swam through if it weren't for Theon's scales shining ahead. His entire body was covered in them now, as though he could move them, coating the walls of the tunnel in shimmering shades of blue. It wasn't long until the other end of the tunnel revealed itself, only by the orange light of the setting sun. Theon waited just past the tunnel opening and watched Ivy exit as gracefully as she could, which turned out to be rather *ungraceful* as she focused on making sure her scuba tank didn't scratch against the rocks. She pointed to the surface and swam up before Theon could react.

As soon as she broke the surface, she spat her mouthpiece out, letting it dangle over her shoulder, and moved her goggles to her head. Theon appeared not long after, only stopping once his eyes were above the surface. His eyes darted across the water.

'What are you doing?' she asked.

Theon broke the surface up to his shoulders, treading water in a sea painted orange by the setting sun. 'Can't have any humans seeing me.'

Ivy's brows furrowed. 'Why not?'

He chuckled, but stopped when she didn't laugh with him. 'Wait, you really don't know?'

'I mean, I know that you're not from our world. But is it so bad if a human sees you? I saw you.'

The corner of his lips turned up in a cheeky smirk. 'And I'm glad you did.'

Ivy sighed and rolled her eyes, but she couldn't control the smile forming. 'You're a bit of a flirt.'

'Is that bad?'

'No,' she answered, slightly out of breath from keeping herself above the water. 'Just ... confident.'

His next smile was contagious, and she watched his eyes flitter between her own before flicking up. Her stomach tightened; she had goggles on her head—what must she look like to him? Her face heated despite the cool breeze icing the water on her face.

His smile turned into a smirk, but he quickly looked away, his eyes finding the beach, and asked, 'What's that?'

She followed his gaze to a small structure up the shore and smiled. 'That's my home.'

'Really? It's so strange.'

'Not as strange as living underwater,' Ivy remarked. Theon laughed, and she revelled in the sound. Then, as curiosity encased her, she said, 'You don't have a tail. My mum always told me merfolk had tails.' His smile dropped, and she instantly realised she must have said something rather personal. 'Sorry,' she said quickly. 'I didn't mean to—'

'No, it's fine,' he interrupted, yet the tone of his voice told her it wasn't entirely fine. 'You're right. Merfolk have tails, I don't. I'm usually referred to as an unknown race.'

Silence stung the air. Before either of them could say anything further, the sun officially completed its descent, hiding beneath the waves and shadowing Theon and Ivy in complete darkness, save for the slight shine of his scales. Her mum would be worried sick; she had to get home.

'I should go,' she said, her smile fading and eyes softening. 'I know this is real, but a part of me keeps thinking that I'll just wake up in my bed.'

'Why?'

'Because ...' That was an excellent question. She'd known while getting changed in Alvaro's home that Harukai couldn't possibly be a dream, and yet ... 'Because I was raised to believe people like you are just myth. Fauns, centaurs, merfolk. None of them exist here.'

'Well, it's definitely not a dream,' Theon confirmed.

Ivy nodded. 'I know.' They stayed there in comfortable silence. She wasn't sure why, but she didn't particularly want to leave. Maybe because of the possibility that she would never see Theon again. She had never seen that tunnel before today; it could easily vanish overnight. 'In case I don't see you again ... I'm really glad I met you.'

'Me, too. But I'm sure we'll see each other again,' he added with a slight smirk.

Something bloomed in her chest at his smirk, and she returned it with a smile of her own. 'Bye, Theon.'

'Goodbye, Ivy.'

She turned and made her way to the shore, back home, leaving Theon, Alvaro, and Harukai behind.

NINE

How could someone so beautiful, so electric, so magnetic even exist? And that's not even mentioning the fact he lived and breathed underwater. How utterly incredible. Ivy carved his smile, his eyes, his voice into her mind so he could linger with her as long as she allowed. The way his hair hugged his face, outlining the scales along his jaw. His subtle smirk, and the way her name sounded from his lips.

The sandbank Ivy swam into jolted her from her thoughts. As she waded out of the crashing waves, she turned back, hoping to see his red hair in the distance despite the darkness.

She couldn't see him.

Ivy spat out her mouthpiece and sighed, stripping herself of her flippers and goggles, and carrying them to the house. The small building was painted a beautiful sapphire blue and emerald green. Her mother's choice—the colour of her and Ivy's eyes.

'Ivy!' A woman who could easily be mistaken for Ivy's older

sister ran towards the water and crashed into her. 'I've been so worried!'

'Sorry, Mum.' Ivy slumped into her mother's arms, exhaustion starting to take over.

'Where were you?'

Ivy chuckled. 'You'll never believe me.'

Her mum pulled back and held Ivy at arm's length. 'Ivy, where were you?'

Surely her mother wouldn't believe her—'I swam into a world that looked exactly like the bedtime stories you used to tell me, filled with mythical creatures'—but what else could she say? Those bedtime stories, told by her mother all throughout her childhood, flashed in her mind. The worlds she described resembled Harukai almost too accurately.

'Do you remember the bedtime stories you used to tell me? About the forest and underwater lands, and the mermaids and fauns and fairies?' Even saying it out loud sounded ridiculous.

'Of course,' her mother said, deep blue eyes twinkling under the moonlight. 'Why do you ask?'

'Well, this sounds crazy, but ... I think I went there.' Ivy waited silently for her mother to laugh, cry, tell her she was crazy, dreaming, anything.

But instead, her mother's eyes widened. 'You found Harukai?'

Ivy wracked her brain for those bedtime stories she loved while growing up—and still loved. Had her mum ever mentioned the name of the land? If so, surely she would have recognised it when Alvaro had told her. Then again, she hadn't been told those stories in six or seven years, so she could easily have forgotten.

Right?

But the way her mother's face turned a shade of longing, of hope, tears brimming in her eyes, told Ivy otherwise. 'Mum,' she started. 'How do you know the name of the land?' She didn't need to wait for her answer—it was as clear as the night sky, but Ivy couldn't quite place the pieces together. Harukai was real, she knew this, but the bedtime stories were just that—stories.

Or were they one and the same?

Her mum had never told her the name of the world.

'Because ... those stories I told you are real,' she said. Then, she smiled. 'I can't believe you found it! What happened? You need to tell me everything.'

Ivy opened her mouth to speak, but she found her voice had completely and utterly abandoned her. Where to start? She was still trying to wrap her head around the fact that this place with fauns and fairies and merfolk was *real*, let alone manage to talk about it.

'Don't worry about it. Let's get you inside. Gosh, you must be freezing.' Her mum guided her to the house, wrapping her arms around her shoulders and rubbing her arms, but Ivy couldn't focus on whether she was actually cold or not. The stories were real. Did that mean just the place was real, or everything that happened in those stories? And how did her mother know about Harukai?

Ivy's mum stopped them at the door, but before either of them could step inside, her mum turned to her and said with a voice as cold as Ivy most likely was—again, she couldn't entirely focus on that fact—from the brisk wind against her wet skin, 'Don't tell your father about this.'

Ivy followed her mum in a daze as she entered the house, carrying her flippers and goggles with her, which would usually be left on the porch. The room was completely dark except for a streak of moonlight across the floor from the window, and beside that streak of moonlight, in a chair by the fireplace, was the silhouette of the exact person her mum had referred to.

'Don't tell me about what?' Ivy's father asked.

'Hi, Dad.'

Her mum ushered her inside. 'Let's get you cleaned up.'

'Don't tell me about what?' her dad repeated.

'It's nothing, Elias.' Ivy's mother tried guiding her through the house, her arm wrapped around Ivy's shoulders, but Elias's voice froze her.

'I don't think it's nothing.' He stood and slowly ambled to where Ivy and her mother waited in the entryway. 'Dorothea, what are you hiding from me?'

'Mum,' Ivy started, 'it's fine—'

'No, Ivy, you don't understand.'

Elias stepped closer until he was inches away from Dorothea. 'Tell me,' he demanded.

Ivy's thumb grazed the twigs of her ring, spinning the band until the sapphire gemstone sat underneath her fingers.

Dorothea raised her head and glared at Elias. 'No.'

Elias returned her steely glare, searching for an answer in Dorothea's eyes. His own softened as he said, 'So, it's finally happened.'

'You can't stop us,' Dorothea stated. 'It was easy to keep quiet when we were trapped here like everyone else. But I won't keep silent any longer.'

Ivy was transfixed, too focused on the words and wondering what they meant to notice Dorothea's subtle movements. Suddenly, something swung into the side of Elias's head, the clunk against his skull ringing in Ivy's ears.

'Dad!' Ivy screamed.

Elias staggered sideways with the blow. Before Ivy had a chance to move, her mother grabbed her arm and ran out the front door.

They blurred through the night, making a direct path for the water. Ivy's scuba tank thumped against her back, attempting to slow them down, but Dorothea continued dragging her along. Ivy could hardly feel each *thunk* of the tank, the sand flicking beneath her feet, or the tightness in her chest. 'Mum,' she called, but Dorothea's grip did not lighten. She did not slow down.

'Mum!' Closer and closer to the ocean they ran. Ivy stumbled, the ground rising to meet her, flippers and goggles flinging out of her grasp, now lost to the sand. Arms wrapped beneath her shoulders and hoisted her up. Dorothea made to run again, but Ivy grabbed her. 'What the hell is happening?'

'I'll explain everything once we're safe. You just have to trust me.'

'What are you talking about? You just smacked Dad over the head!'

Dorothea pulled Ivy close, their foreheads pressing together. 'Listen,' she whispered. 'That man is not—'

'Ahh!' Some unseen force behind Ivy pulled her back.

Elias gripped her arm, holding her to his side. 'I'm not what, Dorothea?'

'Let her go,' her mother demanded.

'I knew this day would come eventually,' Elias started, still holding Ivy. 'But I hoped you would see what I have done for you and choose to stay.'

Ivy knew her dad wasn't a danger to her, but as his grip on her arm tightened, she instinctively writhed against it. 'Dad, you're hurting me.'

The glare Elias held on Dorothea switched to her but instantly softened when he noticed her face twitching in pain. When his arm remained, Ivy thought for a moment that he wouldn't let go and ignore her. But thankfully, he released her.

'You can't leave,' he said to Dorothea.

'I have been complaisant,' Dorothea said. 'I have stayed, I have listened, I have done everything you asked of me.' She sniffled, and Ivy could see the tears streaming down her mother's cheeks. 'I have longed for my home, for my family.'

'What ...' Ivy muttered. She couldn't understand what her mother was talking about. This was her home. Ivy was her family. 'Mum, what are you—'

'You can't keep us here forever, Elias,' her mother exclaimed, interrupting her. 'We don't belong here.'

Ivy was sick of sitting on the sidelines. She was certain her mum had never lied to her, that she'd told her everything about her life. But could that not be true? She easily believed anything she was told, but only because she believed whoever spoke.

'What are you talking about?' she shouted. Waves lingering at the edge of the shore fell back into the ocean and rushed their next approach, each wave overlapping the next.

Both her parents looked at her, then back to each other, completely ignoring her.

'She can't go back,' Elias whispered.

'That's her home,' Dorothea told him.

Ivy grunted. 'I'm right here!'

'If she goes back,' Elias explained, 'then *they* will know.'

Dorothea's brows scrunched, and she opened her mouth to say something then shut it, before opening her mouth again and saying, 'I don't care what you have to say. My daughter and I are leaving. Let's go, Ivy.' She grabbed Ivy's arm and once again ran towards the ocean. There was no boat or any means of travel nearby. If they were going somewhere, they should be going the opposite way, towards the road. Except ...

There was *one* means of travel in the ocean.

They only managed a few steps, their feet running into the overlapping waves, before Elias's hand wrapped around Ivy's other arm and yanked her back, her shoulder joint pulling taut with the effort.

Ivy screamed.

Dorothea lunged.

And a blade flew.

TEN

A squelching signified the blade's burial in someone's flesh.

Elias's grip on Ivy's arm was released with the blade's impact and she fell to the ground, landing right where the waves crashed on the shore. She looked up, wondering where on earth the flying blade had come from. And storming towards them from the ocean, covered in blue scales that shimmered under the moonlight, copper hair shadowing his contorted features ...

Theon.

Ivy's brows scrunched. What was he doing here?

It was only due to the shining scales outlining his face that Ivy could see his lips drawn in a tight line, his eyebrows pulled together, and eyes homed in on the scene of her and her parents. Earlier, his entire body had been covered in scales as they swam through the tunnel, but now they only partially covered his torso and arms, although his legs were still completely scaled.

Ivy's eyes searched the brown leather straps across his body until she found the now empty thigh strap that housed his dagger earlier. The dagger that was now embedded in ...

Her head snapped to her parents. Elias groaned, sprawled on the sand, the dagger buried in his shoulder.

'Dad,' Ivy cried. Before she had a chance to crawl to him, a large hand wrapped around her arm and pulled. Red hair glinted in her periphery, and she spun around to face the culprit. 'What the hell have you done?' she yelled at Theon, attempting to rip her arm from him, but he held firm.

Another groan sounded. Elias staggered to his feet, blood dripping from the wound and staining his light grey shirt. Ivy tried to run to him, but Theon refused to let her go. '*Let go of me,*' she growled.

Theon flinched and released her.

What the hell is happening? her mind repeated as she stumbled to her wounded father. 'Dad?' A hand on her arm tugged her back. Not the strong hand that belonged to Theon, but a different one. Gentle, soft. Ivy turned and faced Dorothea. 'Mum,' she whispered, her face now wet with tears. 'What's happening?'

Her mother brushed away loose strands of hair from Ivy's tear-stricken face. 'I promise, I will tell you everything,' she whispered. 'But we need to go.'

Ivy sniffled. 'Go where?'

Dorothea's lips parted, but before she could speak, her eyes darted behind Ivy. Instead of answering her question, Dorothea threw her to the side. Hands wrapped around Ivy's upper arms, holding her in place. She watched as Elias snatched Dorothea and spun her, pulling her to his chest and pressing his arm across her throat.

'Mum!' Ivy lunged for her parents, but Theon's grip did not waver. Water aggressively crashed against her legs. 'Let me go!'

He did not let go.

'I don't want to do this,' her father explained, his eyes shadowed in sorrow. 'But I can't let you leave. I can't let you go back there.'

Go back where? To Harukai? Ivy was perfectly happy staying here if it meant keeping her life the way it had been that morning, but she knew that after this, nothing would be the same again.

Unlike Ivy's squirming, Dorothea was unmoving in Elias's grasp. Her eyes drifted to the spot above Ivy's right shoulder, where she assumed Theon was. 'Take her,' she said to him.

Ivy paused, salty tears falling between her lips and stinging her tongue. 'What?'

Why would she say that?

Why would her own mother want her to leave?

It was Elias's turn to address Theon. 'Give her to me.'

'See, he's asking for me. Just let me go!' Ivy writhed, almost breaking free, until Theon wrapped both arms around her and pinned her to him. As desperately as she wanted to be freed, it was difficult to determine which of her parents she should listen to in this moment. Surely her mum, for Elias was acting irrationally, yet she wanted Ivy to leave.

Why did there have to be a choice? Why was this happening, when they had all been perfectly fine before today?

'Please, Theon,' Dorothea begged. 'Take her.'

'You know me?' Theon asked. And at the same moment, Ivy froze and said, 'You know him?'

Dorothea ignored them both. 'It's not me he needs. It's Ivy.' She choked on the last word as Elias pressed his arm further against her throat.

'Mum!' Ivy squirmed again. The sound of waves fighting each other, crashing ferociously, could be heard from behind, but she didn't dare turn around. A rough wind rushed past, freezing her water-soaked legs.

'I don't want to hurt you, Dorothea,' Elias started, then turned to Theon and continued, 'They will know if Ivy returns. She'll be safe with me.'

Who was he talking about? Who was this *they* he'd mentioned more than once?

'Don't listen to him,' Dorothea choked.

'Can someone just tell me what's going on?' Ivy yelled above the angry sea.

Dorothea mouthed to Theon, *Go*. He hesitated, the only movement from him caused by Ivy trying to escape his hold.

'Don't,' Ivy begged him. 'Please, just let me go. Let me stay with my parents.'

She felt his body move as he leant to her ear and whispered, 'I'm sorry,' and slowly walked backwards.

'*No!*' Ivy thrashed, elbows finding Theon's ribs, feet striking his shins.

Elias opened his mouth to speak, but instead, a grunt fell from his lips. He rolled his shoulders and twisted his neck, his face contorting in the process. The sorrow in his eyes turned to fury; his lopsided lips became a snarl. The arm across Dorothea's throat reached to his shoulder and gripped the hilt of Theon's blade, pulling it free with a loud squelch, before pressing it against the delicate skin of Dorothea's throat.

'Mum!' Ivy wailed.

'I will find you, Ivy.' Elias said. Even his voice had changed ever-so-slightly, a deep and unnaturally calm cadence. 'Unless you find me first.'

'Find Alvaro,' Dorothea called. 'He will keep you safe.' When her sentence finished, she finally moved, her arms rushing to grip the hand holding Theon's dagger.

Ivy floundered in Theon's arms as he dragged her into the ocean. 'Let me go! Mum!' She screamed and cried and wailed and flopped around like a fish on land, continuing to hit every inch of Theon she could. But his scales covering all those inches of him made sure no damage was done.

Ivy watched through teary eyes and screamed through broken cries as Elias dragged Dorothea away, back towards the house, the dagger still to her throat. '*Mum!*'

Theon traipsed into the ocean, water splashing Ivy as she thrashed against him. Each agonising step into the sea had the waves thrashing higher and higher, barrelling into her and Theon and nearly toppling them over. Her loose strands of hair gushed in front of her face, landing in her open mouth.

'*Let me go!*'

He pushed the mouthpiece from her scuba tank into her mouth and held it there before repeating, 'I'm sorry,' and shoving her underwater.

The ocean was like a pressure chamber. Pressing against her, squishing her flesh against her bones. Ivy couldn't breathe, despite the fact that she actually could breathe because of her scuba tank.

She struggled against Theon's hold, thrashing and thrashing and—

She slipped from his arms.

Up and up and up, straight to the surface. Her fingers grazed the top, grazed the cool night air.

A hand wrapped around her shin and pulled.

Down and down and down they went. Towards the open tunnel. Away from her parents. Her family. Her home. The ocean hugged her on all sides, squeezing out the life she was leaving behind. Each ripple she passed taunted her.

Her kicking slowed, most of her energy having been expended; she could only fight for so long. She couldn't scream, but that didn't stop her from trying. Her cries escaped in bubbles that floated to the surface.

At least a part of her got away.

With his hand still gripping her leg, Theon pulled Ivy through the tunnel. A shaft of moonlight through the rippling water revealed the tunnel entrance as she passed through its gaping jaws. One last attempt at escape had her reaching for the opening and latching on, pulling herself away from Theon. But his grip was too strong. She slipped, her hands scraping against the inner walls and tearing the palms of her hands; the cuts instantly started stinging from the salt water. And as they travelled further into the tunnel, the single streak of moonlight vanished from her vision, burying her in complete darkness.

Ivy slumped, her head tapping the bottom of the tunnel before bobbing back up. The burning in her palms was the only indication that any of this were real.

She looked behind her and found Theon's scales partially lighting the front of the tunnel. Despite everything that had happened, she felt a comfort in his presence, like his very existence, his way of life, was balm for her emotions. His grip on her leg was gentle yet strong, that hand the only part of his body not covered in scales. The softness of his skin was calming, welcoming—

No. That hand was what pulled her away from her family.

She kicked and squirmed, but it was no use: her energy was gone.

New rippling moonlight told her they had exited the tunnel. Further away from freedom Theon swam, a frozen Ivy being dragged behind, her only movements caused by his continuous pull. That same moonlight revealed the sand bank below Ivy just as Theon slowed and finally released her.

As if his very touch dampened her spirit, she kicked off the sand bank, propelling herself through the ocean, back towards the tunnel, her escape, her mother. She knew she wouldn't make it, but she needed to try.

Scaled arms wrapped around her and pulled her away.

Ivy remained limp in Theon's arms until he stood on the sand bank and lifted her above the water. She squirmed in his hold and spat her mouthpiece out. 'Put me down!' she screamed, salty water from either her eyes or the ocean running into her mouth.

Theon carried her towards the shore, and she throttled against him until they were away from the waves.

'What is happening?' a deep voice asked. Ivy didn't care to check who spoke. The second Theon released her she ran back to the ocean.

'Shit,' Theon swore.

Ivy sprinted through the crashing waves, Theon's footsteps following her into the ocean and splashing behind her. Once the water was at her knees, she put her mouthpiece in place and dove.

Her legs kicked relentlessly, tirelessly, towards the tunnel. A streak of moonlight illuminated the space before her. The shine of Theon's scales could be seen in her periphery; he was close enough to grab her, but he didn't need to. She faced the tunnel again, but as she swam closer, it became smaller.

It was shrinking.

Closing.

No ...

She kicked as hard as she could, but she could only swim so fast. She was only human.

The tunnel closed completely just before she got there.

NO! She screamed into her mouthpiece, bubbles bursting into the water rushing around her. Her cries continued until her mouthpiece fell out. She quickly closed her lips against the rush of water entering her.

Theon's scales illuminated the rock wall, helping her see what she decided to throw herself against. She slammed her fists and feet against the rocks, each thud reverberating throughout her body—a welcoming pain—but the wall did not budge.

Water fought its way into her lungs. Her chest expanded; her throat began to collapse.

She desperately needed to keep attacking that same spot on the wall where the tunnel had been—it had opened once, surely it could open again—but more than that, she needed to breathe. She swam to the surface and coughed the water back into its home.

Now that Ivy was above water, however, it was easier to continue her attempts at breaking the wall. Over and over again she threw herself against the rocks, welcoming the agonising pain. When that clearly refused to work, she started pulling at them, the fresh cuts on her palms tearing further. Blood dripped down her arms and the rocks, creating a bloody splotch in the ocean barely visible under the silver light of the moon.

'Mum!' Her voice cracked, hoarse from all her screaming and the lingering saltiness of the water that had been trapped in her throat.

She gripped the rocks and pulled herself up, screaming at the pain in her hands, but pushing through, only to slip due to her lack of energy. She'd spent her entire life climbing these same rocks on *her* side of the rock wall, all while wearing scuba gear, but now, her attempts were futile. Her muscles strained as she tried to pull herself again, but her open wounds had her falling to the water.

'Ivy,' Theon whispered beside her. He reached for her, his fingers grazing her arm—

'Don't touch me,' she snapped, jolting away from his grasp. Theon flinched, his blue eyes shadowed with his earlier apologies. Words that meant nothing to Ivy. 'This is all your fault.'

Was it, though?

She hadn't yet had a chance to analyse everything, but what she did know in this moment was that Theon took her away and brought her back to this foreign land. She didn't want to think about whether all of this was truly his fault. She needed someone to blame, someone to throw her anger at like she threw herself against the wall. And, thankfully, Theon didn't correct her.

In fact, he didn't utter a word as she said again, 'This is *all your fault!*'

Ivy hit the wall again but lacked the energy she previously had. Instead, she held on to the rocks and cried. Exhaustion overcame her, a blanket made of water encompassing her in its embrace. There was nothing else she could do. Her tears mixed with droplets of the salty ocean. She slipped from the wall, her scuba tank threatening to pull her under, fully into exhaustion's hold. She tried to tread water, tried to float, but her limbs were tired. The cuts on her palms burned from the salt water—a beautiful, welcoming pain. A physical pain that would distract her from the emotional heartache.

Theon grabbed her, and this time, she didn't object. His scaled, muscular arms wrapped around her weak form and her burdening scuba tank before he kicked off the rock wall towards the shore. As the pair made their way to the beach, the faint, warm beating inside her began once more.

When they arrived at the Thidin Kingdom, Theon kept an arm around her shoulders—even in her current state, she couldn't ignore how it seamlessly fit like a tailored jacket around her—and guided her onto the beach, her feet dragging through the sand.

A figure ran towards her, blurred by her watery vision. 'Miss Ivy,' they said, their hands cupping her cheeks. Ivy blinked and the person came into focus. 'Are you all right?' Alvaro asked in a panicked tone.

Ivy couldn't speak, even if she wanted to. All her screaming and crying had made her throat drier than ... Well, everything was drenched at the moment. Her throat was the driest thing around.

'Let us get this off you,' Alvaro said. The weight of Theon's arm around her vanished as Alvaro's hands found the straps of her scuba tank, pushing it off her shoulders. It *thunked* onto the sand.

Ivy whipped her head towards the sound. A silver cylinder with thick black straps and a black cord that attached to the mouthpiece. How much oxygen was left? How much had she wasted? When she first travelled through the tunnel to Harukai she knew there was roughly four hours of oxygen left. But now she didn't even know how much time had passed since she arrived here earlier that day, let alone how much time she had spent using said oxygen.

Now, the tank lay like a corpse on the sand, the black straps acting as skeletal arms. Scratches marred the cylinder. It was the only thing she still had from home, other than her swimmers. The tank was a reminder of everything that had happened. The lack of flippers and goggles, lost to the sandy shore at home, was a reminder of everything she had now lost.

The death of her old life.

And with death comes grief to claim the essence of her young spirit.

'Here,' Theon said. 'I'll get that.'

His leaning frame came into view as Ivy watched him grab the silver corpse, holding its skeletal straps like it was merely a piece of metal and not the only remnants of her life she managed to sneak into this world. He slipped one strap over his shoulder and placed his other hand against her back to guide her forward. She looked up, his hair now hanging in dried clumps either side of his face. He may have been what she believed was a perfect specimen, but all she could see was his dagger pushing against Dorothea's throat. All she could hear was his apology before he dragged her away. All she could feel beneath his hand on her back was the same hand gripping her leg and pulling her into the tunnel.

Ivy stepped out of his touch and wrapped her arms around herself, turning away before she could witness his reaction.

'Here,' Alvaro said, stepping forward and taking the scuba tank. 'Thank you, Theon.' Alvaro guided Ivy away from the ocean and towards the forest.

Away from her home. Her mother. Her life.

PART TWO

THE GIRL WHO FELL

'How much worse can it get?' you ask.
I turn to the person beside me, and in time
with the pulsing of space around us, we
sigh and roll our eyes.

ELEVEN

Sunlight cast her glow through the open window and across the bed, bathing Ivy in a golden luminescence. She opened her eyes, squinting against the sun's rays as a cool breeze glided alongside the streak of sunlight.

Last night's events flashed in her mind.

'I don't want to do this,' her father explained, his eyes shadowed in sorrow. 'But I can't let you leave. I can't let you go back there.'

Ivy watched through teary eyes and screamed through broken cries as Elias dragged Dorothea away, back towards the house, the dagger still to her throat.

'I will find you, Ivy.' Even his voice had changed ever-so-slightly, a deep and unnaturally calm cadence. 'Unless you find me first.'

Ivy sat up, pushing on her hands to do so and causing her palms to sting. 'Ah.' She looked down and found her hands wrapped in a white cloth.

Over and over again she threw herself against the rocks …

She started pulling at them, the fresh cuts on her palms tearing further. Blood dripped down her arms and the rocks ...

Salty tears stained her tongue as they fell into her partly open mouth. 'Why ...' she whispered, gently running her thumb across the bandages.

On instinct, she made to touch her ring, but she couldn't feel the band or the gemstone through the wrappings. Panic encroached on her sorrow. She was wearing the ring yesterday. Had it slipped off her finger while her mum was pulling her towards the water? Or maybe when Theon dragged her underwater through the tunnel?

She looked around the room, her heart beating rapidly. Light leaves drenched the walls like spindly fingers clawing at the tree trunk; potted plants resembling gargoyles watched her eerily with pistils like beady eyes. With nowhere else to go last night, Ivy had let Alvaro take her back to his place. She supposed she would stay here for the foreseeable future.

Next to the bed, a cup of water sat on a bedside table, her mother's ring waiting for her beside it.

The bandage around her fingers was thin, allowing her to slip the ring on her middle finger. Ivy flexed her hand to admire her mother's jewellery, a reminder of home she could carry with her at all times, but the slight stretching of her palm pulled the cuts beneath the bandage.

Out the open window, leaves swayed with the strong breeze that dried her tears. And above the treetops of the lush forest surrounding Alvaro's clearing was a strip of crisp, blue ocean. The sound of water scratching against a sandy beach could be heard, taunting her.

It was the ocean that brought her here, and she glared at it now, knowing it would be that same vile sea that could take her home.

Ivy rolled off the bed and stood by the window, marvelling at the whimsical beauty of Harukai. But the ethereal nature of the flowers and mushrooms that grew on the edge of the clearing were no match for her newfound emotional wounds bleeding within her. Distress rolled like crashing waves against her organs, her bones, her flesh. She was like a scratched disc that could only play one scene, a single memory replaying: *Elias dragged Dorothea away, back towards the house, the dagger still to her throat.*

Memories, thoughts, and questions flooded her mind. What had he done with her? *Why* had he taken her? Was she safe, sitting in their family home, trying to find a way back here? Or had Elias taken her elsewhere?

'It's not me he needs. It's Ivy.' What did that mean? *'I will find you, Ivy ... Unless you find me first.'* He'd had her for sixteen and a half years. If he needed her for something, why hadn't he done so already?

And her mum ... She knew about Harukai, had told her to find Alvaro. She'd even called Theon by his name. *How* did her mother know about Harukai? *How* did she know Alvaro? *How* did she know Theon's name?

Theon ...

Theon traipsed into the ocean, water splashing Ivy as she thrashed against him ... He pushed the mouthpiece from her scuba tank into her mouth and held it there before repeating, 'I'm sorry,' and shoving her underwater. Why did he take her away? He could've left her there. He *should've* left her there. But instead, he took a young girl from her parents and trapped her alone in a foreign land. She shouldn't be here, didn't *want* to be here, knowing her mum was clearly in some sort of danger.

Elias dragged Dorothea away, back towards the house, the dagger still to her throat.

And yet, despite her incessant begging and thrashing, Theon had still brought her here.

Why?

Because her mother had told him to? Why would he listen to someone he didn't even know as opposed to someone he ... well, barely knew? Whatever the reason, Ivy being here was his fault. Yes, her mother had told him to take her, but he'd *listened*. And if it weren't for *his* dagger, her mother wouldn't be ... captive? A prisoner? She had no idea what had happened to her mum. Was she even—

Ivy stopped that thought before it could finish.

The emotional waves sparked into flames that burned her insides. She needed someone to scream at, someone to blame, someone to throw all her anger and frustration and sorrow at. Someone who was a part of this, whether he was entirely to blame or not.

She screamed, releasing what she could into the suffocating world, but it wasn't enough. She wiped her dried tears on the cloth around her hands, careful not to irritate her injuries. She didn't know how to find him, but she'd figure it out. Perhaps if she just waited at the beach and screamed his name, he'd hear her.

With the bed blocking her path, Ivy walked around and stormed towards the stairs leading to the main room of the house, an orange flame appearing in her periphery as she passed the dresser mirror—

She paused.

Walked back to the dresser.

Looked in the mirror.

Emerald eyes looked back at her. She could have sworn her eyes were flaming orange, but it must have been the reflection of one of the many vibrant flowers in the room. She sighed, rubbed her eyes, and once the stars cleared her vision, she gave herself a moment to look at her appearance.

Ivy hadn't bathed after last night's events; her braided hair now dried in a knotted mess and her black swimsuit caused her dark skin to itch with saltwater residue. She took a deep breath in through her nose and out through her mouth, then scrunched her face. The flame inside her dwindled. She'd yelled at Theon last night, and doing so now wouldn't make a difference. She ached to know why he'd brought her back here, and she'd find him soon for those answers, but her body was screaming at her to take care of herself.

Her emotions abandoned her, leaving her aching body tired and drained and empty. Her face formed into a neutral expression, her red eyes the only sign that she had released any emotions. Ivy was trapped in this world. Her mother had been taken by her dad for an unknown reason. She needed to be strong so she could find a way home and find her mum.

Ivy sighed again and said, 'Guess I'll clean up.' She searched the dresser drawers and found the same clothes she'd worn the day before. Was it really only yesterday? So much had happened it felt as though a few days had passed.

She chose the same shirt, skirt, and boots, trying to keep any sort of familiarity (however small it may be), then continued rummaging through the drawers for a towel and toiletries, only to come up empty handed. Was there even a bathroom in this house? It was a *tree*—how could there be a shower or a bath? From what she'd seen, the entire kingdom was a forest. Perhaps they didn't clean themselves? *No,* Ivy thought. *There must be a way for me to clean up.* Hopefully Alvaro was awake to help her, and as the thought crossed her mind, clopping hooves sounded from downstairs.

She awkwardly carried the boots and bundle of clothing, and climbed down the ladder, landing in the main room with a soft *thump*.

'Ahh, Miss Ivy,' Alvaro greeted. 'How are you feeling this morning? Would you like a cup of tea? Some fruit?' He sat in the same chair he had the day before holding a saucer and teacup with steam wafting from the top. A bowl of fruit sat on the table beside him.

'Um … I just want to have a bath. Or shower, or something,' Ivy replied.

'I do not know what a … *shower* is,' he said, overly enunciating the word, 'but I do have a space for you to bathe. Let me get you a towel and soap.'

Ivy watched Alvaro clop to a cupboard built into the tree wall next to the kitchenette and fumble for a towel. The cupboard also housed bed linen, cushions, and blankets. He then opened one of the kitchenette cupboards, revealing multiple bars of soap. Once he had the items, he made his way back to Ivy, but in her nervous state, she instinctively took a step back.

Although he'd been nothing but kind to her, Alvaro was a *stranger*. But was he? *'Find Alvaro. He will keep you safe.'* Despite what her mother had told her, Ivy couldn't help feeling uncomfortable at the thought of having slept here. She couldn't help feeling nervous at the prospect of having no one else to turn to in this strange world.

Alvaro's lips turned down at her retreat. He opened his mouth to speak, then closed it, looking like one of those puffer fish Ivy encountered on her regular swims. The reminder of home had her heart falling, the memory of her mother with a dagger to her throat replaying in her mind. Those waves inside her started building slowly, but she quickly pushed them away before her emotions could completely take over.

'Follow me, Miss Ivy.' Alvaro clopped to the front door and stepped outside.

Outside? Ivy thought. *Why on earth should I bathe out here?* Nevertheless, she didn't object. After all, she had assumed there wouldn't be a bathroom inside the tree.

They veered left off the stone footpath that led to the wondrous garden tunnel and walked to the forest entrance—the opposite side of the clearing to where they had entered the day before. Alvaro guided her through a twisting soil path of tall trees until they arrived at a pond, the blue water so still Ivy thought it was frozen over. Once more, those vibrant flowers bloomed, scattered around the edge of the pond. Mushrooms grew in jumbled patches at the roots of the surrounding trees, all in varying heights and patterns.

'This is my bathing pond,' Alvaro started, breaking the silence. Although, it wasn't entirely silent; the faint tweeting of birds could be heard. 'No one comes through here as it is my private territory, so I can assure you, you will be utterly alone.' He handed Ivy the items and pointed to the soap. 'This is the wash. It can be used for hair, body, and face. I made it myself,' he added with a small smile. 'When you are done, come back to the house, and I will have a warm cup of tea waiting for you.' He then gave her a polite nod and left.

Ivy looked around, noticing all the trees stood close together—almost touching—with the only visible gap being the path back to Alvaro's home. Her gaze followed the path to the cosy tree. Alvaro was nowhere to be seen, but the window at the front of the home was closed. She stood at the edge of the pond, underneath one of those tall trees and its overhanging vines for some time, unsure whether undressing and bathing in a pond in the middle of the forest was the best idea. But she couldn't very well stay in her swimmers ... could she? No, she couldn't. Her skin was sticky and itchy, and her hair was just one large clump of tangles. Ivy decided a wash was exactly what she needed.

She left her clothes and towel on a nearby mushroom top and brought the soap to the edge of the pond, then scanned the vicinity one more time. As far as she could tell, no one was lurking nearby. Ivy removed her swimmers as quickly as she could and waded into the water. Her body tensed, expecting it to be as cold as the ice it resembled, but as her toes graced the surface, a neutral warmth enveloped her.

The water felt like ... home.

She dove in and cascaded down, down, down, until she couldn't go any further and pushed herself to the surface. It was the most divine water she had ever swum in. Silky and soft and refreshing. And it wasn't even for swimming. She untied her braid and pulled apart the course strands, careful not to damage her hair, then made her way to the edge of the pond and grabbed the soap, bringing the bar to her nose.

Coconut and lime.

Her muscles instantly relaxed from the scent alone, and she soaked the soap before rubbing the bar across her body. With each scrub, saltwater washed away. The same saltwater from her home. Another part of her gone, as though this soap was scrubbing her clean of her old life.

Alvaro had said the soap could be used for hair, body, and face, and although she wasn't sure how well it would work in her curly hair, she didn't particularly have another option. She lathered the soap in her hands and scrubbed away more of herself, massaging her scalp in the process. The bar of soap floated on the surface of the pond while she leant back and rinsed the suds from her hair. She then washed her face and took a moment to relax in the water, abandoning the soap on the edge of the pond.

Despite what the ocean's water had done to her, the calm water of the bathing pond cleared her mind, allowing her to properly assess everything from yesterday. So many things had been said, yet more had been left unsaid.

Elias dragged Dorothea away, back towards the house, the dagger still to her throat.

Ivy shook her head, hoping that final image of her mother would fall from her mind and into the water. She needed to push past the memory and think about everything else that had happened.

'I'll explain everything once we're safe.'

'That man is not—'

'I promise, I will tell you everything. But we need to go.'

Tell her what? Go *where*? How did her mum know Harukai, and why would she only tell Ivy of this world's existence through bedtime stories, making her believe it was nothing more than a fairytale? Was this where she planned to take Ivy as they sprinted towards the ocean in the black of night? Why else would her mum choose to run *into* the water? Was Harukai where she thought they would both be safe?

'I have longed for my home, for my family ... You can't keep us here forever, Elias. We don't belong here ... That's her home.'

Ivy fell beneath the pond's surface, that final line following her down: *'That's her home.'*

She sunk to the floor, attempting to escape the line echoing around her.

'That's her home.'

'That's her home.'

Her feet pushed into the floor, sending her to the surface, and as she broke through the water, she took in a deep breath of fresh air. Her mum believed Harukai was Ivy's *home*. That couldn't be true; she had only been to this world for the first time yesterday. But her father hadn't disagreed, hadn't argued. Had spoken as though he believed it too. *'She can't go back,'* Elias whispered. *'... I can't let you leave. I can't let you go back there.'*

This was getting too much. There were too many questions with not enough answers. Too many memories attacking her from all sides.

'I will find you, Ivy. Unless you find me first.' His voice, his de-meanour, everything about him had transformed in that final mo-ment. He'd become someone Ivy didn't recognise. Someone who

desperately needed Ivy for something now but hadn't needed her for the last sixteen years of her life. What had he been waiting for? And what had changed now that caused him to act this way?

Her mother had told her to trust her. She'd always trusted her mother, and that wouldn't change now, but trust her with what? Trust her *about* what? Dorothea never got her chance to explain, and now Ivy was left alone with all these questions.

Ivy looked through the trees, her eyes following that footpath to the clearing of Alvaro's home. The large tree encompassed only a small portion of the grassy circle. A house in a *tree.* How marvellous. *'Find Alvaro. He will keep you safe.'*

Perhaps staying with him wasn't such a bad thing after all.

Twelve

Ivy spent the remainder of her bath crying in the pond, her tears becoming the water she would most likely bathe herself in again. Her life had well and truly been changed forever. She was bathing in a pond in the middle of a forest with whimsical trees and flowers—she was living in a fairytale—yet all she wished for was to be back home with her mother.

Could she wish for such a thing? Could the wish come true? After all, she was clearly in some magical fantasy world—at least, she assumed it was magical, what with the tunnel to her home disappearing on its own.

But how would she go about making a wish come true?

Movies and books always had people wishing to the stars at night, and it was currently morning. So, she would just have to wait.

She climbed out of the pond and dried herself in a hurry, still cautious of unseen eyes watching her. The copse of trees close together only did so much to assure her of her privacy. Once safely in her undergarments, Ivy stepped into the green skirt and pulled on the orange shirt, attaching the leather belt around her waist. She slipped one foot into a boot and laced it up, then did the other, but something inside the second boot stabbed her toe. 'Ow.' She pulled her foot out and tipped the boot upside down. A small pile of seashells fell to the ground.

She'd completely forgotten about her collection of shells, but now, her heart swelled at the sight of them. Something from the very waters of her home that had travelled with her to Harukai and never left. And now, it was another piece of her old life she could hold onto. She fell to her knees and gathered the shells, tears falling. Why Ivy was crying, she didn't know. These shells were her home, the physical nature of where she lived, and she would keep them with her until she returned.

Ivy put the shells back in her boot and scrunched her curly hair with the towel, noticing how silky each strand was. The soap had done wonders to her usually difficult hair—better than any product from home.

Rather than walking with one shoe on, she decided to take the other off and carry them both. She gathered the rest of her things and stumbled up the soft footpath. At the edge of the forest, she breathed deeply and took a moment to admire the clearing. The sprawling grass, the large tree, the entrance to the tunnel, the flowers and mushrooms, the garden behind Alvaro's home. With no way back to the human realm, this place would act as her temporary solitude.

Ivy took another deep breath and made her way to the front door, dusting her soil-coated feet with the towel before stepping inside. Eucalyptus and forest fruits welcomed her, just as they had the day before. Alvaro was back in what she now realised must be his usual seat, the bowl of fruit still on the side table with a cup of tea waiting for her, just as he promised.

'Ahh, Miss Ivy.' Alvaro rushed over and took her towel, soap, and swimmers. 'Sit down and have something to eat,' he said, and left through the front door.

She did as he told, placing the boots beside the chair. She hadn't realised she was hungry, but the sight of those delicious fruits had her stomach grumbling. Steam from the tea wafted into her nose as she sat in the opposite chair.

When Alvaro returned, Ivy said, 'You can just call me Ivy.'

'Oh, my apologies. A force of habit, I am afraid.'

Ivy found that a strange thing to say not once, but twice—the first being when he had collected her from the beach after she had bolted from the library and met Theon. He'd only known her the same amount of time she'd known him, yet he already had a habit of calling her "Miss Ivy"? There were enough questions rattling around in her head that she didn't have any answers to: she didn't need any more. She chose to ignore the statement and instead grabbed a few pieces of fruit and chucked them in her mouth.

'Have some tea,' Alvaro calmy interrupted. 'It will soothe your sorrows.'

Ivy picked up the steaming cup beside her and brought it close, that welcoming eucalyptus scent returning. It was the same tea as yesterday, the delectable liquid warming her throat and calming her soul. And although it didn't entirely soothe her sorrows, it did help her relax ever-so-slightly.

'So,' Alvaro started, 'I know you have just been through an ... eventful experience. I can only imagine how you are feeling at this time. But while the memories are still fresh in your mind, I feel we must see Lady Eira to discuss everything that has transpired. She may offer guidance, or advice.'

'Who's Lady Eira?'

'Oh, of course, you do not know. How silly of me.' He took a sip of his tea and placed the cup on the side table. 'She is the Lady of the Thidin Kingdom, and it is essential she understands your ... situation.'

Her situation. Ivy didn't want to admit it yet, but she knew the truth: she was stuck here. And now she had to talk about what happened, which was the last thing she wanted to do. But maybe that would also give her some answers.

'Find Alvaro. He will keep you safe.'

As long as she stayed with Alvaro, he would keep her safe. At least, according to her mother.

That brief memory—one of the final ones of her mother—had her eyes brimming with tears. 'I ... I'll be back,' Ivy stammered before setting her half-drunk tea on the table, collecting the boots, and climbing upstairs.

Once in the spare room, she sat on the bed and allowed the tears to silently fall. She wanted to stay there and cry for as long as she needed to, but Alvaro had said this Lady Eira could give her some advice. Maybe she would also miraculously have all the answers she needed. So, Ivy only gave herself a few short moments to cry before she sniffled and wiped her tears away.

She poured her seashells out of the boot and laid them on the dresser in a line, almost exactly how she would have placed them back home. They all sparkled, looking right at home in this room. Then, she rummaged for a comb in the drawers and pulled it through her silky curls, marvelling at how well the soap had worked.

She ruffled her hair and let it fall naturally over her shoulders, then looked at herself in the mirror. These clothes, made for a folk of Harukai, fit her perfectly—aside from those pants she tried yesterday—and she wondered how strange of a coincidence that was. Flowers in potted homes framing the room faced her, seemingly watching as she analysed herself and her broken life like she was nothing more than some homework. They greeted her, as though she was one of them—one of the flowers or one of the folk, Ivy wasn't quite sure. A singular flower in a pot on the bedside table faced her, their petals only half-open. She reached over and grazed their purple doors, and at the touch of her fingers, the flower bloomed, their petals opening wide. A strange, warm sensation flooded her, as though the flowers were right in their assessment: she was one of them. But one of the flowers or one of the folk? Both? Neither?

'This is her home.'

Ivy released the petals and shook the memory from her mind. She didn't belong here, wasn't one of anyone or anything in this land. She was human.

Sunlight from the open window reflected on the mirror, casting Ivy in a bright glow and causing the embroidery on her clothing to shimmer.

Everything about this world, from the flowers and mushrooms to the forest and the ocean, all the way down to the clothing and accessories, was utterly beautiful.

But it wasn't home.

Ivy put the boots on and laced them up, then made her way back downstairs.

Alvaro was exactly where she'd left him, looking at her in awe. 'You look beautiful, Miss Ivy.'

'Thank you,' she said, noting he once again called her "Miss Ivy."
'For the clothes, for the bed. For letting me stay here.'

'Oh, there is no need to thank me. It is my pleasure.'

Ivy stayed near the staircase fiddling with her skirt and trailing her fingers across the embroidery on her clothes.

'Is everything all right, Miss Ivy? Are you still hungry?' Alvaro asked.

In the short time she had been in Harukai, she'd never properly looked at Alvaro. Yes, she'd noticed he was a faun, but past his antlers and legs were eyes of deep green, and hair that wasn't quite curly but not quite straight. Yes, he was a faun, but he was also a person, who was friendly and kind and clearly quite caring. He wore the same sapphire kilt he'd been wearing the day before—or perhaps he had multiple kilts in the same colour. His hands were wrapped in bandages similar to hers.

He smiled, but it didn't reach his eyes.

'Ah, no, thank you.' Ivy shuffled. She barely knew Alvaro, but she was starting to feel more comfortable around him. She trusted her mother's words that he would keep her safe. But despite all of that, she needed to get home, back to her mother, back to the familiarity of her life. Except, all of that was gone. Her life had been changed irrevocably. 'We should go see Lady Eira.'

'Oh. Are you sure you would like to do that now?'

Ivy nodded. 'I want to know how the hell I'm going to get back home and find my mum.'

Thirteen

Sunlight seemed to be forbidden in the tunnel of flowers and vines. Light leaves curled around the roots of trees framing the walkway and tangled in hanging vines was the only light source, aside from tiny dots of sunlight that managed to break through the cage of leaves and branches and vines. Those gaps allowed a cool breeze to brush past, creating a song on its way through. A song like a whistled lullaby.

Beside Ivy, Alvaro ducked beneath the higher-hanging vines that stopped far above her head. He towered over her, and his green eyes shimmered against the golden light from the leaves.

Flowers framed the footpath, their pistils watching the pair as they walked past. Or rather, watching *Ivy*. She turned back to see them, but each time she looked their way, they were merely gently blowing in the wind, looking anywhere but at her.

Hustling and bustling sounded as they reached the end of the tunnel, streaks of sunlight highlighting the small grassy mounds decorated with flowers and mushrooms. Ivy and Alvaro followed the path as it snaked to the right and through more trees, the sensation inside her building its faint rhythm, until they entered the main area of the Thidin Kingdom.

Folk milled about, shopping at stalls, smiling, chatting, children laughing and playing. Wings fluttered, tails swished, and claws dug through the soil. They were beautiful. Magnificent. Every single one of them.

'Good morning, Alvaro,' a harpy greeted as he made his way towards them. His feathered wings, which replaced his arms, were a light brown that matched his skin, feathered legs, and faun antlers.

'Oh, good morning, Jaxan,' Alvaro replied in kind.

Jaxan looked Ivy's way, his eyes glazing over her form, possibly searching for any folk-like identifying feature. When he realised she had none, he blinked, then flinched, before quietly gasping. His eyes widened and he glanced to Alvaro, whispering, 'Is she ...?'

Instead of answering Jaxan's unfinished question, Alvaro said, 'My apologies, Jaxan, but we have somewhere to be. Maybe we can catch up another time,' and offered him a friendly smile before quickly guiding Ivy away.

As they walked further into the kingdom, Ivy looked around and noticed all the folk were watching her. Some started mumbling and pointing like they had the previous day. Either this world didn't believe it was rude to stare and point, or they just didn't care, and although she thankfully couldn't hear what they said, she could easily wager a guess.

'Is that who I think ...'
'She looks like ...'

'It's really you …'

They were enthralled by her. Her appearance, her existence … just *her*. A shiver ran down her spine.

'Come along, Miss Ivy.' Alvaro gently rested his hand on her upper back and guided her around the market space and past mesmerised folk, whispers floating in the air and prickling the hairs on her arms, until they arrived at what was definitely the largest tree Ivy had ever seen in her entire life (apologies to Alvaro).

The trunk alone was almost as wide as the clearing of Alvaro's home, and the tree was so tall the top wasn't visible, reaching far above the other treetops. Emerald, purple, and even—Ivy blinked—*white* leaves hung down in vines and were decorated with those shining lights. In the centre was a door adorned in a glittering, golden trail that travelled beyond the doorframe and onto the tree itself, curving around the trunk.

They walked up a small staircase of tree roots and grass, stopping at the front door. Alvaro raised his fist to knock but froze. He looked over his shoulder, not lowering his fist, and Ivy followed. Every folk in the area was staring at them. At Ivy. Muttering and mumbling and whispering and pointing. That sneaking tendril crept around the crevices of her internal organs, grazing her insides but not constricting them. It teased her, like it knew the reason the folk stared, but refused to let her in on the secret. And standing on a higher level, with this cluster of strangers gaping at her in awe, had her feeling like some sort of long-lost ruler, a long-awaited messiah.

It unnerved her.

'Is there a problem?' Alvaro asked in a way that was both authoritative and polite at the same time. Everyone instantly looked away and continued what they were doing, as though they hadn't been almost praying to Ivy.

Alvaro looked down at her, exhaled a sigh, and shrugged his shoulders far too casually, then gently knocked on the door. A few moments passed before the door swung open, revealing a glowing figure.

Golden waves cascaded over her shoulders, reaching past her hips, with vines and leaves twisted among the curls. Her pale brown, golden-tinted skin had a slight glow to it, shimmering under the sunlight. Her eyes were as blue as the ocean, sparkling like freshly cut diamonds, and her wings—oh, her wings—were white with a shining golden thread woven through. She wore a white gown that poured to the ground like a waterfall, with sparkling green and gold embroidery. And the bodice, or rather lack thereof, was made of a sheer fabric that criss-crossed over her breasts and wrapped around her upper arms just below her shoulders.

She wasn't just a fairy.

She was a goddess.

'Good morning, Alvaro,' she said in a singsong, fairytale princess voice.

'Good morning, Lady Eira.' Alvaro bowed, and while doing so, turned his head to Ivy and nodded towards the ground. She quickly followed suit. Once standing, Alvaro said, 'There is something we need to discuss.'

'I see.' Her eyes flicked to Ivy. 'Or rather, some*one* to discuss.'

'May we step inside, please?'

Without answering, Lady Eira stepped back and gestured into her home. Ivy waited and tilted her head back to look at Alvaro, expecting him to enter first. But he was already watching her and said, 'After you.' She gave Lady Eira an awkward but polite smile as she passed and stepped inside the tree.

Based on Lady Eira's appearance and the size of the tree, Ivy was expecting grand elegance, but her home was like a cosy cottage, not unlike Alvaro's. A round table with six chairs took up the centre of the space, with flowers in a vase and a clear jar of light leaves. Ivy followed through to the left, towards the small lounge and two sitting chairs below a window.

On the other side of the dining table was what would have been a corner kitchen if not for the lack of corners in the circular tree home. And next to the not-so-corner kitchen was a winding staircase, the railing lit up with light leaves. Her eyes followed those leaves up the staircase until she was staring at the ceiling, beautifully decorated with more lights.

The door clinked shut, drawing Ivy's attention to Alvaro and Lady Eira. 'Please, have a seat.' Lady Eira gestured to the small sitting area.

Ivy chose one of the sitting chairs closest to the front door, ensuring she didn't feel any more trapped than she already was in this foreign land.

'Would you like something to drink? Or maybe some food?' Lady Eira asked as Alvaro sat on the end of the lounge closest to Ivy.

Alvaro replied for them both, 'Oh, no thank you, Lady Eira. We had some tea and fruit earlier.'

Lady Eira nodded politely and walked across the room, her dress lightly grazing the floor, before taking a seat on the lounge next to

Alvaro. 'So, what is it you wish to speak to me about, Alvaro? Other than the young girl sitting in my home,' she added with a smile.

'Ah, yes. Lady Eira, this is Miss Ivy.' Lady Eira's eyes widened at the mention of her name, a reaction similar to Alvaro's when they first met, and not unlike the rest of the folk in this godforsaken kingdom upon seeing her. Ivy's thumb rubbed the band of her ring. 'She arrived in Harukai yesterday,' Alvaro continued. 'I found her near the beach at the edge of the kingdom and brought her back to my home.'

'How did she get here?' Lady Eira asked.

'A tunnel in the Realm Divider opened.'

Lady Eira's brows furrowed, but she didn't reply.

Alvaro continued, 'When she was ready to leave, I took her to the beach and sent her on her way with Theon of the Noa Kingdom. I thought that was it, but they returned shortly after the sun had gone down. Ivy was ... quite distraught. I am not aware of the details, but what I do know is that Ivy did not plan to return to Harukai.' He looked down at his twiddling fingers. 'And the tunnel is officially closed.'

Officially closed? Ivy thought. *What does he mean by* officially *closed?*

'Are you sure the tunnel is closed?' Lady Eira asked.

'Yes, I am certain. I found a moment early this morning to speak to Theon, and he informed me it closed last night.'

Lady Eira met Ivy's gaze. 'Would you like to explain what happened?'

'Does it matter?' Ivy asked without thinking. 'I just want to get back home.'

'Miss Ivy,' Alvaro answered. 'You tried last night. The tunnel is closed.'

'I know. But can't you just open it again?'

Alvaro and Lady Eira glanced at each other, then turned back to Ivy. 'I am afraid we cannot do that,' Alvaro explained.

Ivy's heart skipped a beat. 'What do you mean? Someone must've opened it. How else did I get here?'

'I do not know how the tunnel appeared. But no one in this world is capable of opening the rock wall.'

Officially closed ...

Her lungs were caught in the tightening tendril, each of her breaths releasing at such a pace they began to overlap. *Officially closed ...* She needed to get home, find her mother. There was no other option for her, no other way of life if she was here without her only family. 'But ... but I need to get back. My mum, she's ...'

'She's what?' Lady Eira interrupted.

'I don't know! I don't know what happened.' Waves roiled inside her, uncontrollable tears escaping and creating a salty path down her cheeks. 'My dad, he ... he took her. Or something. He had a dagger to her throat and took her away. I don't know why.' Those waves washed over the tendril that gripped her organs tight, but it didn't release its hold. 'He said he'll find me, or I'll find him, or something like that. Mum told me to come here, to find Alvaro, that I'd be safe.' Ivy sniffed and wiped her face. 'I don't know where he's taken her or why he's taken her. But she's in trouble. I can feel it.'

Neither Alvaro nor Lady Eira said anything.

'And that stupid merfolk threw a dagger at my dad and brought me back here,' Ivy finished.

No one spoke for quite some time. Ivy needed to get home; there had to be a way. The tunnel opened yesterday—it could open again. But even if it couldn't, there was surely another way for her to return home. She wouldn't accept any other answer. There *had* to be a way back. 'How do I get home?'

'Like Alvaro said, no one here can open the tunnel.'

'That's not what I asked.'

Lady Eira sighed. 'I understand that you have been through quite an ordeal, Ivy, but there is no way for you to return home. I'm sorry.'

Officially closed ...

No, this couldn't be right. 'How does that work? The tunnel opened! It can open again. Just open the damn tunnel!'

'If there is a way for us to open it,' Alvaro said, 'then we do not know of it.'

Short, sharp bursts of oxygen entered Ivy's lungs in an uneven pattern. There had to be a way back. 'So, what? That's it? I'm ... I'm actually stuck here?' More tears threatened to break free at the thought of never being able to return home. Never being able to see her mother again.

A tear fell down Alvaro's cheek. 'I am afraid so.'

'No.' Her familiar tendril found its way into her throat, each uneven gasp of air caught in the tendril's path. She stood. 'No, I won't accept that. The last memory I have of my mum is her being taken away from me with a dagger pressed to her throat.' Alvaro tensed. 'I can't just leave her there.' Neither of them answered. Ivy looked directly at Alvaro and continued, 'Mum told me to find you, Alvaro. That has to mean something. Why would she say that? Do you at least know *why* she was taken? You must know something.'

Alvaro lifted his gaze to her. 'I have been trying to figure that out for over sixteen years. If I knew, I would not withhold the information from you.'

In her frazzled state, Ivy couldn't entirely comprehend what Alvaro said. She instead turned to Lady Eira, who had been silent for some time. 'What about you? You're the lady of this kingdom. Surely you know something, right? About the tunnel, about my mother, anything!'

Lady Eira shook her head. 'I don't ... I don't know.'

Since her mother knew Harukai, knew Alvaro, she had hoped that maybe he or Lady Eira would at least know something that could help. But clearly, she was wrong.

'Miss Ivy.' Alvaro stood and reached for her.

She stepped back, choking on a sob, and asked, 'Can either of you help me?'

'Miss Ivy,' he repeated. 'I have been trying to break through that wall to rescue your mother for sixteen years. I do not know how that tunnel appeared yesterday, but there is no known way for us mere folk to open it. There is no way for us to get to the human realm.'

Ivy took another step back. 'What?' she whispered. What did he mean? He'd been trying to save her mother for sixteen years. What did that *mean*? She reached behind and found the door. There was no way home. *No no no no no no.* 'I need some air,' she managed to mutter through her sobs.

'Miss Ivy, please.'

She opened the door and ran.

FOURTEEN

Fluttering wings. Hooves and claws smooshing the soil. Mounds of moss and grass. Mushrooms large and small, rainbow flowers. Towering trees, falling vines.

Everything blurred past.

The tendril coiled tighter around Ivy's insides, constricting the flow of oxygen. There were only two locations in this kingdom Ivy was remotely familiar with: Alvaro's home and the beach. And she certainly wasn't going back to Alvaro's home.

Heads turned. Folk jumped out of the way for the terrified human girl running through the kingdom. She swerved through the market stalls. That beating rhythm rode alongside each of her steps. It was difficult for folk to move out of the way in such a tight space, but Ivy had no remorse for whoever she ran into. She just kept running.

Based on yesterday's journey through the kingdom, she assumed she was moving in the general direction of the beach.

This can't be happening. Her feet sunk into the terrain. With each step, the crashing of waves got louder, assuring her she was going the right way. More waves roiled inside her, thrashing against her bones, searching for escape.

I'm not trapped here. Leaves crunched beneath her feet as she entered the forest, finding herself on a path similar to the one she met Alvaro on. That was definitely near the beach, so she must be close. Flowers watched her breeze past them, but she paid them no mind.

Tighter and tighter the tendril coiled until white sand revealed itself at the end of the pathway, clear blue water crashing against the shore, mimicking her emotions. She broke free of the forest and the watchful gazes of the flowers. Her feet thumped across the sand as she sprinted closer to the comfort of the ocean. She needed to escape this spacious enclosure, this outdoor prison.

Her heart beat rapidly. Those waves screaming inside her began to climb up her throat. Ivy fell to her knees at the water's edge and released the ocean within. The water shuddered at her cries. She choked on her screams. Salty tears stained her face.

That tendril inside her finally loosened its grip and she was able to breathe in the salty sea air. She buried her hands in the sand and released fistfuls across the water, the white crystals seeping beneath her bandages and into her cuts, but she pushed through the pain. Again she threw more sand, aiming for the indestructible wall. Of course, the sand landed nowhere near the rocks, but she didn't care.

Waves lashed in response to her aggression, smacking against the rock wall to show they were on her side. She kept throwing sand until her tears dried. Until her arms ached. Until her throat was hoarse.

Ivy never believed in deities, or Gods, or warlords. But now, she threw her flaming anger at the monstrous force before her. The rocks she used to climb and dive off every weekend back home. The rocks that were once a comforting presence, now turned into a malignant beast.

Over and over again, Ivy grabbed fistfuls of sand and threw them across the water. 'Screw you!' What more could she say to a towering pile of rocks? 'Why would you do this? What is wrong with you? Why would you split apart a mother and daughter? How heartless can you be?'

Apparently, a lot more.

'I will break you!' Ivy grunted and threw one last handful of sand.

Ivy wasn't entirely sure who she was threatening. She was well aware that the rocks were not sentient, that the rocks did not force her away from her mother. But something, or rather, some*one*, had. And whoever that was, that's who she was speaking to. There had to be a way back—she wouldn't accept any other answer. She could try climbing the wall again, but what was the point? Her hands were bandaged with fresh cuts that wouldn't allow her to grip the wall. And even if she could climb to the top now, what would she find? If it was truly that simple, wouldn't everyone know? Wouldn't Alvaro know?

'Miss Ivy.' Ivy turned to the voice, away from the rock wall. As if summoned, Alvaro approached from the trees and the path of fallen leaves. 'I thought I would find you here.'

Her breathing slowed; air rushed into her lungs. People tend to forget how much breath you lose when crying until it's over.

Alvaro sat beside her. 'Unfortunately, threatening the wall will not help you. Trust me, I have tried. Although, it is always good to express your emotions, in any form they take.'

Ivy sniffled.

'Even if that form is throwing sand across the ocean hoping to injure the towering rock wall that divides the realms.' He sighed. Waves lapped against his hooves and the skirt covering Ivy's knees. 'I am deeply sorry for what has happened to you. I ...' He swallowed, then continued, 'I can only imagine how ... heart-wrenching this must be. How overwhelmed with emotions you must feel. I know how difficult it is to accept that there is no way through that wall.'

Ivy choked as another tear fell.

'But you are right, Miss Ivy. Although us folk may not willingly be able to open that tunnel, it did open. And it has opened before. Which implies there must be a way to open it again. And if you let me, I will do whatever I can to help you get back home and find your mother.'

I have been trying to break through that wall to rescue your mother for sixteen years.' She looked at Alvaro, who was looking out across the now calm ocean. *'Find Alvaro. He will keep you safe.'*

'You know my mum.'

He looked down at her. 'Yes, I do.' His gaze wandered across her features; a smile formed. 'And you look just like her.'

Her mother knew Alvaro. She knew Harukai. Had clearly *been* to this land if she and Alvaro knew each other. And Alvaro had spent almost all of Ivy's life trying to bring her mother back to this world.

She wasn't sure she *wanted* the answer to her next question, but she knew she *needed* the answer. She asked, her voice trembling, 'How? How do you know her?'

Alvaro took a deep breath. 'She comes from this world. We ... we spent a lot of time together.'

Ivy turned away and watched the waves soaking her skirt. He must be lying. Dorothea was from the human world, just as she was. Her mother would've told her if she was from here. But why would Alvaro lie about something like that?

'I have longed for my home, for my family ... You can't keep us here forever, Elias. We don't belong here ... That's her home.'

Was that why he was being so nice to her? Did that mean her mother was a folk? But she looked so ... human. And if her mother was a folk, did that mean ...

Ivy shook her head and chuckled, looking across the ocean to one of the two islands in the distance. 'No, she's not. She's human.' Alvaro didn't confirm nor deny. She felt his gaze on her, assessing her. 'She's not from here.'

Was she telling Alvaro that, or herself? Her mother knew Harukai. She and Alvaro knew each other. And Alvaro had apparently spent sixteen years trying to bring her mum back from the human realm. What did that mean? Had her mum been trapped over there all that time, just as Ivy was trapped here now?

She knew she should ask Alvaro all those questions and gain some sort of insight, but there was something else she desperately wanted to know. It certainly wasn't as important, and the seed of guilt was planted in her at the thought of wanting to know this particular thing as opposed to more about her mum's situation. But despite that, she wiped her tear-stricken face and asked, 'Hypothetically, if Mum was from here, what would that mean for me?'

Alvaro sighed and followed Ivy's gaze across the water. 'It means you are also from this world. It means you are not human, Miss Ivy.'

'That's her home.'

Ivy allowed the information to seep into her pores and weigh her down as if she were still carrying her scuba tank. *This isn't true,* her thoughts lied. She was born and raised on the other side of that wall, where her mother was currently being held captive by her father. Or at least, she assumed she was captive.

'I don't believe you,' she told Alvaro. 'I've spent my entire life on the other side of that rock wall. A rock wall I've dived off more times than I can count. A rock wall I thought was just a damn rock wall and nothing more. I am *human.* I mean, I don't even have wings or hooves or anything.' She gestured around herself. 'I don't *look* like I'm from here, so clearly I'm not.'

Alvaro merely nodded and said, 'If that is what you believe.'

'It is what I believe,' Ivy tried to convince herself.

But was it truly what she believed? Her mum and Alvaro *knew* each other. How else could that be if her mother wasn't from here? She supposed she could have visited Harukai, just as Ivy had yesterday. But that didn't explain why Alvaro had spent sixteen years trying to figure out why she was taken when that only happened last night.

Questions stumbled over each other in their rush to the front of her mind. 'I'm not saying I believe you, because I don't,' she said to Alvaro while lying to herself. She faced him, and he followed suit. 'But ... You say you've spent sixteen years trying to figure out why she was taken. What does that mean? She was taken last night, and I only told you today.' And then, the line of questions broke through the gates like a stampede. 'What happened sixteen years ago? Was she taken from here? Has she been trapped over there all my life? Who took her? Why did they take her? *How* did they take her?' She took another deep breath of the delicious salty sea air and swallowed. 'Tell me everything you know.'

The corner of his lips tilted up as he released a breathy chuckle through his nose. 'You are quite the inquisitive type, just like your mother.' Ivy's heart swelled at his mention of her mum and how he could easily tell their similarities. 'I do know how she was taken; however, you will be disappointed to learn that I do not know much else beyond that.' He looked down, then returned his gaze to the sea. 'For as long as Harukai has thrived, we have been at war with humankind. They have a way to open the rock wall so they can enter our land and ... and abduct our kind.'

'What?'

Alvaro continued, 'This happens every few years, and we still do not know how they have the capability of opening the wall when we do not.' He paused, tears slipping from his eyes. 'Around sixteen years ago, they again entered our home and ...' He choked, before finally finishing, 'and took you and your mother.'

Ivy's breathing slowed. *I have longed for my home, for my family ... You can't keep us here forever, Elias.'* That meant ... It meant Alvaro hadn't lied. Her and her mother were from Harukai. And yet she'd been forced to spend her entire life living as a human because of a war she knew nothing about. Ivy shook her head, hoping the truth would fall out in the tears tumbling down her face and escape her mind.

'This is all too much,' she cried. She didn't want to believe it, but she knew it was true.

'I know. I held off from telling you immediately because I knew it would be a lot for you to take in.'

He was right. This was way too much for anyone to have thrown onto them. But then Ivy remembered how neither him nor Lady Eira had mentioned this earlier. 'Were you ever going to tell me?'

'Of course. But I wanted you to settle in this world first. In all honesty, I did not expect to ever see you again and was quite surprised with your sudden appearance yesterday morning. And when I finally gained the courage to tell you, you wanted to leave.'

'You really thought you would never see us again?'

'Do not get me wrong, Miss Ivy, I certainly tried. But out of all the folk who have been abducted over the years, no one has ever returned. Except you.'

How could that be? For as long as this world had existed, folk had been taken, and yet no one had ever returned. No one knew what happened to them, or why they were taken, or how to bring them back. Everyone gone forever, lost to time. And if that tunnel had never mysteriously appeared yesterday, Ivy and her mum would have been given the same fate.

It didn't make sense.

There was no other way to describe it. It just *didn't make sense.*

And that made Ivy furious, her blood sizzling with anger. 'How have none of you found a way to break through that wall in all the time this world has existed? That's *thousands of years* and no one knows what's happening. Did any of you even *try?*' Ivy stood, now towering over Alvaro, and gestured to the rocks. 'How have *they* managed to get through and you haven't? What have you all been doing?' All her thoughts tumbled out with her rage, causing her to miss the way Alvaro's fists clenched. 'How has this continued for all of existence? Do you not fight them? You said there was a war, yet they keep coming through and doing whatever they want. That's not a war. That sounds like a damn sacrifice or something.'

'I told you—'

'Yeah, I know. You've been trying to bring us back. But that tunnel was open yesterday. You could have gone through and brought my mum back if you care so much.'

Alvaro stood, hunching to match her height—although he still managed to remain taller than her—and raised his voice. 'You have no idea how desperately I longed to do that! But there is no way for me to make it through underwater. I would have died before I even got to the tunnel.'

Ivy flinched at his anger, but it didn't dull hers. 'Isn't there an entire kingdom *underwater*? Why could none of them go through?'

'Because it is *dangerous,* Miss Ivy!' He stood to his full height and ran his hands through his hair. 'These humans are ruthless. We have tried to fight them, but they will slaughter anyone who gets in their way. We have never been on the other side of the wall and lived to tell the tale, so it is not surprising that if anyone had known the tunnel was open that they chose not to go through on the chance their lives would end.'

'I don't know how your world works, Alvaro, but if you're fighting a war, you kind of have to risk your life. Do you not have armies? Soldiers trained to fight and rescue and all that crap?'

'Yes, Miss Ivy, you are right. But we also have to be strategic, and being the general of the Thidin Kingdom's militia, I can say for absolute certainty that we cannot go through mysterious tunnels we have never been through before, not knowing what lies in wait on the other side, without a plan. And a plan takes time to build. That tunnel was only open for a short time, certainly not long enough for such a plan to be created and enacted.'

Ivy's anger slowly dispersed in heaving breaths, as did Alvaro's. She had no more retorts. It was strange arguing with him like that. In the short time she'd known him, he'd been so polite and kind; she hadn't guessed he could speak to anyone in such a way. But there was also passion in his words, his tone, his voice. It wasn't fair for her to question him like that, and yelling at him wouldn't get her the answers she desired.

What had been flaming anger was now dampened sorrow. Ivy flopped on the sand and hugged her legs, crying into her knees. 'I don't know what to do. I'm scared and confused and I ... I just want to be with my mum.' She choked on the last words.

Alvaro sat beside her, and neither of them spoke for some time. The ocean's melody was a comforting tune which reminded her of home, of the waters her mother had taught her to swim in. It brought her back to her eighth birthday, when she had been given her first scuba diving set. Her parents knelt before her and guided her feet into the flippers while she braced herself on their shoulders.

She'd stumbled to the water, unable to run because the flippers were too big for her small feet.

Alvaro's voice brought her back to reality. 'Do you want to know why I was on my way to this beach yesterday when you arrived?'

Her muffled voice mumbled into her knees, 'Why?'

'I was preparing to swim to the rock wall and tear it apart. I had a dagger I was planning on stabbing the wall with. And when that inevitably did not work, I was ready to throw my entire form against those rotten rocks, bruising myself head to toe and tearing my palms until they bled. Just as you did yesterday evening. Just as I do every single day.'

Ivy's heart swelled, her eyes welling with more tears. She looked at him and asked, 'You do that every day, for me and Mum?'

He nodded.

Her eyes found his hands, wrapped in bandages just like hers were. 'Why?' she asked, returning her gaze to his. 'If you know it won't work, why do you still do it?'

'If I stop trying, it means I have given up. And I refuse to give up.'

Ivy didn't know what else to say. Her heart was full. This man, who she barely knew, cared so deeply for her and her mother. So deeply that he physically destroyed himself every day trying to bring them back.

She shuffled onto her knees and threw her arms around his neck. Alvaro flinched at the sudden contact, but did not pull away. 'Thank you,' she mumbled. Then, she felt his arms tighten around her. 'I don't know what to do, Alvaro,' she whispered.

'Neither do I, Miss Ivy. But whatever we do, we will do it together.'

'*H*ow much water?'

'*Ahh ...*' *Her mother reads the box instructions.* 'One hundred millilitres.'

Six-year-old Ivy fills the measuring jug and carefully carries the water to their workstation. Her mum has stepped out of the kitchen but calls out, 'Put it in the bowl and start mixing.' Ivy lifts the heavy jug and pours it into their brownie batter, careful not to spill any. She grabs the spoon and starts mixing the sludge.

Dorothea comes back and looks at the liquified mixture. 'Ivy, how much water did you put in?'

Ivy points to the mark on the jug with a one and three zeros. You read that right: three zeros.

'Oh, no. It was meant to be there.' Her mother points to the mark on the jug with a one and two zeros. One hundred millilitres.

Ivy freezes, looking at the space between one hundred and one thousand millilitres. That's a lot of extra water.

The beautiful sound of her mother's laughter pushes through the concern. 'Well, it's our only box. We may as well bake it.'

Half an hour later, her mum pulls the tray from the oven. Where beautiful brownies are meant to be is actually just a tray of brown water with crispy, burnt edges. Mother and daughter look at the unappealing liquid, then look at each other, and burst into a fit of laughter.

'What's all the fuss?' Her father's voice sneaks through just as he does, a soft smile on his lips.

'We made brownies!' Ivy cheered.

He looks at the sludge. 'Hm. Have you tried them yet?'

Ivy laughs some more. 'No!'

'Well, how will you know if they're any good?' Her father grabs a knife and starts cutting the liquid brownies. And, of course, it doesn't work. 'Hm, let me try something.' He grabs a spoon from the drawer and scoops a water-brownie, offering it to Ivy. She seals her lips and shakes her head. Her father shrugs, and brings the spoon to his lips, immediately spitting the brownie back into the tray. Laughter coats the room.

FIFTEEN

Ivy spent the next three days inside a tree.

She slept on a tear-stained pillow at night and spent her days resting on that same pillow, looking out the open window to the trees surrounding the empty clearing, the strip of ocean teasing her from above the treetops. Alvaro brought her food and water and tea, and every time he did, he would ask if she wanted to sit with him downstairs or go for a walk. Or even just bathe.

She did not.

The only time she left the room was to use the bathroom. Or rather, *not* use the bathroom, since apparently, they didn't exist in this world. At least, they didn't exist in Alvaro's home. The forest was her bathroom, but she had barely eaten or drunk enough these last few days to warrant going more than once or twice a day.

On the first of those three nights, after she had screamed at the God-like rock wall, she stared out the open window of the spare room and wished to the stars. Wished to be brought home, wished to be with her mother, wished for them both to be safe, wherever that was. Yet here she stayed, three days later, still trapped in this foreign land. A foreign land that was her home, according to her mother and Alvaro, but that didn't feel like such a place.

She didn't want to eat or drink or talk or even sleep. She *especially* didn't want to sleep. Sleep brought the memories of that night to the surface without her control, forcing her to drown in the memory of her mother with a dagger to her throat, before she woke choking on air. The only thing Ivy wanted was the one thing she didn't have: her mother. Well, other than her home, her phone, her clothes, and all her belongings. But none of that mattered anymore.

If she didn't have her own family, her own blood, then what was the point? She was trapped in a wondrous world—a world she longed to explore if the circumstances weren't so dour. She wished to tell her mum about the beautiful flowers, the tunnel leading to the kingdom's sector, the fauns and fairies and harpies and centaurs, and the fact that there was an entire kingdom underwater. She wanted to tell her how she was currently living in a tree of all places. But did her mum already know all those details about this world? Had she once lived in a tree, just as Alvaro did?

Those questions didn't matter. She couldn't bring herself to feel excited, to see this unique world. All she could do was cry.

It wasn't until what she believed was mid-afternoon on the third day (she hadn't found any clocks and wasn't particularly well-trained in telling time based on the sun) that Ivy finally decided to leave the bedroom—for reasons other than relieving herself. She was still wearing the same clothes she wore the day after she lost her mother, and they held her like a straitjacket, clinging to her like sweat clings to skin. Her muscles fidgeted, itching to escape the fabric cage. Her breathing quickened like she was trapped in a corset; although, Ivy wouldn't know what that felt like aside from portrayals in movies.

She rushed to strip, the shirt tangling in her curls. The skirt would have been easier if not for the belt; her fingers fumbled on the clasp. Her heart beat wildly. But after a few attempts, the belt finally released, and Ivy threw the skirt to the ground. The undergarments were the last items to free her. The boots were already gone, the only thing she managed to remove three days ago before her wallowing began.

Now completely naked, she faced the mirror. Sunlight streamed in through the open window behind her, bathing her in its rays. She'd been staring out that window for three consecutive days and knew no one would ever be walking past, so she didn't care to close it now.

Although her figure was practically the same as it was a few short days ago, her lack of substance was noticeable. Her cheeks had started to cave—although, the dimple in her left cheek re-mained—and dark circles shadowed her eyes. Lips, once a bright pink, now blended into her paler-than-usual dark skin. The tendril inside her that had lingered these few days caressed her flesh. It didn't suffocate or choke her, but it was present, reminding her it wasn't leaving anytime soon. Reminding her it had never appeared before she visited Harukai, as though this world had birthed her grief, her fear, her sorrow.

What was she like before Harukai? She spent her weekends ex-ploring the ocean, always eager to make new discoveries. That urge to explore still lingered, but it twisted with the friendly, comforting tendril inside her. Both warring with each other, attempting to pull Ivy to their side: live her old life and explore this fantastical world, or step into her new one coated in loss and trauma? Surely, she could do both, but the gauntness in her features told her otherwise. Each aspect of her old life, her *human* life, had faded like the colour in her skin, had slimmed like the plumpness in her cheeks. Now all that was left was a husk, each fragment of her being vanishing and leaving her empty like the shells that lined the dresser. Her entire life, she'd been nothing more than human, but that belief had been taken from her like her mother had been taken. Like both *her* and her mother had been taken.

Her eyes travelled past her face, past her breasts, to the small plumpness of her lower belly that still remained. Ivy turned and noticed the roundness in her backside had also seemingly stayed the same. Her lips formed a smile. That was where her old life lived, still within her, still a part of her, but now accompanied by her new experiences. Despite everything she had gone through in such a short time, despite all she had lost, some of her would always stay the same.

A clean towel lay folded on the drawers; Alvaro had left it for when she was ready to bathe. She wrapped it around herself, then rummaged for some clean clothes, hoping to find something less constricting; she was unsuccessful. Ivy settled for a similar skirt to the previous one, the pattern a gradient colour of autumn leaves, and a small brown linen top, hoping that wouldn't be as suffocating as the other shirt. She refused to add a belt to the ensemble.

Her hair fell in her face as she leant forward to stuff the clothes—along with some undergarments—into a linen bag that was discarded in the closet. She grabbed her hair band that lay amongst the seashells and made to pull her hair into a low ponytail, but as she pushed her hands over her scalp, she felt something pointy on either side of her head. She released her hair, letting it fall over her shoulders, and grasped the pointy things, feeling whatever they were until her fingers stopped at ears. Then, her fingers moved up her ears until they reached ...

She stepped closer to the mirror and pushed her hair aside until her ear was in full view. And right where the top of her ear should be rounded, was a long, pointed tip. A single tear slipped down her cheek. Alvaro had told her she was from this land, but she supposed some hidden part of her that even she couldn't access had believed she was still human because she didn't have any folk-like features. But now, there was no denying she was a folk. Would other features slowly appear? She hoped so, to at least know exactly who she was. Of course, she could ask Alvaro—since he'd known her and her mother, Ivy assumed he would know what race she was. But she'd barely adjusted to the fact that she wasn't human; did she really want to know *exactly* who she was just yet?

Ivy slung the linen bag over her shoulder, leaving her hair unbound and her new identity partially unwound, before looking downstairs and climbing down the ladder. The corner of the towel was tucked in tight, but she was wearing nothing underneath, so needed visual confirmation that no one was nearby. She made a mental note to always wear something underneath a towel.

Her feet lightly thudded as she landed on the heartwood floor, and she turned around, expecting a greeting from Alvaro, but he was nowhere to be seen. She knew he'd been leaving during the day, but didn't know when. He'd mentioned he was the general of the militia; she supposed he had responsibilities in that regard.

Ivy opened the cupboard where the soap bars were kept and found the one she had used the other day sitting beside another, very used soap bar. She grabbed the soap and headed outside. Ivy was still cautious about the possibility of people noticing her, despite how secluded Alvaro's home and bathing pond were. She scanned the clearing, but couldn't see any lurking eyes, so continued on her way. The grass was soft beneath her feet, nothing like the dry grass at home. Every small detail about this place had her thinking of home, but she needed to push those thoughts aside. Yes, she would find a way back to her mother, but this was her home now—whether temporary or permanent.

Soft grass led to even softer soil. Walking through a forest wearing nothing but a bath towel was something Ivy wasn't sure she would ever get used to. Flowers and mushrooms lined the mushy path, always watching her. She took deep breaths in through her nose and out through her mouth, breathing in the rich scents of soil, leaves, and water. The small part of this world she had seen so far was truly magnificent. The ocean was her true place of comfort—at least, it had been before that dreaded night—but now, the elements of this forest land seeped into her core.

Once again, the pond looked like a thin layer of ice rested atop it. Ivy threw a pebble and watched the ripples travel in a circle out towards the edge. She placed the bag of clothes on a nearby mushroom top and found another taller mushroom to lean against while she untied her bandages. After she'd thrown sand at the rock wall the other day, Alvaro had cleaned and rebandaged her wounds, removing the sand from her cuts. Deep cuts remained with some scabbing starting to form that ached to be scratched—a constant reminder of what had happened.

Ivy grabbed the soap with just her fingers, careful not to grasp it in her palm and irritate her injuries, and only let her towel fall once she was sure no one was watching. Her toes graced the water, perfect coolness coating her skin. It wasn't the ocean, but it was close enough. She dove beneath the surface, staying underneath as water held her in a mother's embrace that she never thought she'd crave so dearly. She wanted to stay there, in the water's comforting hold; anything was better than the reality of her mother's absence. But she broke through the surface and took a deep breath.

Aside from her breathing, the only sounds were the rustling of leaves and the rippling of water. The surrounding trees were like natural privacy, providing a sense of ease that she was truly safe and alone. And as Ivy bathed in solitude, her muscles relaxed, and a feeling she couldn't quite place overcame her, spreading like a comforting warmth, as though the water were spiked with it.

A trail of soil followed Ivy into Alvaro's home, up the ladder, and across the spare room until it stopped in front of the dresser, where

Ivy stood clad in the new outfit she had picked. The skirt was marvellous, just like the last one—loose and billowy but still form-fitting and comfortable, with the gradient colours of deep red and orange dancing together across the fabric. The brown linen top she wore hugged her breasts and loosely gripped her bodice, stopping just above the skirt. Frilled sleeves rested below her shoulders.

Ivy wondered again how these clothes fit her almost perfectly, and now that thought escalated: Why did Alvaro have them? Who did they belong to? Where were they now? She sighed; more questions she didn't need clogging her mind at the moment. She let the mystery curl away like a sleeping cat, patiently waiting for its reveal.

Her damp hair dangled like vines, stopping past the waistline of her skirt and covering her pointed ears. Earlier, she had been desperate to free herself from the confines of her last outfit, but now that she was clean and dressed, she had no idea what to do. She needed to find a way out of this land, but Alvaro wasn't here to help, and she didn't know where to start on her own. However, no matter what she did, what she needed now was to leave this suffocating tree and clearing.

Ivy slipped on the same brown boots from the other day, found a cloth downstairs, and cleaned her path of soil. Then, she rummaged through the kitchen cupboards until she found bandages to wrap her hands. Once she was done, she decided to make her way towards the kingdom. As she followed the path of nature through the tunnel made from trees, she remembered a stone building she had stumbled upon her first day in Harukai, filled with books lining scattered shelves. She supposed books were a great place to start with finding information.

Lavender-coloured vines poured down from overhanging trees, petals and leaves falling into her hair and clinging to her curls as she brushed them aside. Sounds of the kingdom slowly filtered in from the end of the tunnel—chatting, clattering, bustling, music. Ivy's steps slowed, fluttering encasing her stomach.

'Is that who I think …'

'We've waited years …'

'It's really you …'

The few times she'd entered the kingdom, the folk had watched her as though she were a goddess, some magnificent being for them to pray to. It was strange, uncomfortable, eerie, unnerving. And why had they spoken as though they'd been expecting her arrival?

More questions. No answers. Her tendril snaked around her lungs without touching them, hovering, ready to squeeze at any moment. Ivy took a step back, deciding to wait for Alvaro to return, but she froze. When would he be back? She hadn't paid attention to the spaces of time between each moment he brought her food. It could be hours before he returned. And she refused to stay in that room any longer, refused to keep looking at the same clearing and trees. She took a deep breath and walked the rest of the way through the tunnel.

A few moments later, Ivy was entering the Thidin Kingdom's market centre. The second she stepped off the path and into the open terrain, heads turned, and eyes widened. She swallowed, trying her best to ignore their gawking, pushing aside the frustratingly calm rhythm in her blood, and instead focused on remembering how to get to the library. But their eyes followed her, seeping beneath her skin as she wandered between the grassy mounds and mushrooms and trees. Ivy couldn't help but look at their ears; all of them were pointed, just like hers, except for centaurs, who's ears resembled that of horses. Faun ears also had tufts of fur at the tips. What could she be? Centaur seemed to be out of the question—and a part of her was thankful for that—but she supposed fairy, harpy, and perhaps even faun were still on the table.

She kept her head down to avoid their stares and ignore their features, following her footsteps and whatever was in her peripheral, until she somehow tripped over nothing and fell straight into a tree.

She stepped back and rubbed her forehead. Her foot fumbled along the grass and leaves in search of whatever had tripped her, but nothing could be found. She really had just tripped over nothing. How embarrassing. She looked up, ready to step around the tree, only to find a folk standing before her, righting himself from his own stumbling.

'Oh, I'm so sorry,' Ivy said.

Brown feathers partially obscured her vision, sprouting from magnificent ruffling wings that sprawled from the folk's back. He folded them in and glared at Ivy, light brown curls hanging in front of his dark eyes. 'Watch where you're going,' he mumbled, before storming away. Despite the slight rudeness in his tone, she smiled. He hadn't gasped at her appearance or made some strange comment about her existence.

Ivy instinctively brushed down her clothes and made her way into the cluster of market stalls, soon finding the spot where the folk had surrounded her in a claustrophobic frenzy just a few days prior. And surrounding her now were folk muttering to themselves or others, pointing and staring at her. Would they ever stop? Or would she have to endure their strange impoliteness for as long as she stayed here?

Not wanting to be their focal point any longer, Ivy quickly charged out of the market and into the forest, their eyes carving into her spine.

Sixteen

Ivy traipsed through the forest, hoping she was going the right way. The only time she had gone through this part of the land was while frantically escaping the folk after her first encounter. Now, she attempted to remember every detail of her journey to the library. That tree had a bloom of five flowers around the roots—two pink, two blue, and a violet—while that one over there had only three flowers with two mushrooms that stood just above Ivy's knees.

It didn't take long for her to find the forest's edge and the cliff that housed the library. She marvelled at the marble structure, crammed into the cavernous cliff face, and made her way towards the grand staircase. But a few steps into the clearing she was pulled away by the sound of soft rainfall and light splashing.

To the right of the library at the edge of the cliff face was a small pond, a waterfall gently pouring down. Stones, saplings, mushrooms, and flowers surrounded the water. She walked over to it, the waterfall calming her. The pond was clearer than a glass of water from home, with seagrass and sand easily visible. Large fish of varying oranges, blacks, and whites swam about, reminding Ivy of Japanese koi from ancient history books. She sat by the water for a moment, watching them live peacefully in their home, with no outside forces controlling what happened next. She dipped her fingers in the water and they instantly swam to her intrusion, greeting her like an old friend.

After some time, Ivy noticed new fish had appeared and some of the older ones had left. She scrunched her brows and looked up the waterfall. Had they really fallen from the top of the cliff? Surely she would have seen them splash into the pond. She watched the fish closely, and sure enough, she spotted another fish—and it certainly didn't fall. It swam out from behind the waterfall. She moved to the back of the pond and there, almost hidden by the waterfall, was a tunnel entrance carved into the cliff, just like the one that brought her to Harukai. Were these fish trapped, too? Or did their tunnel remain open, giving them free access to both sides whenever they felt so inclined?

Memories from the other night flashed in her mind at the sight of that tunnel, of Theon pulling her through the one in the rock wall. Of her swimming for the tunnel only to watch it close right before her eyes.

Ivy abandoned the pond and the memories that resurfaced and walked up the library staircase. As she ascended the stairs, she admired the magnitude of those female statues. Who were they meant to represent? Historical figures, goddesses, or something else entirely?

Beyond the mahogany door, a cylindrical shaft of sunlight shone from the dome ceiling in the centre, highlighting folk scattered across the space reading quietly. Since the library was built *into* the cliff wall, she wondered how much more of it there was to be discovered beyond this main section. Utterly magnificent.

Knock knock.

The same faun stood behind the counter waiting patiently with a smile on her face. *I was told you would need these ...* Nerves shuddered through Ivy at the faun's—Leyrah's— comment about the stack of books she'd tried to give Ivy.

'Uh, hi,' she greeted. Who had told Leyrah the books were for her? Or a better question: *Why* had she been told to give Ivy those books? Was it the same reason the folk of the kingdom seemingly knew her, praised her, had been expecting her?

The dots connected easily enough: Ivy was clearly *someone* to these people, but she refused to believe she could be anyone, or anything, more than herself. Her little tendril shifted, reminding her she was no longer who she once was. She had already changed, and she would continue to change.

She just didn't know it yet.

Ivy met Leyrah at the counter, took a deep breath, and asked, 'I believe you have some books for me?'

Leyrah's smile grew wider than Ivy thought possible, before she ducked beneath the countertop and returned with the same two books, larger than Ivy had ever seen. 'How ...' she started to say. How what? How would she carry them? How long would it take her to read each book? Her fingers traced the worn, peeling leather of each spine, wrinkled with age. 'How did you know I would need these?' she finally asked.

Leyrah handed Ivy a piece of parchment that read, *I was told you would need them.*

'But who told you?' Ivy dared to ask, her tendril coiling tighter at the suspense of what the answer might be. Who could have possibly known she would need these books to help her return home and find her mum? Her situation was too particular for it to be coincidence or a misunderstanding.

But what if that's not what the books were for?

Are you who I think you are?

'It's really you …'

'We've waited years …'

The tendril tightened; each of her breaths now inhaled in a jagged pattern with no real rhyme or reason. Leyrah was in the midst of scribbling her answer when Ivy asked, 'Why do I need these books?'

Leyrah paused, scanning what she had already written, then nodded and finished her note, handing it to Ivy.

These books have been kept aside for longer than I have been alive. All I know is that they are for you.

So many questions, and a part of Ivy desperately wanted to ask more, but she was also … afraid. Her entire existence had shifted, and it didn't seem to be slowing. What did it all mean? Why had the books been kept aside for so long, specifically for her? And why did everyone seemingly know who she was—or rather, know who she was supposed to be? Did they know her because she was one of them? Or for another reason? Everyone here certainly knew more than she did about herself, and that was what scared her the most.

'Why?' Ivy asked again. 'Why were they left for me?'

Leyrah's smile saddened, and she shrugged.

Ivy sighed, defeated but slightly relieved that not *everyone* knew more about herself than she did. She needed to know, but more than that, she needed to get home. The dagger Elias held to Dorothea's throat was confirmation enough that her mother was in trouble. She needed to find her way back and find her mother. *Then* she could figure out what the hell was happening.

SEVENTEEN

The sound of relaxed waves brushing the sand caressed Ivy's soul. She had spent the remainder of the day in the library reading the books from Leyrah but was yet to figure out why she needed them.

She'd started with one called *The History of the Divided Realms*, hoping for information on the rock wall and how to travel between each world. But rather than read every word on every page from start to finish—Did you see the size of those books? It would have taken her days, perhaps even weeks!—she flipped through the book, reading each title, heading, and subheading, until a section titled 'How the Division Came to Be' stood out, stating:

After the humans caused such destruction among the folk, the Maidens took it upon themselves to erect the Dividing Rocks. Together, they mustered every ounce of their magic and built the Realm Divider. It ascended from beneath the sands of the Noa Kingdom, stopping just shy of the Thidin Kingdom's treetops.

Not only did the Maidens build the wall, but they also imbued it with magic to segment Harukai from Earth. A magic unrelated to the elements. Power that transcends space.

Now, Ivy stood on the shore of the beach, that same wall taunting her. These Maidens—whoever they were—had built the wall using *magic*. She'd prepared to start reading the other book, *A Maiden's History*, to figure out who these Maidens were, when Leyrah informed her the library was closing. Since she'd barely been able to carry the stack around the library, let alone all the way back to Alvaro's home, she'd decided to leave them with Leyrah.

Ivy allowed the picturesque sand to carry her to the water's edge, the ocean reflecting the pinks and oranges of sunset. She needed a moment to herself by the water before returning to Alvaro's home.

As the sea pulled away from the shore, seashells were revealed half-buried in the damp sand. She kicked off her boots away from the water and stepped into the lapping waves, only stopping when the bottom of her skirt was submerged. A breath of salty sea breeze filled her lungs, each particle twirling and embracing, before being freed in an exhale. Fish swam around her feet beneath the clear-blue water. Ivy wanted nothing more than to dive in and twirl with them, but that tendril strangely gripped her lungs at the thought. She hadn't been in the ocean since the night she'd been brought back here, since she'd been dragged through that tunnel, since she'd attacked the rocks after her escape had vanished before her eyes. The ocean had suffocated her then, just as the thought of going back in suffocated her now.

'Hi.'

Ivy gasped and looked towards the voice. A certain merfolk lingered a few metres away, only visible from his shoulders up, his copper hair slicked behind him. He'd looked just like that when they had parted ways on the other side of the rock wall, before he threw a knife at her dad. Before he brought her back here against her will. He didn't move, so Ivy didn't either.

'What are you doing here?' she asked.

'Ah, I live here,' Theon replied, one corner of his lips slowly turning upwards. The beginnings of a smirk.

Fine, Ivy thought. *He wants to be smart; I can be smart, too.* 'Actually, I believe you live down there.' She gestured to the grand ocean behind him.

With half a smirk on his face, he said, 'And how do you know that?'

Ivy did not return the smile. 'It was an educated guess. So, I'll ask again: What are you doing *here*?'

Theon's smile dropped. 'I wanted to see you.'

'Why?'

'It's been a few days. I want to know if you're okay, after ... everything.'

'Ahh, yes. After the'—she assessed Theon, still beneath the water, but remembered the scales that coated his body; from this distance, she could see some speckled along the sides of his face, his fin-like ears poking above his hair—'red-haired fish-man dragged me away from my home, my mother, against my will. And not just dragged me away but took me to a completely different world where I'm now trapped. Oh, and that was all after you *threw a dagger at my dad.* I'm fine, thanks for asking.'

It wasn't until she finished speaking that Ivy realised Theon had moved closer. Clearly having reached the sand bank, he stood, slowly rising above the ocean's surface, water dripping down his scales. Her eyes followed those droplets, marvelling at how they shone against the blues and greens of his scales. Scales that still partially covered his torso, but in a different pattern than the first time they'd met. Could he really move the scales as he saw fit? With the sun setting just to the right and almost completely hidden by the horizon, he was cast in a partial silhouette, but his scales shimmered, allowing her to see some of his features. With his hair slicked back, she could see his fin-like ears: nothing like hers. Even if they were, she knew she wasn't merfolk—she'd spent her entire life in the water and remained human-like.

'I had to bring you back here,' he explained.

'You had to? What's that supposed to mean? You could've just left me there. You *should've* left me there.'

Theon raised his voice and took a step towards Ivy. 'I was protecting you. You were in danger.'

Ivy scoffed. 'And that's why you had to bring me into an entirely different world?'

'Your dad held a dagger to your mum's throat,' he exclaimed. 'Is that not enough danger for you?'

Suddenly, Theon was only inches away. Her breath hitched at the proximity. Ivy stepped backwards, stopping once she was out of the water. He was right, of course, but she couldn't let him know that.

'You were already taking me away before he did that,' she retorted, although the temporary distraction from Theon stole her conviction. 'And besides, he only had that dagger because of you.'

He slowly released a deep sigh. 'I was protecting you from him.'

'And because of that, my mum is most likely in danger now. Thank you so very much,' she added sarcastically. Except, it was the truth. And that thought had the tendril inside her curling around her lungs.

The wind picked up, spinning above the ocean and picking up water in the process. Waves tumbled over each other with no rhyme or reason.

With Theon's face cast in shadow, it was only thanks to the shining scales along the sides of his face that she could see the way his jaw clenched. 'If I had left you there, do you really think you could have saved her?' He was at the edge of the ocean now, dissipating waves gracing the scales on his feet. 'He's a grown man with a weapon. You're nothing but flesh and bones. There's no muscle there, no strength beneath that skin.'

'You know nothing about my strength,' she said, trying to stop her voice from trembling. A trembling voice was the last thing she needed, especially when she was trying to prove her strength. But, again, he was right, and he probably knew it this time.

Now it was Theon's turn to scoff. 'Oh, really? I am captain of the Noa Kingdom's legion. I'm trained to assess someone's strength just by looking at them, to determine whether I can defeat them. And you?' His gaze wandered down her body like she was his prey, a snarl plastered to his lips. He lowered his voice as he said, 'I could put you down quicker than you knew what was happening.' He stepped out of the water, and Ivy walked back up the shore with Theon stalking her until her back was pressed against a tree. 'Tell me, Ivy. If I pulled my dagger out right now and tried to attack you, what would you do? Fight? Or run?' He was mere inches away, but this time Ivy couldn't step back any further.

Heat coursed between them despite the sea breeze brushing against her skin. Ivy had to tilt her head back to look at him, and although the sun was setting, his scales shone enough for her to see his eyes, their blue depths so easy for her to drown in.

But the snarl drenching his lips ... His taunting, and lack of apology for what he'd done. He claimed to care, but she knew he didn't. He claimed he was protecting her—and perhaps he was—but was that the only reason? Or did he secretly have some strange, obscure, delusional ulterior motive?

Her hands found his chest, his scales momentarily bringing her back to when she'd first touched them just a few days ago, and she shoved him back. 'Who do you think you are?' Ivy snapped, internally smiling at the way his brows pulled together, and how his snarl fell from his lips. 'You don't get to bring me back here against my will, claim you were protecting me, and then speak to me like I'm just some filthy, weak human.'

She stalked towards him, just as he had done, anger burning beneath her skin. Whether her assumptions were accurate or not, she didn't care. This rage for Theon had sparked the day she woke after he'd brought her here, and now that she was with him, all she longed to do was let it out.

'I don't need you to remind me of what I went through. In case you forgot, I was there. What I need you to do is leave me alone.' She shoved him again, and he stumbled back to the ocean's edge, waves crashing in their rush to greet him. Her retorts had run dry, but her fury still simmered.

He lingered by the water, his scales illuminating him in soft blues and greens. She expected him to say something, and maybe she wanted him to say something just so she could yell at him more, but he stayed silent.

'Just ...' Ivy watched his waiting form, his facial scales revealing his downturned eyes, which caught her off guard. 'Just leave me alone,' she finished with less conviction than she wanted, before storming through the trees.

Eighteen

'Miss Ivy, there you are.'

Ivy entered the clearing of Alvaro's home, but not from the tunnel of curved trees and flowers. She'd decided to follow the path through the forest Alvaro had taken her down on her first day in Harukai. The walk along the fallen leaves had allowed her time to simmer, the bubbling heat of her fury dissipating with each step.

To her right, a few feet away from where she exited the forest, Alvaro crouched by what she could only assume was a firepit—a bed of kindling surrounded by a circle of rocks with a small spit above.

'I was about to cook dinner,' he continued. 'But since you are up and about still, perhaps we could wander through the Tarad.'

'What's the Tarad?' she asked.

'The area we walked past on our way to see Lady Eira the other day. With all the stalls.'

Ah, the market centre. The same area the folk had stared at Ivy and worshipped her, even when with Alvaro. Her tendril slithered between her organs at the thought of being stared at once more. Beneath her bandages, her palms began to sweat. 'I'm not sure I want to be gawked at anymore,' Ivy said, attempting a light-hearted chuckle, and made her way to the front door.

Alvaro spoke as she passed him, 'I feel that the Tarad would be a great experience for you. We will not be there for long. We can have something to eat and enjoy the festivities for a bit.'

'Festivities?'

'Oh, just some singing and dancing. I feel it would be good for you to truly experience the life of us folk, especially since we do not know how long you will be here for. Besides, you are one ...' He sighed, then finished with, 'It may reduce some of your stress.'

Ivy knew what he almost said: she's one of them, despite her lack of any distinguishing folk-like features. But aside from that, he was right. Although she refused to admit it, the truth was she could be here for weeks. It sounded like it could be a fun evening, and since she really was one of them—which her new pointed ears seemed to confirm—it might be good to experience how they lived. But their eyeballing ...

'Will they stare?' Ivy asked.

Alvaro stood from the firepit and made his way over to her. 'I am not normally a violent type, Miss Ivy. Only when I need to be. But I will *personally* see to it that they do not stare. Even if violence is the only answer,' he added with a small smile.

Ivy laughed—not chuckled but truly laughed. Her first real laugh in Harukai. She hadn't thought that was something she would ever be able to do again. A weight lifted—not too much, but enough to notice—as though some of her worries had in fact already been relieved, just from that small laughter.

'I mean, you could also just tell them not to stare.'

Alvaro leant down, glancing around as though making sure no one else would hear, despite them being the only two people in the vicinity, and whispered, 'That would be too easy.'

He turned towards the garden tunnel, but Ivy stopped him. 'Wait.' She had no one in this world to turn to except him, and she wanted to tell someone about her pointed ears. But what could Alvaro do about it? She knew what it meant: she was a folk. It just didn't tell her *what* folk she was. And she wasn't entirely certain she wanted to know just yet. She was still trying to process the fact she wasn't human; she wasn't sure she was ready to discover just how unhuman she was.

'Miss Ivy?' Alvaro waited for her to continue.

'I, uh ...' Her voice trembled. 'I found something this morning.' Ivy pushed her hair behind her ear and turned her head to the side to reveal the new pointed tip.

'What is it, exactly, that you are showing me, Miss Ivy?'

'My ears. They're ...' She faced him and noticed his own pointed ears either side of his head, with fur covering their tips. Of course, she realised, all folk had pointed ears. 'Human ears aren't pointed,' she explained. 'Mine have always been round, but I noticed this morning they'd changed.'

A sad smile formed on his lips, but he didn't say anything.

'I'm really not human, am I?' She knew the answer already, of course. But she hoped it would be slightly easier for her to accept if someone else confirmed the truth.

That wasn't the case.

'No, Miss Ivy, you are not.'

Tears Ivy didn't know were waiting broke free, and she fell forward, her head landing on Alvaro's chest. She wasn't sure why she sought comfort in him. Perhaps because her mother had told her he would keep her safe, or maybe it was purely because he was *there*, but as his arms wrapped around her, her body fell against him a tiny bit more.

She wasn't human. She'd never been human. But now she was stuck in this strange limbo, because she didn't seem to be entirely folk, either. She assumed if her ears grew in that all her other folk-like features—whatever they may be—would appear, too. But perhaps pointed ears were all she had. Would that at least make her partially human?

That didn't add up. She and her mum had been taken from Harukai, implying she'd been born here. Which meant her father wasn't human.

'That man is not—'

That man was not her father. The man who had raised her—and the same man who had held a dagger to her mum's throat—wasn't her father. Ivy wasn't sure if it was comforting to know that at least her own father hadn't acted that way, or distressing to know that she'd been raised to believe he was her father. And if he wasn't her father, then who was? What race of folk was he? What race of folk was her mother? And what race of folk was she?

She wanted to know, *needed* to know. But right now, more than anything, she needed to cry.

Nineteen

After having stained Alvaro's shirt with tears, Ivy decided she didn't want to destroy her identity any more for the night. In just a few days, she'd been torn apart from her family, learnt she wasn't human—and had grown pointed ears to prove the fact—and discovered her father was not actually her father. She could at least allow herself a night to process her newfound identity.

Since Alvaro knew her and her mother from a time she didn't remember, she knew he would have the answers to who she was. She just wasn't quite ready to learn just yet.

The flowers lining the walkway through the tunnel were barely visible beneath the night sky, only illuminating a pale glow. As they walked towards the Tarad, Ivy told Alvaro about her visit to the library and the books she found, omitting the tiny detail about how they had been kept aside specifically for her. No one else needed to know.

'That book on the Divided Realms ... I have not read it in years,'

Alvaro remarked. 'But perhaps it is a good idea to read it again. After all, sixteen years is a long time. We may find something I had missed the first time I read it.' And so, her and Alvaro had agreed to meet at midday the next day—which, when she'd asked how she would know the time, since there were no clocks in this world, he'd informed her was when the sun was at its peak—to read together.

A few moments later they entered the Tarad, and it was nothing like it had been during the day. Music flowed through the air and ground, pulsing beneath the soil and into Ivy's veins, dampening the lingering beat that seemed to strengthen every time she entered this space. Delicious scents wafted alongside the flow of music. With the sun almost completely set behind them, the only light was from the golden dots woven through leaves and hanging vines. Folk continued to stare, but not in that same gawking way they had pre-viously. They seemed to acknowledge Alvaro shadowing her, and rather than point and watch her in awe, they smiled. Surely it wasn't Alvaro's presence alone that had them changing their demeanour, otherwise they would've stopped the other day when he was with her. But whatever it was—time to adjust to her presence, Alvaro being with her, or something else entirely—Ivy was glad she wasn't the centre of unwanted attention.

Multiple food and goods stalls were open and thriving, while others were closed for the day. The smell of food only grew stronger as they weaved between stalls, and Ivy's mouth began to water. Alvaro stopped at a stall with what appeared to have the longest line in the Tarad, but it moved quickly, and once at the end, he purchased two skewered meat sticks drenched in a delectable sweet and sticky sauce.

'Oh my ...' Ivy said after her first bite. 'Your food is good, Alvaro, but this ...'

He chuckled. 'Oh, I know. This is my favourite delicacy of the kingdom.'

'I think this is one of the best things I've ever eaten.'

'Then you will be sorely disappointed when we continue eating my plain dinners.'

A laugh burst from her. A second one, and so soon after the first. Laughing was healthy—she knew that—but another seed of guilt was planted in her, as though she shouldn't be happy at a time like this.

She and Alvaro continued walking through the Tarad, the pulsing music in her veins growing stronger with each step. It was magnetising. But soon the music dimmed the further they walked while the pulsing remained. That same pulsing beat Ivy felt every other time she'd walked through this place, that had lingered on the edge of her blood since entering Harukai. Only now, it grew stronger, shifting to a vibration, a thrumming of sorts. What *was* that? Higher and higher the beat rose within her, until suddenly it slowed to a gradual hum. Ivy froze, then took a few steps back, leaving Alvaro behind; the pulsing quickened and slowed again. She walked back and forth, following the rise and fall of each strange beat, until she found a small stall hidden between two larger ones.

Stained glass trinkets, dishes, and jewellery decorated the table-top, with more hanging from the top of the stall like windchimes. Deep within the stall, stained glass mirrors and other decorative wall pieces hung in no particular pattern. A harpy stood in the centre, white wings in place of arms tucked behind her, the edges barely touching the sides of her stall. Her black hair was messily cropped just above her chin.

'Hi,' she greeted.

The pulsing settled within Ivy, but didn't stop or slow. 'Uh, hi.'

'Can I help you with anything?' the harpy asked.

'I'm not sure.' Ivy took a closer look at one of the hanging glass pieces. Orange and red glass swirled up a piece of twine, like a burning flame. 'What are these made of?'

The harpy eyed her curiously. 'Glass.'

Ivy touched the hanging glass flame with some unexplainable hope that it would cure the pulsing, but nothing happened. 'They're beautiful,' she told the owner. The harpy nodded her thanks, and Ivy walked off, finding Alvaro waiting for her a few stalls down.

'Did you see anything you like?' he asked.

The pulsing slowed now that she was away from the stall, but it still lingered beneath her skin. 'Ah, I don't know.' Maybe she would come back to that stall later, or tomorrow.

But they rounded a corner, and that darn pulsing grew louder once more. Ivy stretched the imaginary crick in her neck the pulsing thrum now created. Each step was another pulse louder, until it was even stronger than at the glass trinket stall. She allowed the pulsing to guide her, like an invisible thread tied to her waist pulling her to its source. It took her through the Tarad in the same direction Alvaro walked, so at least she didn't have to leave his side. Ivy followed it willingly, paying no mind to other stalls or folk, hoping that if she found its source she could be rid of it.

A few moments later, Ivy stopped at a large stall home to weaponry, the beat lingering in this space. The front bench was cut off at the end to create an entryway. Weapons and armour and shields decorated the walls and tables inside.

'Good evening,' a deep voice said. A centaur took up a large portion of the stall, his coat a honey brown. Blonde hair hung in long braids down his front with flowers woven through, stark against his golden tan skin, while some shorter strands fell loosely around his face. He wore one of those custom tunic-shawls the colour of wine. Glazed grey eyes looked past her. Ivy turned, but no one else was at the stall. Alvaro must not have seen her stop.

'Ah, hi.' Ivy stepped inside the stall, the pulsing continuing to grow with each step. Steel gleamed under light leaves; leathered armour hung on display. Shields in a variety of shapes, sizes, and designs hung alongside the weapons and armour, and stood on the tables and ground, leaning against the walls.

'Is there anything I can help you with?' Now that Ivy was inside the stall, she could see the centaur held a cane. His glazed eyes only looked past her.

'I'm not sure,' she admitted. She slowly wandered through the stall, waiting for some sign of where the pulsing was emanating from. It grew stronger and louder with each step; surely, she was close.

'You're Alvaro's ward, aren't you?'

The question shocked her. From his glazed eyes and cane, she assumed he was blind. 'Um, I guess so,' she answered curiously, uncertain about both his ability to see and what a ward was. The mention of Alvaro had Ivy looking back to find him, but he wasn't there. Hopefully he would find her soon.

The centaur chuckled. 'I may be unable to see, but my senses have only grown stronger with time.'

Ivy ignored his statement, too focused on the thrumming pulse that had started to beat against her muscles, begging to be revealed. She stretched her neck again, only this time the ache wasn't so imaginary.

'Raesor, good evening.' Alvaro's voice travelled through the stall. 'I see Miss Ivy has taken an interest in your stall.'

'Yes, we were just getting acquainted,' the centaur—Raesor—replied. His tail, the same colour as his hair, swished idly against her arm.

The pulsing intensified, Alvaro and Raesor's chatter turning into distant mumblings. Blades littered the table, so many she couldn't see the tabletop. The pulsing screamed inside her, rattling her bones. Whatever caused this incessant, aching thrum must be on this table buried beneath the pile of weaponry.

Ivy shuffled through the mess, grabbing weapons at random. Some were short daggers, others large swords and axes. Each weapon was unique, but none seemed extra special in any kind of way. Her head had started to throb from the pulsing; it vibrated in every pore, every vein, every hair root. So close.

With no success on the table, Ivy looked to the wall, a mural of weapons on display. And there, hanging amongst them, was a sword unlike any of the other weapons in the stall. Its blade had curved, waving edges from hilt to tip made from stained glass of oranges and blues, like fire and water swirling together. The hilt was embossed in trees and leaves and clouds with more of that swirling stained glass in deep green and pale grey.

Ivy wrapped her hand around the hilt—

The pulsing didn't stop, but it dimmed significantly, shrinking into a tiny grain of sand that lay within her core, quieter than it had been the first time she felt it. The aching dispersed and her muscles relaxed. Alvaro and Raesor's voices slowly returned, or maybe she returned to them.

Ivy weighed the sword in her hand; the blade itself was roughly the length of her arm from shoulder to wrist. She'd never held a sword before today, but the hilt fit in her palm perfectly, and the weight was neither too heavy nor too light. Like it was made for her.

She placed it back on the wall, and the moment her fingers released the hilt, the thrumming intensified. Without hesitation, she snatched it off the wall and the pulsing dimmed. Would it ever vanish entirely, or was this now a part of her new identity?

'That is a magnificent sword, Miss Ivy.' Alvaro stopped beside her and admired the weapon in her grasp.

'Yeah ... it's beautiful. How did you make this one?' she asked Raesor. 'It's different from the others.'

Raesor offered his open hands to Ivy, and she placed the sword in his awaiting palms, the pulsing filling her body once more. He gently slid his hand along the blade, while his other rubbed the hilt. 'Ah, you have a good eye. This is my most recent creation. Kali owns a stall nearby with stained glass trinkets, and I asked her to show me her technique. She and I worked together to make this sword. We finished it a few days ago.' He handed the weapon back to Ivy and she admired it once more. She wasn't sure if she adored it purely because it quietened the strange thrumming or because of its beauty. Either way, she wanted it. She *needed* it.

'The glass,' Alvaro started. 'How does it work in combat?'

'Well, it's not made entirely from stained glass,' Raesor began to explain. 'The glass coats one of my standard steel blades, while a thin layer of steel coats the glass. You can't see it, but it may appear as a shine atop the blade. It's strong enough so the glass won't shatter when colliding with other weapons or shields. At least, that is the hope,' he added with a smile. 'However, if the glass does happen to shatter, you're at least not left with a broken, unusable sword.'

'Magnificent.' Alvaro turned to Ivy, who still held the sword. 'Well, Miss Ivy, are you ready to leave?'

How could she explain to Alvaro why she needed to keep this sword? Even in a world with fantastical beings and mysteriously disappearing tunnels, she felt she would sound ridiculous if she told him the truth—mainly because it was unbelievable even to herself that a sword could call to her in this way. But what else could she say?

When she didn't put the sword back on the wall, Alvaro said, 'Miss Ivy?'

'I, um ...'

Alvaro huffed a laugh. 'I see you have grown attached. I do not blame you, it is marvellous.'

Ivy decided that was a good excuse to follow. 'Ah, yeah ... it's amazing.'

Alvaro smiled, then turned to Raesor and said, 'We will take it.'

A few moments later, Ivy was leaving the stall with her first ever sword resting in its home in a leather sheath tied to her waist. At first, she'd told Alvaro that buying it wasn't necessary, but she didn't think that was true. Even though she wasn't holding it, the pulsing didn't ache, quiet in its new home.

They left the Tarad and circled around to the back, Lady Eira's tree looming like a menacing tower nearby, shadowing everything in hanging vines and leaves. Ivy's gaze followed those vines up as far as she could see, but something caught her eye. From a window halfway up the tree, Lady Eira watched over the kingdom, her eyes solely on Ivy.

Ivy looked to Alvaro. 'Why doesn't Lady Eira come out?'

'I wish I knew. I have known Lady Eira all my life, and she always enjoyed these nights,' he explained. 'But when she became Lady of the Thidin Kingdom, that all changed. I assume the weight of her position has affected her in some way, but I cannot imagine why a night like this every so often could be so difficult. When I was—' he swallowed, before asking, 'Why do you ask?'

Ivy turned back to the window, but Lady Eira was gone. 'No reason.'

Behind the Tarad was an open space with small grassy mounds; folk danced to music around fire pits, and logs were used as seats. Children ran past chasing each other with sticks of fire, causing Ivy to jump back lest she get burnt.

'Be careful, Eli!' a parent called.

Squealing and laughter sounded, and Ivy couldn't help but smile. In a world veiled by unsolved abductions, the folk still found a way to have fun and live life. Was Ivy expected to do the same? To forget what happened to her and her mum and just ... move on? Live life without her mum by her side?

She wasn't sure that was possible.

Ivy and Alvaro spent the evening around those fire pits. At one point, Alvaro even managed to get Ivy up and dancing. She was reluctant at first, unsure how the other folk would react to her attempting to mingle with them, but he'd insisted, and the smile on his face when she joined in made it all worth it.

Children of all species ran about screaming and laughing as children do, their parents warning them to be careful of the fires. Even across realms, some things never change. Folk she didn't know danced with her, and she enjoyed it. Her and Alvaro talked and laughed about everything and nothing. Ivy relished the freedom to open up ever-so-slightly and experience Alvaro for who he truly was: a folk of the Thidin Kingdom, just like everyone else ... just like herself. But also a carer and a friend.

Reality was a distant thing, waiting for the new day to make itself known once more. Ivy had been right earlier: she shouldn't be happy at a time like this.

But she was.

'*I* want the love story again.'

'*Again?*'

'*It's my favourite.*'

'*But you already know what happens.*'

'*Pleeeaaase!*' eight-year-old Ivy begs.

Dorothea smiles. '*Fine.*' She sidles up next to Ivy in her bed, wrapping an arm around her shoulders. '*Long ago, a merfolk princess wanted to escape her life.*'

'*Why? She's a princess!*'

Her mother smiles again. '*You already know why.*'

Ivy sighs. '*I know. But just pretend I don't know.*'

'*Okay,*' she says through a chuckle. '*Being a princess comes with a lot of responsibilities. She couldn't have fun, couldn't love who she wanted, couldn't make too many friends. The princess just wanted to live her life on her terms.*

'*One day, she swims to the surface and lays on the sand. It's the only place where she can be who she wants. But she's not alone for long.*'

Ivy takes a quick breath and smiles wide, knowing exactly what happens next.

'*Someone steps out of the trees, interrupting her quiet. "Excuse me," they say. "I believe this beach belongs to my parents." At first, she's annoyed at their presence, but once she sees who it is, that annoyance vanishes, as though it never existed to begin with. He may be a land folk, but he's the most beautiful folk she's ever seen.*'

Dorothea's words soon put Ivy into a deep slumber, where she dreams of merfolk and love and a whimsical forest that she never considers could be a real world.

TWENTY

Last night, after the festivities came to an end, Ivy and Alvaro laughed and chatted all the way back to his home. She hadn't thought it possible to feel any sort of happiness while knowing her mother wasn't safe, but despite her initial guilt, it had been freeing. Talking with Alvaro in such a relaxing way felt like speaking with someone she had known all her life.

As she'd undressed for bed, she'd admired her sword once more. *Her* sword—such a strange yet intriguing occurrence. Why had the weapon called to her? And not just any weapon, but *this* weapon. The one with a stained-glass-and steel blade clearly resembling the four elements of nature. What was she supposed to do with it? Well, that was a stupid question; she could fight. But she didn't know the first thing about wielding a weapon. A better question would be *why* would she need to fight?

Elias dragged Dorothea away, back towards the house, the dagger still to her throat.

'I will find you, Ivy.' Even his voice had changed ever-so-slightly, a deep and unnaturally calm cadence. 'Unless you find me first.'

Surely Ivy wouldn't have to fight her own father, right? But if she were to find a way back to the human realm and rescue her mother—if her mother did in fact need rescuing; she didn't exactly have any confirmation of that fact—then perhaps she would have to fight her dad.

She'd put the matter to the back of her mind and attempted slumber, surprisingly falling into a deep and undisturbed sleep. And now, Ivy once again found herself on the beach, staring out at the vast ocean. The swishing of waves rippling over each other was a familiar song in her veins, yet the crashing of waves against the indestructible rock wall was a harsh, out of tune harmony grating her soul. She wasn't sure why she was here, but it was one of the only places in this kingdom where she felt true freedom and comfort, despite the sea's recent suffocation.

Her boots were by the trees, while her bare toes graced the foamy white tips of the ocean. Salty air tangled in her unbound curls and swirled down her throat. Her soul ached to be submerged, but her cosy tendril crept around her lungs, keeping her stuck at the edge of the sea.

The rock wall loomed like a menacing deity, laughing at what it had done to her, and probably laughing at the way she'd pathetically thrown sand towards it the other day. There was nothing more she could do. She'd tried breaking it that night, and now her palms were torn to pieces while the wall was left without a scratch. Her eyes raked across its form, searching for weak spots that didn't exist—and even if they did, she certainly wasn't close enough to see them—when a familiar head of orange hair made its way into view. The last thing she'd told Theon was to leave her alone and yet here he was, clearly not listening. However, some would argue that he was merely watching her from a distance, which technically classified as leaving her alone.

Ivy opened her mouth to say something, although not quite knowing what, when he ducked beneath the waves. Her blood began to boil, not at him ignoring her request to leave her alone, but at the memory of him bringing her back here despite her desperate attempts to remain in the human realm. She didn't believe that what he told her about his motives was everything, because why would he feel the need to protect someone he barely knew? A deep sigh fell from her lips.

'You don't need to hide,' Ivy called, even though she doubted he could hear. 'I want to talk.' There was no sign of him. 'Whatever,' she mumbled. 'I doubt you can even hear me.'

'I can.'

Ivy jumped and turned away from the rock wall. 'Holy shit,' she blurted.

Theon was a few feet away, standing on the sandbank, his lips painted in a smirk at her startle. He was standing more to the right than usual, blocking himself from her periphery, and she wondered if he'd done so on purpose.

'You wanted to talk,' he said.

Did she jump straight into yelling at him again, accusing him of harbouring ulterior motives? Or would it be better to ask him his true reason for bringing her here before her temper rose too quickly for her to control?

Deciding to let the universe dictate what she said first, she opened her mouth, but her eyes caught on the droplets glistening down his scales. 'You ...' She hated how beautifully distracting he was. 'You didn't leave me alone,' she ended up saying instead.

His smirk only grew. 'Is that really what you wanted to talk about?'

'Well, I uh ...' Ivy attempted confidence but failed miserably, that smirk of his causing heat to wick through her. 'Well, no,' she admitted lamely.

'So?'

'So ...' She assessed him, that ridiculously perfect smirk crinkling his eyes. She sighed and shook her head. 'Stop looking at me like that.' Surprisingly, he listened, his features falling to a neutral expression. And when he didn't say anything, she continued, 'I just want to know why you brought me here.'

'Like I said, I was protecting you.'

'Yeah, I know,' she snapped, her boiling blood rising in temperature. 'But why? Why did you feel the need to protect me? You barely know me. And why were you even there? I thought you would have gone back here as soon as we said goodbye.'

His jaw clenched, and Ivy spotted the way he bit the inside of his cheek. But no answer.

She grunted. 'Seriously? So, you know me for five minutes, and suddenly you have an urge to attack my dad and drag me away to a foreign land all because my mum told you to, and you were "protecting me." Am I really supposed to believe that?'

'Yes, Ivy, you are. Because that's what happened,' he snapped back.

too well what losing a child can do to a mother. But at that point, I knew exactly what the beat was telling me.'

The reminder of that night had her eyes filling with tears. 'Please,' Ivy begged.

'I had to protect you,' he whispered. 'There was no other choice. It was like ... like if I didn't, my organs would shatter. And now, it's as though it doesn't even exist.'

Tears freed themselves, trickling like rain down her cheeks. Theon was right. Ivy had been in danger in the human realm. A part of her already knew that but hearing it in this way solidified the fact. With her eerily similar beat for the sword, she knew how irritating and aching it could be; he had no choice but to listen and protect her.

'You ...' she swallowed and cleared her throat. 'You were protecting me.'

He breathed a sigh of relief. 'Yes, Ivy. You have no idea how much I hated bringing you back here, but I had to.' His hands grasped the sides of her face as his thumbs wiped her tears. Her breath hitched at the intimacy, but she didn't pull away. 'I'm truly sorry for what I've done. I hope ... I hope you can find it in yourself to forgive me.' Their eyes met, and he watched her with an agony she'd never seen in someone but had felt to the depths of her core.

Theon really had been protecting her. And now, she was safe. But Ivy being safe in Harukai didn't mean she should accept her fate. Her father was dangerous, which meant her mum truly was in trouble, and that confirmation only fuelled her determination to find a way home and rescue her mother.

'I will find you, Ivy.' Even his voice had changed ever-so-slightly, a deep and unnaturally calm cadence. 'Unless you find me first.'

It was clear her mother wasn't the only one in danger. The sword had called to her—perhaps this was the reason. Except, she had no idea where to start with learning how to use it. She supposed she could just swing it about until she found a comfortable rhythm, but that wasn't enough. She needed *strength*, and she hated to admit it, but Theon was right yesterday—she was weak. If he pulled his dagger or one of his swords on her, she would have absolutely no clue on how to defend herself. If—no, *when*—she found her mother, she would just get caught in the process, potentially trapping them both.

But Theon was the captain of the Noa Kingdom's legion. Ivy assumed that was their army of sorts, and if that were the case, he knew how to use a weapon—after all, he did carry a dagger. And two swords. She needed to learn how to fight, and here was someone who could do exactly that.

She sniffled and said, 'Train me.'

Theon's brows pulled together. 'What?'

'You were right yesterday. I'm weak.' At her declaration, his lips twitched into a smirk. *Smartass.* 'I don't know how to fight. But once I get out of here, I'll need to be able to save my mother. So ... train me.'

'You want me to teach you how to fight?'

Ivy nodded.

Theon chuckled, and a warmth spread in her chest at the sound. 'Fine. When do you wanna start?'

The sun was low, indicating the day had only just begun. Her and Alvaro would meet at the library when the sun was at its peak. Ivy guessed she still had a few hours.

'Now.'

Twenty-One

Ivy had been left on the beach while Theon dove into the Noa Kingdom to grab some things for their training session. As she waited, she started some basic upper and lower body stretches to get her muscles working. After a while, Theon still hadn't returned, so she pulled her sword from its sheath.

She'd never seen any weapons in her short life until that night on the beach just a few days ago, but compared to everything else in Raesor's stall, she could tell this sword was truly magnificent. The wavy edges of the blade were clearly a unique feature, and the stained glass was mesmerising. She swung the sword around like she'd seen in movies, warding off attacks from an invisible opponent. Her steps fumbled in the sand, but she kept going, parrying a blow only she could see.

'Wow, you *really* need this training.'

Ivy spun towards the sea; water dripped off every surface of Theon as he stood in the low rippling waves.

Morning sunlight reflected against the scales that caressed his pale skin, drenching him in sparkling blues.

Ivy gulped, then shook away her momentary awe. 'You took your time,' she said.

He shrugged. 'Maybe I shouldn't have come back. You seem to really have a knack for fighting techniques,' he said with a smirk.

Ivy glared at him.

Theon chuckled, then waded out of the water carrying a brown bag. 'I was held up by Lord Tullius. He takes priority.'

'Who's Lord Tullius?'

'The Lord of the Noa Kingdom.' Theon dropped the bag on the sand nearby, his eyes flicking briefly to her hand as he did so. 'Nice sword.' Then, his eyes moved back to the weapon and lingered. '*Really* nice sword,' he added with obvious awe.

'Thanks,' she replied. 'I got it from the Tarad last night.' His head tilted to the side as he continued eyeing the weapon. 'Here.' She offered it to him, and when he grabbed the hilt, his fingers brushed hers. Her eyes found his, which were already on her.

His jaw tensed, then he pulled away and admired the sword, holding it at various angles. 'This is ... I've never seen a sword like this.' He stabbed an invisible opponent, just as Ivy had done, but with what she could only assume was a proper technique. (Some would argue that any technique could be considered proper when compared to Ivy's earlier wielding.) 'It's nothing like anything I've ever handled before,' he said as he handed the weapon back to her. She was careful not to touch his hand when she took it from him. 'Put it away.'

'What?'

'The sword. Back in the sheath.'

'I thought we were training.'

'We are.' He circled her, eyeing her from head to toe. 'But training doesn't start with weaponry, especially not with you.'

She whirled on him. 'What's that supposed to mean?'

Theon smirked, which turned into chuckling. An unwelcome warmth spread through her at the sound. 'Your technique is far from perfect. And as you said, when *you* asked *me* to train you, you're weak. So, I'll only ask you this once: Do you still want me to train you?'

Ivy nodded.

'Then you will listen to me and do as I say.' He continued circling her, switching to a commanding voice that she didn't particularly hate. 'I'm Captain of the Noa Kingdom's legion. I train the warriors of the sea. I'm an experienced fighter, not only in training, but in practice.'

Her lips parted. 'Wait, do you mean ...'

'Yes. I've fought in battle. It was just over a year ago now and was the reason I got promoted so early in my years. I know what it's like to fight against an enemy, not just practise with fellow warriors. There's truly no one else in the Noa Kingdom better suited to train you. Consider yourself lucky.'

How old was he? He didn't look much older than her, perhaps only seventeen. And yet, he'd already fought in battle, presumably against humans. She knew he was telling the truth—there was no reason for him to lie since she'd already asked him to train her—but she couldn't help but tease him. 'Up yourself, much.'

Theon grinned. 'Push-ups. Now.'

The sun was nearly at its peak, blaring heat onto Ivy as she hunched over her knees, struggling to breathe. Sweat dripped from every pore on her body, creating damp spots in the sand. Her sword was cast aside near a tree, tucked neatly in its sheath.

She and Theon had been training for hours, and despite Theon's claims to stop, Ivy had insisted they keep going. She wasn't going to waste a second of her time. Every moment in Harukai needed to be spent either preparing to save her mother or finding a way to break through that damn wall. Last night was an exception; she'd had fun, but she couldn't allow herself to do that again.

She'd gone through drills of exercises for her upper body—push-ups, pull-ups on a tree branch, and even weight lifting with some light weights Theon had in his brown bag. They'd run through attacks and blocks with her arms and torso, but mainly focused on stance and posture. It was easy enough for her to manoeuvre in her skirt—although, she did hope she could find a pair of pants that fit her—but the loose linen cropped shirt she wore wasn't as practical. She'd also left her hair strap at Alvaro's home, so her hair kept flying into her face.

But nevertheless, Ivy was exhausted, and rightfully so.

'We're done for the day,' Theon told her. 'You need to rest.'

She nodded, untying her boots and walking knee-deep into the water, not caring about her clothes being wet. The tendril inside her attempted to clench her lungs the deeper she got, but it too was as drained as she was. Exhaustion took hold, and she fell rather ungracefully into the waves, drenching her bandages in the process. Undrinkable, but refreshing, nonetheless. As though the ocean had revived it, her tendril wrapped neatly around her organs, and she quickly leapt from the water.

Theon was right where she left him: on the beach, muscled arms tensed and crossed. His hair was now ratty and untamed after drying in the sun all morning. Her eyes trailed down the scales that carved a path across his torso, over his hips, and down his muscular thighs, every inch of his lower body covered. Something stirred deep within her at the sight of him, and she fell back onto the waves, hoping to rid the feeling.

Floating atop the sea, nothing but a blue sky and fluffy clouds passed her by. Those clouds reminded Ivy of the sky kingdom Alvaro had briefly mentioned. An island in the sky seemed impossible, but so did a world you could only get to through a rock wall. She scanned those clouds in search of something that could be an island, but the only thing she deemed out of the ordinary was a large clump of clouds closer to the two islands across the way. Was that the sky kingdom?

Ivy closed her eyes against the sun, allowing the buoyancy to relax her muscles. Oh, she missed this. Missed the way the waves cradled her, and the way the salt crept beneath her pores. She missed being *under* the water more, but she wasn't sure she could do that just yet.

New waves rippled against her floating form, indicating Theon's presence in the water. 'Ivy.'

Her ears were submerged; she could only just make out his muffled voice. 'Hm?' she replied.

'We'll meet tomorrow. Same time.'

She felt him standing next to her, could hear the waves lightly smacking against his bare skin and scales. 'Mhm.' She wanted to keep her eyes closed, but knowing he was right next to her—something nagged at her to get one more look at him before he departed.

With the sun close to its peak, he was cast in an almost-silhouette, yet strands of his unkempt hair broke through the shadowed darkness. Scales on the edge of his face and arms sparkled under the sun's bright glow. Even covered in shadows, he was still beautiful. Ivy hated it.

She could just make out the corner of his lips turning into a smirk, and she was left wondering what it meant as he dove into the waves without a word.

Twenty-Two

Ivy traipsed through the forest, weaving between trees and mushrooms on her way to the library. Soil and grass attached itself to her wet feet while she carried her boots, the drenched linen shirt she wore gripping her skin. Water dripped down her front and back from her sopping hair, and her precious sword was snug on her left side.

She entered the clearing with the library, once again walking up those grand stairs and feeling too small for this world when beside those statues. Not wanting to drag water into the library, she left her boots by the door, then wrung out her hair and clothes as best she could, before stepping inside.

Ivy went to collect her books from Leyrah, only to find Alvaro had already done so. He sat at a round table to the far left of the library entrance, one of the two massive tomes open before him. She set herself down beside him, *A Maiden's History* closed and resting beside a bowl of fruit.

'Miss Ivy,' Alvaro greeted, turning to face her. 'Leyrah informed me of the books she had set aside for you.' Then, his brows furrowed. 'Why are you wet?'

'Oh, sorry,' Ivy started. 'I shouldn't have gone in with your clothes—'

'No, it is quite all right.' Alvaro chuckled. 'It is merely clothing. They will be fine after a good wash. But why did you not wear your swimming clothes?'

She released a soft chuckle, then proceeded to explain her morning, leaving out the part about the strange beating Theon felt for her safety. It felt private, personal, almost intimate. Something she wanted to keep between the two of them. But she did tell him how Theon had been protecting her that night and about their new regular training schedule.

'Well, that is a rather interesting development. Are you certain this is the right course of action?'

'Of course it is. I need to find a way back home ... I mean, back to the human realm,' she corrected. But that place was still her home—it always would be. 'But what happens once I do?' She spoke with the confidence that there definitely was a way for her to return; she refused to accept any other possibility. Thankfully, Alvaro didn't correct her. 'My life won't be waiting for me as it was. My dad ...' Ivy gulped. '*Elias* is dangerous, and if he's taken Mum somewhere, it won't be easy finding and saving her. I'm weak, and I don't know how to fight. I'll probably just end up trapping us both.'

'Miss Ivy, you are so young. You should not have to be burdened with something such as this.'

'But I am. My dad ...' She mentally cursed herself for calling him that again. 'He said he'll find me, but the way he said it ... It didn't sound like him. But it *was* him. I don't know what's going to happen once I'm there, but I need to be prepared.'

Alvaro sighed. 'You are right. And I trust Theon will train you well. I have seen him fight. He is ... He is no better than the other soldiers in the legion. No more skilled than the other captains. But ... it is as though he can manipulate his opponents to provide himself with a targeted advantage. It is truly quite peculiar. Marvellous, even.'

How could someone manipulate others? Ivy didn't know the first thing about fighting—actually, she did in part after this morning—but even she could tell that was an unusual way to fight.

'But if that is the case,' Alvaro continued, 'then allow me to also train you in my own methods. It would be useful for you to know multiple techniques.'

'Just as long as it's not as strenuous as Theon's training.'

Alvaro smiled. 'I promise I will go easy on you. We can train in the evenings to allow yourself the day to rest.' He turned back to his reading, and Ivy found herself staring at his ears. She instinctively reached for her own; no fur was there, but they were still pointed.

Who was she?

Ivy opened her mouth to ask, but her tendril snatched her lungs. The question caught in her throat. She desperately wanted to know, but a deep part of her feared the answer. Each new experience, each new fact, stripped her of her old self. She wasn't sure how much of herself was left and was afraid that whatever she learnt next would remove everything that remained.

As her eyes slid down, away from his pointed ears, she noticed faded marks splattered along his arms. 'What are those?' she asked.

'Hm?' He followed her gaze to his arms. 'Oh … Never mind about those,' he told her quickly. 'It is nothing for you to worry about.' Then he returned to his reading, a sign she shouldn't say anything more on the matter.

Ivy reached for the bowl and popped a few pieces of fruit in her mouth, then opened *A Maiden's History* to the first page to distract herself from her emotional turmoil. She hoped this book would provide more detailed information on how these Maidens had built the wall—since magic had erected it, perhaps magic could open it. She just needed to know who they were, where they were now, and whether their magic was indeed the answer she was looking for.

The first page of *A Maiden's History* read:

There are three myths surrounding the Maidens.

The first is they were goddesses. Beings who created our world using the elements they wielded. Folk believed they built the Realm Divider, using their magic to the point of sacrifice in order to protect Harukai.

The second myth is they embody each element. Rather than merely wielding the elements as magic, some folk believe the Maidens are in fact the elements, capable of taking on the form of anyone and anything residing in such element, as well as manipulating their own selves to exist as the elements. Meaning, the Maiden of Water could become water, while the Maiden of Air could turn into the breeze. This myth leads to the belief that the Maidens are now a part of the Realm Divider, never leaving their final resting place among the rocks lest the wall fall, and the realms are joined once more.

The final myth is the Maidens are monsters. Still related to the elements, each Maiden is believed to be a creature of the element, hiding in the shadows.

However, the <u>truth</u> is that the Maidens never existed. They are stories passed down through generations to provide hope to the folk that perhaps the ongoing war with humankind may come to an end. Because there is one thing that connects all three myths: the belief that the Maidens will someday return to put an end to the war. Unfortunately, that can never be true.

This book tells the stories of the Maidens in relation to each myth.

Ivy's brows scrunched. Why would a book on the history of the Maidens only speak of myth? History books usually implied accuracy. She flipped the page, starting in *Part I: The Goddesses*, and started reading, but after three short stories, it was clear this book was nothing more than fairytales. Each story was insistent on reminding the reader that these myths were just that: myths.

'That doesn't make sense,' Ivy muttered to herself. She checked the cover, which was just as old and peeling as *The History of the Divided Realms*, and there, in whimsical lettering, *A Maiden's History* was written. But according to this book, the Maidens were only a myth passed down over the years.

'What is it?' Alvaro asked.

Instead of answering, Ivy snatched the book he read and flipped to the section she read yesterday.

After the humans caused such destruction among the folk, the Maidens took it upon themselves to erect the Dividing Rocks. Together, they mustered every ounce of their magic and built the Realm

Divider. It ascended from beneath the sands of the Noa Kingdom, stopping just shy of the Thidin Kingdom's treetops.

Not only did the Maidens build the wall, but they also imbued it with magic to segment Harukai from Earth. A magic unrelated to the elements. Power that transcends space.

This book spoke as though the Maidens had in fact existed. Which was the truth? If the Maidens were myth, how did the wall appear? Or had it always been there? But if the Maidens were real, then why would the history book lie?

'Miss Ivy, what is it?'

A Maiden's History had been set aside specifically for Ivy, yet there was a chance it was lying. What was she supposed to do with information that wasn't real? *What am I supposed to do if the information* is *real?* she thought. The aging leather on the cover was indication enough that the book was older than time itself, but the content sounded as though it had been written far too recently. 'The Maidens ... do you know anything about them?' she asked.

'Probably not much more than that book would tell you.'

'Do you believe they're real?'

'Oh.' He was taken aback, clearly not expecting her to ask that question. 'Well, nobody knows whether the Maidens are real—'

'Do *you* believe they're real?' she asked again.

'I, uh ... Does it matter what I believe? Nobody knows the truth, Miss Ivy. That is why there are myths.'

Ivy stared at the worn pages of *A Maiden's History*. 'But why is there a history book?'

'Well, I suppose ... Actually, I do not have a clue. History books usually imply accuracy.' She smiled at the similarity of their thoughts. 'What does it say?' She showed him the text at the front of the book; his brows scrunched as he read it. 'That cannot be right,' Alvaro mumbled. Then, he followed her exact movements to check the front cover, before opening the book again. He flicked through the pages, skimming content. 'I am certain I have read this book before.'

'Oh.' That's certainly not what she'd expected him to say; he'd seemed just as confused as she had been. 'So, the myths are the history?'

'Ah, not exactly. I do not know. Perhaps.' His brows pulled together. 'But ... I do not believe I read these words in this book.'

'So, there's another history book? Or myth book? Or something?'

'Uh, perhaps ... But it does not matter.'

'Actually, I think it does.' Ivy sidled closer to him, laying the books open between them to compare the texts. 'Here,' she started, pointing to the first page in *The History of the Divided Realms*, 'it says the Maidens built the wall. Nothing about beliefs or myths or anything. Just that they built it. But this book,' she flicked to the front of *A Maiden's History*, 'claims they weren't even real.'

'Well, some people believe the Maidens were not real. It is difficult to know what the truth is when these books were written so long ago.'

'But that's just it. These books look to have been written years and years ago, but the information doesn't align. They're both history books most likely written around the same time. Should the information not be accurate across both texts?'

Alvaro's jaw tensed and he bit the inside of his cheek. 'I suppose ... I suppose you have a point. But perhaps this one is incorrect,' he said as he touched the pages of *The History of the Divided Realms*.

'Maybe. But how do we know for sure?'

'We do not, Miss Ivy,' he snapped. 'There is no way for anyone to know if their existence was ever real or not. And it does not matter either way, because if the Maidens truly are real, they will not be helping us. They will not heed your call.'

Ivy flinched at his raised voice. She moved her seat away, back to where it belonged, and dragged both books with her. 'Sorry,' she said. 'If you don't think it matters, fine. But I do.'

'Miss Ivy, I did not mean—'

'This is all I have!' At her own raised voice, Ivy instantly looked around the library and noticed most of the folk were looking her way. She turned back to Alvaro and lowered her voice. 'I get that you tried this all those years ago, but I haven't. And I can't just go off someone's word that it won't work. I need to *try*. If you don't want to try anymore, that's fine by me. But I'm not going to stop.' She adjusted the books and started reading the text again, but her mind wouldn't focus.

Alvaro slid his chair closer to her. 'I am sorry, Miss Ivy. I did not mean to raise my voice.' He sighed, and continued, 'As you said, I have tried this. I read this passage about the Maidens having built the wall, and I made it a mission to learn everything I could about them. I prayed to them, asking for their service. When that did not work, I begged. And when that, too, failed, I cursed them. Now, it is much easier for me to believe they never existed. Because if what is written is real, if these beings gifted with magic had separated us from an enemy, why would they allow these abductions to contin-ue? Why would they allow us folk to live in constant fear, or to feel a never-ending grief? Why would they sit idly by and watch while folk destroy themselves both internally and externally over something they created?' A tear landed on the table beside Ivy's arm, causing her to face Alvaro; salty lines marred his face. 'I have told you before and I will tell you again: I will not give up. And if you choose to pursue the Maidens, then I will support you in that endeavour. But I cannot allow myself to believe in them wholeheartedly. I cannot rely on them without the proof that they exist. And even then, I do not know if I can ever truly rely on them, for they have abandoned us all these years.'

An empathetic sort of longing lodged itself in her throat. He had every reason to feel that way, and after hearing his story, Ivy wasn't sure what she should believe. 'I'm sorry,' she said, although she didn't know what she was apologising for.

'Oh, it is quite all right,' Alvaro said with a smile, wiping his eyes and face, and taking a deep breath. 'Now, rather than continuing to discuss which text is accurate, it might be beneficial for us to proceed with an assumption. Which information do you believe is true?'

'Alvaro, it's fine—'

He held up his hand. 'As I said, I will support you. So, which text?'

Ivy sighed and answered, 'This one,' while pointing to *The History of the Divided Realms*.

The corner of his lips dropped so slightly that Ivy almost missed it. 'In that case, let us assume they did in fact erect the Realm Divider. Let us also assume that their methods of doing so can help us open the wall to enter the human realm. Firstly, they have vanished from our world, leaving us no means of communicating with them, and no information about their existence other than these myths. Now we could, of course, read these myths with the belief that they are factual, but that then leads me to my other point: both of these texts say the Maidens used magic to erect the wall, something the folk have not seen in …' His gaze moved past Ivy, his pupils dilating in a rhythm independent from their surroundings.

Ivy turned, following his gaze, but there was nothing he could be looking at other than a tree. She turned back to him, waiting for him to finish his sentence, but when he didn't, she said, 'Ah, Alvaro?'

'Hm?' He blinked, his eyes finding hers once more. 'Oh, my apologies. What I meant to say was that the Maidens used their own magic, something the folk have not seen since their existence, if they even existed. We could not open the tunnel using their methods.'

Ivy slumped, defeated. Her eyes scanned the two books. That couldn't be everything. She'd only just started reading these books. Surely there was something hiding within the pages.

'I must go,' Alvaro said suddenly.

'Already? I thought …' What had she thought? They had never specified how long they would read together. He probably needed to get back to the militia.

'I am so sorry, Miss Ivy, but I … I remembered I had to do something. I promise, we will still meet tomorrow. I will see you tonight.'

Before Ivy could say anything else, Alvaro left.

Twenty-Three

I vy stayed in the library, flicking between both books. She briefly wondered why Alvaro had acted strange earlier, but out of all the nagging questions she had, that was one she could hopefully get the answer to soon. For now, she had books to read.

She reread the last section of the introductory text in *A Maiden's History*.

However, the <u>truth</u> is that the Maidens never existed. They are stories passed down through generations to provide hope to the folk that perhaps the ongoing war with humankind may come to an end. Because there is one thing that connects all three myths: the belief that the Maidens will someday return to put an end to the war. Unfortunately, that can never be true.

This book tells the stories of the Maidens in relation to each myth.

She supposed the myths about the Maidens could be real, but if that was the case, why would the passage emphasise their nonexistence?

Ivy moved back to *The History of the Divided Realms.* There was no specification of the Maidens being goddesses, embodiment of the elements, or monsters. It only specified the magic they used for the Realm Divider wasn't elemental. As though whoever read the book should know the truth.

But what *was* the truth?

Since the Maidens allegedly built the wall, she decided it was best to continue reading the myths about their existence in the hope she would find some hidden truth within the stories. But as she flipped to the next story, the first page slipped from its binding—a common occurrence with books as old as these, but how odd that only the first page had broken free. Out of mere curiosity, she fanned the pages through her hand, but none joined the first in freedom. How odd indeed. She realigned the loose page, and that was when she noticed ...

The handwriting didn't match the text on the next page. However, that was only the heading *Part 1: The Goddesses.* She turned to the first page of the first story and compared the text with the handwriting on the fallen page. Again, it didn't match. They were similar enough that no one would notice when casually reading the book, just as she hadn't. But once both styles of handwriting had been in view, the differences were clear.

No authors were listed; perhaps multiple people wrote the book. Ivy flicked to the end of the first story and bent the last page just enough to align the text with that in the next story—they were exactly the same. She turned to random sections in the book and did the same thing, comparing handwriting with different stories, but every single page aligned. So, coincidentally, the singular page that had fallen loose from the book was also written in someone else's handwriting. Could it be just a coincidence?

She stared at the odd page as it lay loose and askew in its home, revealing the page underneath. There was a stark difference between both those pages. Her brows scrunched. Were her eyes playing tricks on her? Both pages were stained brown with all the years they had existed, but the one on top was much lighter, newer. Ivy compared that page with others throughout the book, and again, it remained the odd one out. That surely couldn't be a coincidence.

No matter the reason, Ivy supposed she should tell the librarian.

She slid the page where it belonged—allegedly—and closed both books, stacking them together and carrying them to the counter where Leyrah waited. When she saw Ivy making her way over, she smiled and started writing a message. The parchment was waiting for her when she arrived: *Are you done for the day? Did you find what you were looking for?*

'Not exactly,' Ivy replied, carefully laying the books on the counter. 'There's something wrong with this book.' Leyrah's brows furrowed, and Ivy showed the loose page. 'But it's not just that. I noticed the handwriting is different. So is the paper. See?' She aligned the odd page with another in the book to compare and show Leyrah. 'Do you see the difference?'

Leyrah didn't move to write and instead gave Ivy a questioning look. Maybe her eyes *were* playing tricks on her. She sighed and shut the book, then flicked her gaze between both tomes. Perhaps Leyrah would know which information was accurate.

'There's something else. I think ...' Ivy knew how ridiculous she would sound. She wasn't even from this world—no, she *was* from this world; her newly-formed pointed ears told her as much. But she hadn't been raised here, had never read the texts or learnt the history or heard the stories, and yet she had the audacity to question their historical texts. 'I think there's a problem with the information in these books.'

Leyrah's quill ran along the parchment. *How do you mean?*

'This book'—she pointed to *A Maiden's History*—'is supposed to be about the history of the Maidens, right?' Leyrah nodded slowly. 'But it doesn't talk about the history. It talks about myth. About stories passed down through generations.'

Leyrah scribbled another message. *There are many stories about the Maidens, which are believed to be their history.*

Ivy shook her head. 'But it doesn't say anything about history.' She opened the book again and pointed to one of the last passages on the loose page. 'Here. It says, "... the *truth* is that the Maidens never existed." And see, right there.' She pointed to the word 'truth'. 'Why is it emphasised? This is a historical text, but myth isn't history. Myth is myth, and history is fact. Right?'

Leyrah's brows pulled together, her quill hovering over the parchment, unmoving.

Her lack of response had Ivy continuing. 'I don't think the information in this book is correct. I think ...' What did she think? A page had fallen. The handwriting belonged to someone else. The page was newer. And the information didn't align with what the book was labelled as. 'I think it's been tampered with.'

Leyrah's eyes widened. She brought her finger to her lips, motioning silence, then fumbled with a new piece of parchment and dipped her quill in the ink pot. But as she leant over to start writing, her hand shook. She looked up to Ivy and brought her finger to her lips again, but this time, with a sharp look in her eyes. Just as the quill hit the parchment, she glanced to Ivy's left.

Ivy followed her gaze, but Leyrah cleared her throat. She turned back and watched her quill scribble along the parchment. *I'm sorry,* she wrote, *I don't know what you're talking about.*

'But—' Ivy began, but Leyrah lifted her eyes to her and shot that same look, ultimately cutting off her sentence.

However, Leyrah continued, *We have a huge collection of books about the history of Harukai. Let me show you.* Without a moment of hesitation, Leyrah made her way around the desk, leaving her parchment and quill behind.

Ivy followed Leyrah's clopping hooves through the library. Sunlight dimmed, a reminder that the library was built into a cavernous wall. More trees lived in the darkened space, with the leaves being the same light leaves seen throughout the rest of the kingdom. Ivy wondered how the trees thrived with such little sunlight. They continued down deserted nooks and abandoned crannies, until the light leaves could travel no more. Darkness consumed them, but Leyrah kept walking.

Ivy's vision had barely adjusted to the darkness when they turned down a crammed aisle, where she could just make out Leyrah proceeding to search through the books. Only, she wasn't actually searching. She dragged her finger lightly against the spines, but her eyes didn't travel with it. She glanced past Ivy to where they entered the aisle, and after a few moments of not searching, Leyrah gestured for Ivy to keep following.

What the hell is she doing? Ivy questioned. 'Ah, Leyrah?'

Leyrah swivelled back and brought her finger to her lips. Her eyes darted behind Ivy, before she turned back around and kept walking.

Ivy shivered, but she wasn't sure if it was from the cold seeping in from the cavern the deeper they walked, or because of Leyrah's strange behaviour. Either way, she wrapped her arms around herself, the hairs on them standing on end.

After a few more minutes of silent walking and clopping, they finally stopped. Ivy's skin pricked from the freezing air. Leyrah had led them to an old and cold corner of the library. But where the walls throughout the building were stone like the outside, the back wall in this space was like the inside of a cave.

Are we at the back of the library? Ivy wondered.

Leyrah studied the cave wall, where no books lived, her hands feeling along the rocks. Ivy was tempted to inform her there were in fact no books there despite the apparent need for silence, when something clicked.

To Ivy's left, a section of the rock wall slowly swung open. Nothing but darkness swirled within. She wasn't sure if it was a corridor or a room or ... something else.

Leyrah stepped inside and gestured for Ivy to follow, not waiting to see if she obeyed before wandering through.

'Leyrah,' Ivy whispered. But the sound of clopping faun hooves quietened, so she had no choice but to follow.

A few steps in and the door closed behind them, casting them in complete and utter darkness. Ivy gasped. Not that there was any light to begin with, but now Ivy's eyesight had to readjust.

Except, it didn't. It was only the sound of Leyrah's hooves hitting the rocky steps that told Ivy she was still ahead of her. She stuck her hands out to the side, hoping the walls could guide her, but as her hands grazed the rocks, she was transported to that night in the tunnel between realms.

One last attempt at escape had her reaching for the opening and latching on, pulling herself away from Theon. But his grip was too strong. She slipped, her hands scraping against the inner walls and tearing the palms of her hands…

Elias dragged Dorothea away, back towards the house, the dagger still to her throat.

Her tendril made itself known, sneaking around her lungs and squeezing. 'Leyrah,' Ivy breathed, despite knowing she couldn't respond.

Her hooves kept moving.

'Leyrah,' she called, louder this time, hoping she would stop and turn around. Ivy's heart thumped in her ears. Her tendril snaked around each of her breaths, catching them in her throat. 'Leyrah,' she cried, tears now marring her cheeks.

It's not that night, Ivy reminded herself. Deep breath in through her nose. Out through her mouth. Again. And just as the third breath released, an orange glow appeared up ahead. Ivy breathed a sigh of relief, her tendril releasing its grip.

The glow expanded the closer they walked, and Leyrah's silhouette came into view. It wasn't long until Leyrah was stepping down into an open cavern.

Stone braziers about the same height as Ivy stood around the edge of the circular room, each with a ripe flame atop it, burning a bright orange. A wide tree grew in the centre of the cavern and straight through an opening in the rocky ceiling. Flowing water cascaded down the curving wall, leading into a moat than ran behind the braziers. Steps at the entrance carried Ivy over the moat and into the cavern.

She made slow steps through the space, marvelling at nature's beauty. 'What is this place?' she asked before remembering Leyrah had left her parchment and quill behind. She looked around the room and found Leyrah at the tree trunk watching her. 'Sorry,' Ivy amended.

Leyrah smiled and nodded once, then gestured her hand in a 'come here' motion. As Ivy walked closer to the tree, she noticed the trunk wasn't a trunk at all. Hundreds of tree roots twisted together to form the shape of a tree trunk. And in the gaps of those roots ...

Leyrah pulled a book free from the roots and handed it to Ivy, but she didn't take it. She circled the tree, admiring the books buried inside. They rested between the roots, their withered spines blending in with the tree.

Ivy reached for the roots and ran her hand along the tree as she walked around. 'It's beautiful,' she mumbled, before finding her way back to Leyrah.

Ivy took the book from her awaiting grasp, *Real or Myth? Beliefs of the Maidens Across Time*, embossed on the cover. She ran her fingers over the lettering, then looked up at Leyrah. 'I was right, wasn't I? The book was tampered with.'

All of Leyrah's features fell as she nodded; her eyes welled with tears. Ivy remembered the way Leyrah had acted when she'd mentioned the tampering, glancing to the side and motioning for her to be quiet. Had someone made her tamper with the books? She watched the tears fall down Leyrah's face; she clearly hadn't done this willingly.

'Don't worry,' Ivy said. 'I won't tell anyone.' She offered Leyrah a smile, who gave her one in return.

The pair made their way back up the cavernous corridor and through the labyrinth of books, the scent of leather spines and parchment pages musty from years of living inside a cavern. They walked without pause until light leaves appeared to guide them. Leyrah cut into an aisle of books, stopping halfway down. She properly scanned the spines this time and pulled a book from its home, laying it gently on top of the new book in Ivy's hands. Before she had a chance to read the cover, Leyrah was leading them out of the aisle.

As they walked through the foyer towards the front desk, Ivy decided to glance where Leyrah's eyes had flicked to earlier.

Multiple lounge chairs circled a low-lying table scattered with books. Light leaves danced across the chairs and edge of the table. Only two folk sat in the space, seemingly unfamiliar with each other: a faun and a harpy, both reading.

Except, the harpy's book was upside down.

If reading upside down was an ability of the folk, Ivy thought it a strange one. But she doubted that was the case. She tried not to stare, but she couldn't help but find the harpy familiar, despite having only had an interaction with one harpy so far who ran a stained-glass trinket stall at the Tarad. And this harpy was not her. But there was definitely something familiar about this harpy. Their wings were folded behind them, deep brown feathers protruding from behind their shoulders. Light brown curls obscured part of their face. They turned to Ivy, their hair moving to reveal dark eyes.

He folded them in and glared at Ivy, light brown curls hanging in front of his dark eyes. 'Watch where you're going.'

It was the same folk she bumped into yesterday when walking to the library, just after she had entered the Tarad. She was certain of it.

Ivy bumped into the desk, causing her to break eye contact with the harpy. Leyrah was already on the other side waiting for her to place the two new books on the counter. 'Who is that?' she whispered, nodding her head towards the harpy.

Leyrah glanced to the sitting area and stiffened, then scribbled a note on a piece of parchment and slid it across the desk. *Would you like to take these books home?*

'Oh, I, um ...' Ivy stammered, thrown off by the sudden change of subject. *Home ...* She didn't currently have a home to take these books to. And besides, she couldn't carry all of them back to Alvaro's. 'No, I think it's easier to leave them here.'

Leyrah slid another parchment note to her. *You're staying with Alvaro, right?* Ivy nodded. *You can check them out under his name.* Leyrah fumbled with the books and parchment and quill, searching under the desk for whatever she needed to complete the borrowing process.

'But I won't be able to take them back,' Ivy explained. 'They're too heavy. I can't carry them all. Is it okay if I leave them here with you?'

Leyrah paused, glancing at the sitting area again, before writing another note. *I really think it's best if you take them with you. I have a trolley you can use.* And before Ivy could say anything more, Leyrah was wheeling a trolley over and stacking the books inside—the first two she already had, plus the two new ones.

Ivy felt the eyes of the harpy digging into her spine. She desperately wanted to turn around, but while she might have been a bit naive at times, she certainly wasn't stupid. There was something clearly *off* about the harpy and their looming presence; Leyrah's glancing, shushing, and hiding in aisles told her as much. So instead, she tapped her foot incessantly.

Leyrah wheeled the trolley—which Ivy now realised was made of tree bark—around the counter to Ivy, a smile plastered on her face. She pointed to a note on the counter. *There's a ramp outside to the right at the end of the walkway. I hope you find what you're looking for.*

'Thank you.' Ivy smiled, returning the one Leyrah gave her, and walked to the door. Just as she was leaving the library, she took one final look at the sitting area.

The harpy continued to read upside down.

Twenty-Four

Ivy struggled to wheel the trolley through the kingdom since there was no solid ground, only grass and soil. Her clothes were still damp, but her feet were dry enough for her to wear her boots. After last night's festivities, most of the folk paid her no mind or gave her a friendly smile. It was good to finally not be gawked at, to feel accepted.

Alvaro wasn't home when she arrived, and although she'd expected as much, she'd hoped he'd be here so she could try and ask about her identity again. Ivy left the trolley downstairs and set herself up on one of the two chairs below the window with the book titled *Real or Myth? Beliefs of the Maidens Across Time*, the official copy of *A Maiden's History*.

Long ago, elements lived in the dark abyss, before colliding to create what we know as the universe. Planets formed, sprouting from the elemental, energetic collision. And from this display of colourful power, Harukai arose.

Water formed the ocean, the base of our world and home to the Noa Kingdom.

Next was Flame, who created the molten heat in the centre of our planet.

Then Earth built the islands, trees, and plants of the Thidin Kingdom.

Finally, Air become the wind that carries heat and moisture and encapsulates the Savan Kingdom.

These elements are known across Harukai as the Maidens.

This certainly read more like an accurate historical text. Ivy thought back to the library entrance with those goddess-like statues. They each held and were embodied in an element; they must be a representation of the Maidens. As curious as she was to learn more about them, she didn't think it wise to read the entire book. Instead, she flipped through the pages, searching for headings like she had with the book on the divided realms. A section titled 'Building the Realm Divider' was at the end of the book.

There were many attempts made by the folk to stop the war with humankind, to try and understand their motives. But when all else failed, when the humans threatened the folk of Harukai, there was only one option remaining. Together, the Maidens gathered their elemental magic and forged a wall that split the world in two.

Ivy turned the page, but the next few paragraphs spoke of joy spreading through Harukai at being saved. 'That's it?' she exclaimed. 'One measly paragraph that tells me nothing?'

She already knew magic built the wall; *The History of the Divided Realms* told her as much. But she needed to know if the Maidens still existed. Did their magic linger somewhere? Was there a way for

Ivy to use it to open the tunnel? Gosh, how unreal that sounded in her mind—Ivy using magic. The thought of actual *magic* existing was something she needed to see to believe.

But that thrumming she'd felt for the sword, which now lay as an inconspicuous grain of sand in her core, had her wondering: was that magic?

The last paragraph of the book stole her attention.

After the wall was formed, the Maidens vanished. Most believe they used all their energy to protect the folk of Harukai, thus destroying themselves. Others believe their essence became the land, that they will forever reside among their creation. But there is one, named the Oracle, who believes the Maidens will return in a time of great need, in the form of an unknown, unwilling being.

Through the other beliefs of the Maidens' existence, there was one folk who believed they would return. And if that belief held true, the question was *when* would they return? Did this mean the Maidens were in fact real, or was it just more myth? Once again, there were too many questions—only this time, someone may be able to answer them.

Ivy needed to find the Oracle.

The front door swung open, startling Ivy.

'Miss Ivy,' Alvaro said, sounding out of breath. 'I was not expecting you home so soon.' His clothes were soaked, and a dark substance dripped onto the floor through the bandages on his hands.

'Alvaro, are you okay?' She closed her book and left it on the side table before walking over to him and grabbing his hand for her to inspect. She unwrapped the bandage; his palm was shredded with deep slices not unlike the ones bandaged and healing on her own hands. She spotted a purple bruise marring his wrist, causing her eyes to follow up his arm where fresh bruises covered his dark skin, overlapping with the old ones. 'Oh my God, what happened?'

He pulled his hand out of her grasp and walked around her towards the kitchenette. 'I told you,' he started, still out of breath, 'every day I try to break that damned wall. Today was no exception.' He unbandaged his other hand and dipped a cloth in a bucket of water to clean his wounds. So that's what those bruises were from. 'Although, if I am being honest, I have not done so since you have been here.'

'Here, let me get that.' Ivy rushed over to him and took the cloth from his hand. 'Alvaro ...' She didn't know what to say. He *had* told her he'd been doing this every day since she and her mother had been taken. Nearly seventeen years. But she never considered the pain he put himself through. Had he really hurt himself this badly every time? 'Alvaro, why do you do this to yourself if you know it won't work?'

'I cannot give up, Miss Ivy.'

'But you haven't done it since I've been here. That's like, what ... three days? Four?'

'Six,' Alvaro corrected.

'*Six?*' That couldn't be right. Had it really been six days already? She quickly counted the days on her fingers ... and he was right. Including the day she first arrived, today was currently her sixth day in Harukai. Six days and no sign of being able to open the tunnel. Six days since Elias held a dagger to her mother's throat. That tendril coiled inside her, but she pushed those worries aside and focused on Alvaro for the moment, gently wiping his shredded palms with the cloth. 'You hadn't done it in six days. Well, five, since you did it today. But why now? What changed?'

Alvaro hesitated, before saying, 'Anything I can do to help, Miss Ivy.'

Ivy shook her head. 'No. If that's all it is, why did you stop? You stopped for five days, Alvaro. So, why did you do it again?' Ivy soaked the cloth in the bucket of water and drained the excess before moving to his other hand. The wounds on his first hand kept bleeding, but at least the initial mess was clean.

'I stopped because you had returned. After all this time, I finally had hope that your mother could also return. But our talking and reading earlier reminded me ...' He stopped himself and swallowed. Was he hiding something? Before she could ask, he continued, 'It reminded me how impossible it truly is to open that tunnel. It was built using magic, Miss Ivy, something the folk ...' He paused again. 'I was reminded that the only thing I can possibly do is what I have always done, because at least I am trying.'

Ivy couldn't tell if he was outright lying, if he was omitting information, or if he had in fact told her the entire truth. If he knew something about how they could open the rock wall, would he not tell her? Would he not have tried doing so already?

'Alvaro ...' she started. 'Are you telling me the truth?' She met his gaze.

His jaw tensed, and he nodded.

'Find Alvaro. He will keep you safe.' He may be keeping her safe, but could she trust him? Could she believe everything he told her?

Her brows furrowed with uncertainty, but instead of focusing on those thoughts, she allowed them to curl in the shadows of her mind for the time being. 'Well, I'm not letting you do this again, all right? No more nearly killing yourself doing something you *know* won't work. I won't let you.' Ivy finished cleaning his wounds and placed the blood-soaked cloth in the bucket. 'Besides, I think I've found something in one of the books.'

Alvaro's eyes widened. 'Really?'

'But before I show you, let's bandage you up.'

Ivy got to work cleaning and rebandaging his hands, just as he had done for her a few nights ago, and just as she'd been doing for herself every evening after her baths. In that moment, when there was nothing but silence and the sounds of her cleaning his hands, she almost asked about her identity. And perhaps she should have, for her tendril didn't claim her voice, but she was excited to tell Alvaro about her new discovery, and how they were another step closer to opening the tunnel in the rock wall.

When she was done, he made them some tea—he insisted, despite his fresh wounds—before sitting beside her in his usual chair. Ivy opened the book to the very end and showed Alvaro the passage.

'So,' she began, 'we just need to find this Oracle person. They can tell us what they believe about the Maidens, why they believe it, whatever, and maybe that can help us.'

Alvaro didn't seem nearly as excited as she felt when he asked, 'What makes you think this will help? To me, it sounds like another belief, another myth. There is no fact here.'

'But it's something, right? There must be a reason the Oracle thinks the Maidens will return. Everything else just says they're gone or never existed. This can at least lead us somewhere. Perhaps even lead us to the Maidens.'

Alvaro read the paragraph again and mumbled, 'Unknown, un-willing being ...' His brows pulled together but his eyes widened slightly. He kept his finger in place as he shut the book and read the cover. 'Where did you get this book?'

'Oh, I, um ...' She'd promised Leyrah she wouldn't tell anyone. 'There was a mix up with some of the books. *This* is the history of the Maidens.'

'Hmm.' He opened it back to where they'd been reading, his eyes skimming the words. Then, he closed his eyes and sighed. 'Miss Ivy, the Oracle is no one you, or anyone for that matter, should concern yourself with.'

Ivy didn't know what she'd been expecting, but it certainly wasn't a cryptic answer like that. 'Why?' she asked, taking a sip of her tea.

'Well ...' His jaw tensed as he swallowed. 'For starters, I presume they are gone from this world. Stories speak of their existence hun-dreds of years ago. Perhaps close to a thousand years. Mind you, us folk only live to three hundred, so the Oracle should be long gone.'

Ivy choked on her tea. '*Three hundred?*'

Alvaro's brows furrowed. 'Of course. Do humans not live that long?'

'The average human lifespan is like eighty or ninety. A hundred if you're really lucky.'

'Oh my. That is so ... young.'

Ivy reached for her ears hidden beneath her hair and stroked their pointed tips. Other than her ears, she had no other folk-defining features. But Alvaro had said she was a folk, had said that her and her mother had been taken from here. Would she live to be three hundred? That was certainly an interesting thought. What could one person do with three hundred years? The possibilities were endless, but she could plan the rest of her life once her mother was safe.

'As for the other reason,' Alvaro said, 'the Oracle is a dangerous being. And while I believe their life has ended, they were unlike any other folk in Harukai. There is a chance their lifespan may differ from ours.'

'How were they different?'

'They were born ... *unwell*, is the only correct term to use, I suppose. They were gifted with the ability to see and predict things.'

'Predict? See things? Like, predict the future? Wait, can they *see* the future?' she asked with a spark of excitement in her tone. If they could see the future, then they could see the Maidens' return.

Alvaro eyed her, curiosity painting his expression. 'Yes. But that is nothing to be excited about, Miss Ivy. Seeing and predicting the future is a dangerous gift to hold. The Oracle is most known for lying about the future and sending folk into danger.'

Her excitement dwindled, but didn't vanish entirely. 'Why?'

'Because they can. That is what is most dangerous. They have no motive other than the thrill of risking someone's life.'

Ivy didn't say anything, her excitement fading into nothing. Why would the Oracle choose evil when seeing the future could be used for so much good?

'The folk are not gifted with magic,' Alvaro continued, 'yet the Oracle was born with this ability. Thankfully, no one has been born with such powers since. Powers of the mind ... a dangerous ability, and a rare occurrence that shall hopefully not happen again.'

Out of all the folk in all of history, how was it that the Oracle was the only one gifted with magic? Whatever the reason, Ivy assumed the Oracle could see the Maidens' return, meaning their belief was true. She just needed to know when it would happen.

'Do you know where the Oracle is now?' she asked.

Alvaro shook his head. 'No one in Harukai does. It is believed they were banished somewhere they cannot escape. They have not been seen in many, many years, which is also why I believe them to have passed.'

Ivy nodded. A running theme in this world; no answers to a never-ending list of questions.

'Miss Ivy.' Alvaro held her arm gently. 'Do not go looking for the Oracle. Even if they have the answers we seek, there is no way to trust they will tell you. There is no way to trust *what* they will tell you.' He released a slow breath. 'Stories claim the Oracle sent folk to their deaths and laughed afterwards. They could easily give you false answers and send you to your death as well. I will not allow that to happen.'

Ivy didn't want to lie to him. But something told her he was hiding things from her. And while he'd shown his willingness to help in her endeavours—that were also his own—the Oracle was clearly the only way to find the information she needed, despite the strong possibility they were no longer alive. There didn't seem to be any alternative. And she was just as stubborn as Alvaro when it came to not giving up. He threw himself against the rock wall every day—Ivy could throw herself against something too.

'Okay,' she lied.

That evening, Alvaro insisted on training her, despite his injuries. 'I am not the one who is training,' he had explained. 'My injuries are of no concern.' They stood in the clearing behind Alvaro's home, beside the huge vegetable and herb garden planted directly below Ivy's window, filled with tomatoes, zucchinis, carrots, cucumbers, cauliflower—just like her mum's garden. Next to the vegetables were green stalks of herbs, and beyond that, trees for the delectable fruits.

'You can lay your sword to the side,' Alvaro told her. 'You will not be needing it today.'

A part of Ivy wanted to argue; she hadn't been able to use her sword that morning, either. But she knew Alvaro would have good reasons, just as Theon probably did. As she cast her sword aside, Alvaro's eyes followed and lingered on the weapon discarded near the vegetable patch. He walked over and pulled it from its sheath, his brows furrowing as he admired the stained-glass detailing.

'Why did you choose this sword?' he asked.

'I, um ...' Did she tell him the truth? It sounded ridiculous, but that could potentially be because she hadn't been raised here. For all she knew, strange pulses for weapons were normal—despite how *abnormal* it sounded. Although, the way Theon explained his similar beat for her safety seemed as though it was not, in fact, a normal occurrence. 'I just really liked it,' she finally said.

His head snapped to her. '*Why* did you choose *this* sword?'

'I dunno. I just—'

'Tell me, Miss Ivy.'

'I had to!' she said, repeating what Theon had told her. 'I don't know why, but I just had to. I've been feeling this strange rhythm in my veins the second I got here, and it grew stronger every time I was near the Tarad. Last night it called to me, screamed at me to take it. The closer I got, the louder it became, until it started hurting me. And once I found it, I couldn't let it go.'

Alvaro had no response. He brought the sword close and ran his fingers along the blade of flame and water, his brows remaining furrowed.

'Alvaro?' Ivy demanded. But his lack of response confirmed her suspicions; there was something he wasn't telling her. 'Are you hiding things from me?'

'No,' he said without hesitation.

But Ivy didn't believe him, and that realisation had her questioning everything he'd told her. 'Are you ... are you lying to me?'

He pulled his gaze from her sword. 'I am not lying to you, Miss Ivy. I have never lied to you. I just ...' His eyes flicked around the space before returning to her. 'I do not know what the truth is. And rather than telling you something that may possibly be inaccurate, I feel it is better to withhold the information until I know the truth.'

The logic was there, but she wasn't sure she wanted the information kept from her, whether it was true or not. She knew if she asked him to tell her, he would. But was it wise, learning something that could easily be false? Was it better to let Alvaro investigate? Would knowing whatever he kept from her only distract her from finding a way home?

Alvaro stepped closer. 'I know it is a big ask, but I need you to trust me, Miss Ivy. I will learn what I can and once I know the truth, I will tell you immediately. But I would rather you focus on finding a way through the Realm Divider.'

'Find Alvaro. He will keep you safe.'

Was this his way of keeping her safe? Her mother wouldn't tell her only daughter to find just anyone. Dorothea trusted Alvaro, so Ivy should do the same.

She nodded.

Alvaro gave her a small smile. 'Thank you.'

She took her sword from him, but as she pulled it from his grasp, Alvaro grabbed her hand and held it in front of him. 'This ring ...' he muttered, admiring the ring that had once belonged to her mother. The sapphire gemstone glinted in the sun. 'It is beautiful.'

'It was my mum's,' Ivy said cautiously. 'Did you not see it when you cleaned my hands the other night?'

'Yes, I did. And I had noticed its beauty then, too. Although, I was more concerned with your wounds rather than your accessories.' His finger stroked the gemstone. 'Sorry.' He quickly dropped her hand and took a few steps back, while she placed her sword back in its sheath by the vegetable garden. 'Take a deep breath, and close your eyes,' he said, his sudden curiosity about her mother's ring cast aside like her sword. Ivy closed her eyes and followed his direction: in through her nose, out through her mouth. 'Clear your mind,' he continued. 'Imagine your thoughts are clouds passing you by. You will see them again, but for now, they will travel along.'

Ivy continued her breathing, watching her thoughts pass her by. The Maidens, the Oracle, Theon wiping her tears, his hand touching hers, being dragged through the tunnel, a knife to her mum's throat, Theon throwing a dagger at her dad—

'Miss Ivy,' Alvaro's soothing voice interrupted. 'Control your breathing.' Without realising, her breathing had turned ragged. She tried again: in through her nose, out through her mouth. She placed her memories in the passing clouds. 'Concentrate on what is around you.'

She had assumed there would be differences in Alvaro's and Theon's fighting techniques, but she also assumed there would be actual training involved. 'Will we be training soon?' she asked.

'Normally there would be more physical exercise involved. But I presume you have done similarly with Theon this morning, and I do not want to overwork your body. Now, control your breathing. And listen.'

In through her nose, out through her mouth.

'Concentrate on your surroundings. Feel the breeze against your skin. Hear the rustling of the leaves. This will ground you.'

Ivy did as he commanded. She'd braided her hair for this training session, but stray hairs that had broken free blew against her cheeks. She breathed in the slightly sweet scent of fresh grass, the musty smell of soil and tree bark, vegetables and herbs from the garden, and ... saltwater. *The ocean must be close,* Ivy thought. Without knowing why and still keeping her eyes closed, she slowly knelt, untying her boots and removing her socks, before planting her feet in the grass. Her toes wriggled until they dug beneath the grassy roots. She stood, her lips parting on instinct. A variety of tastes entered her mouth: musty soil, fresh grass, crisp leaves, rough bark, and vegetables.

'Open your eyes.' Alvaro's green eyes were wide, the corners of his lips turned up. 'Eyes on me. Follow my movements.' His right leg slid back; hers did the same. His arms moved up in front of him; hers did the same. And together, silently, they moved.

Thoughts passed her by on their clouds. Wind brushed her skin, the scents of nature entering through each breath. Every sense was activated, grounding her. Without knowing the next step, she followed Alvaro through gentle motions and stretches. Neither of them spoke until they stopped an hour later.

'How do you feel?' Alvaro asked.

Ivy took a deep breath and blinked back to reality. Her cloudy thoughts returned, but now without the stress each one caused weighing her down. 'Relaxed,' she answered honestly. 'What was that?'

'A form of meditation. Grounding you in nature helps with patience and enhances your senses. With time, you will learn how to harness this while fighting an opponent. Although, I pray you never have to.'

'It felt ... freeing.'

'Good. Now, I believe you need some rest. You have had a big day, and I have no doubt you will have another tomorrow. But first, would you like to help me prepare some dinner?'

'Ah, sure.'

'Excellent. You pick some vegetables, and I will get the fire started.'

Ivy nodded, then grabbed her sword and did exactly as he said.

Twenty-Five

Ivy sat by the firepit while Alvaro showed her how to light the fire. He scraped two rocks together until a spark lit and landed on the bed of twigs. A large sack of meat sat beside him, while the bag of vegetables she'd picked—cauliflower, carrots, and zucchini—was next to her. Once the spark was lit, he showed her how to skewer the vegetables, and he then did the same to the chopped-up meat while they waited for the spark to turn into flame.

She enjoyed the peace and quiet as she threaded vegetables onto a stick, but her mind was plagued with thoughts and questions. The meditation hadn't helped as much as she'd thought. Her pointed ears held a large space of her crowded mind. Who was she? Would she ever develop new features, or would she remain some abnormal humanoid version of a folk?

Alvaro knew her. Surely he knew who she truly was.

'Alvaro,' she started, pulling his attention away from the meat he carefully skewered. 'I, uh …' Her tendril snaked between the crevices of her internal organs, but she ignored its presence. 'Who am I?'

Alvaro opened his mouth, but no words came out. He closed his lips as he finished skewering the meat, then placed it above the fire. 'I presume you are asking about your folk identity.'

Ivy swallowed and nodded.

'Your mother,' he started with a smile. 'There is a secluded beach through the trees behind my home. That is where her and I first met. You see, she is from the Noa Kingdom.'

'What?' That's certainly not what she was expecting. If her mother was a merfolk, that meant she was too. Except, she didn't have any merfolk features. And her ears weren't that of a merfolk. Though her question was answered, it still left her unknowing of who she was. What kind of merfolk was she supposed to be? What race was her mother? Waves crashed inside her, swirling with the tendril hovering nearby. More of her old self was pulled away, but it wasn't replaced with anything new. She was incomplete. 'But ... but I don't have scales or anything. And I can't breathe underwater. What ... what does that make me?'

'Hm.' His brows pulled together. 'Theoretically, you should be able to breathe underwater.' He removed the skewered meat from the fire and transferred them to a cooling rack. 'No, that is not right. You *can* breathe underwater.'

'No, I can't,' Ivy told him.

'Miss Ivy, I witnessed your first few months of existence. Believe me when I tell you I saw you breathe underwater. I saw ...' He sighed. 'I saw your scales, and your gills, and your tail. I do not know what happened to you in the human realm for those features to have been removed from you. But there is no doubt in my mind of who you are.'

None of that made sense. If he spoke the truth—which there was no reason for him to lie—then what happened to her? Just when her new identity was within reach, it was ripped from her grasp. She was ... She was ... She was broken. The thought had her eyes filling with salty water as ocean waves roiled beneath her flesh.

'Alvaro ...' Her tears spilled before she could even ask her next question. 'What's wrong with me?'

He stood and walked around the cooling rack to sit on her other side. 'There is absolutely nothing wrong with you, Miss Ivy. You are not defined by what is visible on the outside.' He put his hand on her shoulder, the waves inside her quieting. 'You are deeply caring and openly curious. You do not shy away from your emotions, no matter what they are. You are determined and courageous and brave. You are unequivocally *you*.'

Her only response was a sniffle.

'Do you understand?'

She nodded.

He offered her a sad smile and glanced to where the vegetable sticks waited in her hands. 'Here.' He showed her how to add them to the fire. Once they were in place, he said, 'There is more I can tell you, if you like.'

She dried her tears with her bandaged hands and nodded again.

'You are actually not entirely merfolk. You are ...' His jaw tensed and he bit the inside of his cheek before looking at her with wide eyes lined with tears. Not entirely merfolk? It explained her pointed ears, but it just left her feeling even less like a folk than before. Ivy was already inhuman and a merfolk incapable of breathing underwater. Was she ready to learn how else she was broken?

She gave him a third nod to let him know it was okay to continue. 'You are also a faun.'

'What?' Before she had even a second to process this new part of herself, she screamed.

Something pounded against her skull. It throbbed with a headache so intense she genuinely thought her head would explode. Her hands grasped her hair as she doubled over in absolute agony.

'AHHHHHHHH!' Her face was drenched with new tears that poured into her open mouth. The waves and tendril that usually claimed her emotions were no match for whatever this was.

'Miss Ivy?' Alvaro's muffled voice was barely discernible.

She thought he might have grabbed her, but she couldn't tell. All she could feel was her skin starting to tear as whatever it was tried to break through her skull. She started pulling her hair, hoping to ease some of the pain with one that was familiar, but she couldn't feel her roots being pulled from their homes.

'AHHHHHHHH!' Her skin stretched and stretched until it finally tore apart, thick liquid dripping from the wounds. She gasped with relief as the pounding eased. Her head still throbbed, but now other sensations could be felt. Like Alvaro's hands grasping her upper arms, and her hair being pulled from the roots, and ... something pushing through her head.

Her hands found the area at the top of her head, liquid coating her fingers ... Rough bone protruded on the left and right sides. They moved through her fingers on their journey out until they finally stopped. She fumbled her fingers up their slim forms. They felt like … She wasn't quite sure what they felt like. Bone, she supposed, but with pointed ends and smaller pieces branching out.

'Miss Ivy …'

Ivy inhaled ragged breaths and slowly lifted her head.

Alvaro watched her in awe, his eyes travelling up whatever it was she still held in her hands. 'Marvellous …' he whispered. He'd told her she was a faun. Her gaze found his antlers in the same place as the things now on her head.

Without a word, she ran to the house, stumbling with the weight of the bone-like things on her head. Once inside, she climbed the ladder until she was on the top floor and ran the few steps to the dresser.

She didn't know where to look first.

Either side of the centre of her head, curving in no specific way, were antlers. Brown antlers, kind of resembling tree bark. The main stems curved up and back while a smaller stem on each antler curved out to the sides, with tines growing sporadically along their forms.

Antlers. She had *antlers.*

But there was no time to register them, for her skin had also changed. Small white freckles lined her eyes, spreading around her eyebrows, onto her cheekbones, and along the edge of her face. Her arms were dotted with them. She removed her shirt—thankfully there were buttons on the front—only to find more of those freckles splattered across her dark skin.

Her heart beat wildly, her breaths catching in the tendril making itself known once more.

She was a faun.

Ivy lifted her skirt and breathed a sigh of relief; her legs remained the same, only now they were speckled with those freckles. She faced the mirror once more and reached for her antlers. *Antlers.* Her fingers trailed along their smooth yet rough stems. She knew she wasn't human, but something about her features changing so drastically in the span of a few seconds had her tendril clinging onto her organs for dear life.

And her freckles, so stark against her dark skin. She was a *faun.* She leant over the dresser until her nose nearly touched the mirror. Tears slipped from her eyes, and she watched how their transparency changed as they rolled over the different colours of her skin.

Was it merely coincidence that these features had only revealed themselves now, mere seconds after Alvaro told her of her identity? Would her merfolk features do the same the next time she touched water?

Her fingers slid down the slender forms of her antlers—*her* antlers—until they landed in the lingering liquid at their base. She pulled away; blood stained her fingers. Her skin was sticky with sweat and saltwater. She needed to bathe.

'Miss Ivy?' Alvaro called from downstairs. 'Are you all right?'

She hadn't heard him enter, too distracted by her new ... everything. 'I, um ...' She was a *faun*; of course she wasn't all right. 'I'm gonna have a bath.' Her tendril strangled her lungs, causing her to choke on the words.

Silence. Then, 'Would you like to eat first?'

More tears broke free, but she didn't want to break down just yet. She needed to feel everything on her own first before seeking comfort from others. She held the wave of emotions back as she asked, 'Can I eat it later?'

'Of course,' Alvaro said without pause. 'We can heat it on the coals for you when you are ready.' Clopping hooves lead the way to the front door before it closed behind him.

TWENTY-SIX

I vy stood by the pond surrounded by luscious trees, flowers, and mushrooms, the gentle song of rustling leaves echoing through the space. From the edge of the pond, Alvaro and the firepit couldn't be seen. There was nothing but nature everywhere she looked.

She'd stumbled multiple times on her way to the pond because of the unnatural weight of her antlers—or rather, *natural* weight that was merely unnatural to her—and even just standing was difficult. It was like learning to walk all over again. She would need to ask Alvaro for help.

She removed her clothes and stepped towards the pond but stopped before her toes could disturb the still water. Would her merfolk features reveal themselves? She still hadn't gotten used to her antlers and freckles, had barely adjusted to her pointed ears—was she ready to see another side of herself?

Her tendril snuck through and grazed her organs, but she pushed it aside. She needed to know.

Ivy stepped into the water and dove.

It was an ungraceful dive, her antlers throwing her off her natural balance, but she still made it beneath the surface. She tried to stay under for as long as she could hold her breath, but water filtered between the tines and stems of her antlers, causing her to shuffle about with their jolted movements.

She pushed to the surface, and as soon as she was out of the water, kicking her legs to stay afloat, her hands flew to her neck. She gasped—both at what she felt and the sensitivity. She couldn't be certain without a mirror, but her fingers lightly rubbed along three slits on either side of her neck. They had to be gills; what else could they be?

Suddenly, her kicking legs started moving with a mind of their own. The movement slowed until they came together, flowing in a singular rhythm. Ivy ducked beneath the water, and where a pair of legs once were, was ...

She screamed and broke the surface, instantly swimming to the edge. She had to have imagined it. After all, the water was a bit murky. But she knew it wasn't imaginary.

She struggled to swim with her singular leg movements, her arms using all her strength to carry her through the water. Once at the edge of the pond, she pulled herself up the soil and rolled onto her back, sitting up to fully view what had changed with her legs. Her legs hadn't just changed, however—they'd completely vanished. And in their place was a sparkling emerald tail.

It was ... It was beautiful. She reached for it, her fingers grazing the scales; they felt just like Theon's. Above her hips, some of the scales continued, fanning out across her torso and around her back, not unlike the way Theon's did. More speckled her arms, mixing with her white freckles, before falling over her shoulders and grouping across her chest.

Her tendril suffocated her lungs. Ivy pulled her shaking hands away from her tail. She had … She had a *tail*. And gills, and antlers. The cries she'd held back while in the spare room broke free. So much of herself had been stripped away, she wasn't sure there was anything left. What remained? *Who* remained? Everything she once was didn't exist anymore, and everything that existed now wasn't who she was. Her body merely existed in this smoky in-between, inhabited by a lost soul.

Who was she? And why had her mother kept this from her?

Her mother, who was a merfolk—who had been a merfolk all her life. Why had she not told Ivy who she really was? All those years of bedtime stories could have been better spent explaining her true identity.

With her mum most likely in danger, the last thing she wanted to do was be angry or upset with her, but she couldn't help it. Water rippled inside her, encasing the tendril that hugged her organs. Her mother had lied to her all her life, and now she was being stripped of everything that made her who she was. Now she was sitting on the edge of a pond with antlers and white freckles and a tail and gills, and she had no idea what to do. All because her mum hadn't told her.

'*That man is not—*'

She hadn't even told her who her real father was. Instead, she'd told her fictional bedtime stories about a merfolk who fell in love with a faun—

Oh, God. Was that story about her parents? It had been her favourite story growing up; maybe that was because she had some familial connection to it. She had no idea who her father was, but she could only assume he was a faun. What else had the story been about? She racked her brain, but she hadn't heard it in years. All she remembered was a whimsical forest kingdom, an enchanting underwater kingdom, a faun and a merfolk who fell in love, and ... And that was it.

Ivy made to hug her knees, but her tail was too heavy for the movement, which only caused her to cry more. Why hadn't her mum just told her everything? Why was she left picking up the shattered pieces of who she was while simultaneously trying to find a way through the tunnel to find her mum?

And what about Elias? Had he known who she was? Or was keeping this secret her mother's way of protecting her from him, before she had to resort to sending her to Harukai?

'That man is not—'

'It's not me he needs. It's Ivy.'

Who was he? Why did he need Ivy? Or better yet, why did he only need her *now* as opposed to any other time during her life? All those questions fought to be answered, but there was one question that ruled them all.

If he wasn't her dad, then who was?

After bathing, Ivy made her way to the firepit. Her tail had vanished after she'd dried herself, revealing her legs once more. However, some of her scales remained, scattered like her freckles. Her pyjamas consisted of a large button-up shirt and another of those long skirts—she'd never worn the skirt to bed, but she certainly wasn't going to leave her bottom half uncovered.

She sat beside Alvaro, her dinner now laying on the hot coals. Surely he would know who her father was. But did she really want to know just yet?

Alvaro turned to her. 'How are you feeling?'

What a loaded question that was. In the span of, what, thirty minutes? She'd grown antlers and freckles and gills and scales and an entire tail. At this point, to say she was going through an identity crisis was absolutely an understatement. She opened her mouth to answer, but then she looked at him. *Properly* looked at him. Not just his antlers or freckles or his dark ruffled hair. But his eyes, which reflected a deep green. His permanent dimple in his left cheek that she'd never noticed until now. The sapphire flowers on his shirt—he always wore sapphire.

And then, she tried to see past that. Tried to see through to the fact that he knew her mother. Had spent time with her, had even known Ivy as a baby. How he'd spent every day for the last sixteen years destroying himself against the rock wall despite knowing it wouldn't work just to try and bring them back.

'Find Alvaro. He will keep you safe.'

What if ...

She'd learnt enough about herself tonight. She knew Elias wasn't her father—at least, she assumed, but honestly, what else could her mum have been about to say that night? The memory of him had already been tampered with after he'd held that dagger to her mum's throat. But to Ivy, he was still her father. He'd been there when she'd gotten her first pair of flippers and had been the one to teach her how to swim. He'd snuggled her when she couldn't sleep and laughed with her and her mum when they'd failed at baking something as simple as brownies.

She didn't want those memories to be replaced with someone else. Not yet.

Elias dragged Dorothea away, back towards the house, the dagger still to her throat.

Had that only been a few nights ago? So much had changed in such a short time.

In these small moments where she wasn't training or looking for a way through the tunnel, she needed to distract herself.

And Alvaro knew her mum.

Instead of answering his question, she asked one of her own, her fingers twiddling her ring. Her mother's ring. 'Can you tell me about Mum?'

'Oh.' He turned to the skewers on the coals and rolled them over, then asked, 'What do you wish to know?'

'I don't know. Anything. Everything.'

'Well, Miss Ivy, there is quite a lot I could say, but it would take a tremendous amount of time. We would both be sleeping before I could finish,' he added with a smile. 'Is there something specific you wish to know?'

The only thing she wished to know was who her dad was, but she wasn't ready to learn that just yet. All she wanted—no, *need-*

ed—right now was a distraction from everything that plagued her. 'I don't know. Just tell me something. Anything, Alvaro. Please.'

He hesitated, as if he didn't want to tell her anything. Or perhaps he merely didn't know what to tell her. But then he sighed and said, 'As I told you, your mother and I met on a secluded beach behind my home.' He looked across the clearing to that part of the forest. 'She had been trying to escape her life momentarily, just as I was. After that, it became a regular spot for us to meet and sit and talk in peace, without the weight of the world on our shoulders.'

Ivy watched him reminiscing, his memory reminding her of her favourite bedtime story. She noticed those familiar features of his again, and her tendril carefully hugged her organs. She wouldn't learn anything else about her identity tonight. It was a strange yet beautiful thing to hear someone else talk about her mother. It dampened her current reality.

'Tell me something else,' she said without thinking.

'Something else?' he asked, turning back to her. His eyes roamed her face, and he smiled. 'One day, after many suns and moons of us meeting on that beach, she asked me to show her the Thidin Kingdom. Actually, that is not quite right.' He chuckled as he corrected himself and said, 'She *told* me to take her. As long as I have known her, she has always been quite demanding. Mind you, merfolk never enter the Thidin Kingdom. There is no need.'

Alvaro continued his story, and when he was done, Ivy asked him for another. And another. And another. They stayed by the fire long after the sun went down, passing stories and memories between them of Dorothea. They laughed and giggled and reminisced until everything from that day had vanished. Until Ivy was yawning and couldn't keep her eyes open. She was only reminded of her new identity and the questions she still had yet to ask when she stood to go to bed, but by then she was so exhausted that her worries were nothing more than clouds passing her by.

'What are you doing awake?' Elias asks.

'I had a bad dream,' seven-year-old Ivy says.

He sighs. 'Come here, darling.' She sits with him on the lounge, whatever movie he was watching now paused. A container filled with lollies and chocolates rests on his lap. He puts his arm around her, and she snuggles into his side. 'What was the dream?'

She tries to remember, but as dreams do, it was already starting to fade. 'There was lots of darkness. And a scary lady was talking to me.'

'What was she saying?'

'Something about ... flowers, I think. Leaves. Something about a sword and nature. Women becoming flowers, maybe. It was all very weird. And there was a storm. Lightning and dark clouds. Lots of water and fire.'

Her dad pulls her close. 'That sounds very scary. But luckily, it was only a dream.' They sit in silence for a moment, before he asks, 'Do you want to stay out here with me?'

Ivy nods. Her father smiles and plays the movie, then tilts the container of sweets her way. She grabs a red liquorice and a chocolate-coated sultana, and it's not long until she's fast asleep.

Twenty-Seven

Low-hanging tree branches smacked into Ivy's antlers, while vines twisted between the tines. It was bad enough not being able to walk straight with their new weight, but now she also had to account for the extra height.

At least she didn't have hooves.

She'd gone around the Tarad on her way to the beach, through the path of fallen leaves, hoping to avoid being gawked at by the folk once more for her newly formed folk-like features. Her tendril curled like a sleeping cat, squeezing itself into any crevice it could fit.

Water caressed a rocky shore nearby; she'd heard the same sound the first time she'd walked this path with Alvaro. Maybe one day when her life wasn't falling apart at the seams she would see where that music resonated.

But the seams of her life weren't currently sewn together.

So, she walked through a whimsical, ethereal forest on her way to meet a merfolk so he could teach her how to fight with a sword that had ached to be hers. Only now, she also had to learn to fight while balancing a pair of antlers on her head. Would she then also have to learn how to use her sword underwater? Perhaps, if she ever allowed herself to freely swim amongst the waves again.

The path curved to the right, and up ahead, blue water could be seen carving a line against the white crystal shore. Leaves crunched beneath her boots, and she stumbled forward, falling into hanging vines that again tangled around her antlers. She flicked her head around and brushed them away, then checked the ground for whatever she'd tripped over. Only leaves and soil marred the path, her useless feet having stumbled over nothing.

Once her antlers were free and she was righted, her gaze found Theon at the end of the path exiting the water. Without a thought, she ducked off the footpath and hid behind a tree. However, the trees were skinny enough where both of her sides could be seen if he bothered to look. Which, thankfully, he didn't.

Now, why was she hiding from Theon?

Well, her sleeping tendril had woken at the sight of him, cradling her organs like a mother cradles her baby. She didn't want anyone to see her new form. Not even Alvaro, yet he'd been there when she'd changed, so there had been no hiding it. She also lived with him and couldn't very well hide a pair of antlers. Sure, she could avoid the Tarad as much as possible, but she couldn't avoid Theon—unless she stopped their training, which she couldn't do, since she needed the skills for when she finally made it back to the human realm.

He walked up the sand and dropped his brown bag at the tree line, then knelt to open it. Even if she stopped training—which, again, she didn't want to do—she was certain she would see him again. She couldn't very well hide from him forever. And she wasn't sure she *wanted* to hide from him forever.

She stepped out of the trees, and just as she did so, her foot landed on a stick, ultimately snapping it in two.

'Finally decided to show up—' Theon stood and turned around, cutting his sentence short once he saw her. On instinct, her hands found her arms, trying and failing to cover the scales and freckles dotting her skin. 'You, ah, um,' he stuttered, his wide eyes flicking between all her new features. A redness crept onto his cheeks. 'Wow, I, ah, you're, um ... What, ah, what happened?' he finally asked.

'Well,' she started, slowly walking along the sand and trying to ignore the way he looked at her. Not just looked at her but marvelled at her. 'I ... I found out I'm not ... I'm not actually human.' Of course, she knew that already, but when the words were spoken out loud—and from her own lips, no less—they carried an additional weight that had her shoulders hunching forward. Theon didn't say anything, but his gaze flicked to her antlers once more, and she chuckled. 'I'm, um ...' she continued. 'I'm actually *part* faun.'

His brows pulled together. 'Part?' he asked. She lifted her skirt to reveal her humanoid legs—no hooves or fur in sight. 'Hm.' He squatted by his bag again and started rummaging through it. 'Do you, ah, know what your other part is?'

Her tendril crept up her throat, but she swallowed it down. Had he not noticed her scales? 'Yeah. I'm, uh ... I'm a merfolk.'

He stopped his rummaging. 'Yeah, I saw the scales. But, uh ... Have you been underwater? Do you know exactly what you are?'

His head tilted her way, but he didn't entirely look at her. Was he nervous?

'I ... I'm a merfolk,' she said.

He sighed, then resumed his movements—which consisted of continuously rummaging through his bag but never removing anything, as though he were purely trying to look busy. 'I thought ... I *hoped* that if you were half land folk and half sea folk, that perhaps ...' He shook his head. 'It doesn't matter.'

Her tendril loosened its restriction, hiding somewhere she wouldn't find it. He sounded ... disappointed. 'You hoped I'd be like you,' she finished for him.

'It doesn't matter,' he repeated. 'I've gone this long being the only one of my kind. What's another few hundred years?'

Whatever weight she'd been carrying since being in Harukai, having only grown heavier since yesterday evening, didn't feel quite so monumental in this moment. She was afraid of the identity she was rediscovering, but Theon longed to discover his own identity. Their paths were connected, but not entirely intertwined. A silver thread twisting between them and guiding them forward. Perhaps one day she could return the favour of his training and help him discover himself.

But that day would have to wait. Right now, she could barely keep herself upright with her antlers and everything they meant. She feared submerging herself in the ocean which had once been her comfort. And she was trapped in a land that was foreign but was apparently her home. Not apparently—it *was* her home. But that word meant nothing without her mother. It didn't mean too much without Elias, either, but that view was slowly starting to shift.

Despite all of this, all Ivy could do was practise fighting techniques and read books. But she didn't want to just exercise and use weights. She had a sword, and she needed to know how to use it.

'I want to use my sword,' she said.

While she was lost in her thoughts, Theon had started removing some of those said weights. Without hesitation, without stopping or slowing his movements, he replied, 'No.'

Her jaw tensed; she'd had a feeling he would say that. 'I'm not asking.'

That got his attention. Theon slowly stood, rising from the ground like a phoenix rises from the ashes, and turned around. 'No. We've had one training session, Ivy. *One*. You can barely do pull-ups, and I see you struggling to stand straight with those antlers. How do you expect to wield a weapon?'

Her blood started to boil. 'I'm not asking,' she repeated. 'The only way I'm going to learn how to use a weapon is if I *use it*.' She pulled her sword from her sheath and stepped forward, aiming the blade at him. Each step closer had her boiling blood rising. 'You brought me here against my will. You claim to be protecting me. Teaching me how to use this sword, how to fight with it, *is* protecting me.' She was close enough now where the tip of her blade touched the centre of his chest. 'I'm using this sword today, whether you want me to or not.'

Her eyes met his, which glared at her like steel blades cutting emeralds. Not a word was spoken, but heat simmered. Heat that wasn't from her boiling fury. Strands of his copper hair sliced his face, mimicking threads of a setting sun atop a rippling ocean. He raised his arm and gently brushed aside her sword with his fingers.

'Fine.' Then he stepped back and removed his own shortsword from his sheath at his side. 'Show me what you got.'

Ivy fumbled through her mind for the techniques he'd shown her the previous morning, and ended up striking a defence blow, stepping forward and tapping his blade with her own in a failed attempt to push him back.

He sighed. 'Are you sure you want to do this?'

She ignored his question and struck forward again, this time aiming near his torso, which he easily deflected with a simple swing of his arm. Yes, she'd only had one training session with him, but she was determined to try and accomplish something with this weapon today. For all she knew, she could find a way to the human realm tomorrow—she needed to at least know how to defend herself.

Another strike, this one towards his arm. Another one. And another. Each time she struck forward, he easily blocked her shot. Which was completely understandable but still caused that simmering fury of hers to bubble further.

Elias dragged Dorothea away, back towards the house, the dagger still to her throat.

She continued her useless attempts, stepping forward with each failed blow. Her tendril tightened around any and all internal organs, disrupting the flow of oxygen. Deep breaths—in through her nose, out through her mouth.

'That man is not—'

The clanging of their blades rung in her ears. Water rushed inside her, rushed up the shore of the beach. Waves overlapped each other as the tide strengthened.

'Is that who I think ...'

Another strike, another clang.

'Find Alvaro. He will keep you safe.'

She stepped around Theon, aiming for his exposed back, but he quickly spun and blocked her attack.

'We've waited years…'

Each new attack had more strength added to it, causing Theon to properly spar with her rather than merely push each blow aside. They danced along the beach, closer to the waves crashing against the shore. Flaming fury filled her blood; water washed alongside it, coating her flesh in salt water.

'I will find you, Ivy.' Even his voice had changed ever-so-slightly, a deep and unnaturally calm cadence. *'Unless you find me first.'*

On her next swing, Ivy released every ounce of energy, frustration, grief, and torment she had stored away. All those internal flames and waves broke free of their hold inside her, until they weren't merely emotional. Flame coated her stained-glass blade while a gush of water rushed out, splashing into Theon's face.

She gasped and dropped the flaming, water-wielding sword. The second it was released from her grasp, those elements vanished, as if it was nothing more than her imagination. But the way Theon stared at her, frozen in time, fresh water soaking his hair and face, confirmed it wasn't imaginary. 'What…' Theon started.

Her breathing had no rhythm. Slowly, Ivy crouched and touched the hilt of her sword; no fire nor water revealed themselves.

'What,' Theon repeated, but like her, he seemed to be at a complete loss for speech.

With shaking hands, Ivy placed her sword back in its sheath and stood. She assessed him for injuries—perhaps the flame had also struck him—and once she could tell he was fine, she turned and ran into the forest.

Twenty-Eight

Ivy sprinted through the dense forest, her antlers catching on vines and branches, but that didn't stop her. She ran from the beach, from Theon, from all the emotions shrouding her mind and soul.

It wasn't real. It wasn't real. It wasn't real.

But the way her internal flames and waves had poured out of her soul *felt* real. The way her blade had turned to fire and water had drowned Theon *looked* real. Her tendril twisted between her organs and the threads of her nervous system, but she kept running. Kept running until her foot caught beneath a protruding tree root.

It wasn't real.

She flew to the ground, flowers following her falling form. Soil and grass collided with her, and she stayed there, allowing her tears to stain the earth. It wasn't real. But it *was* real. Everything she felt had fallen from her and into her sword.

What did it mean? What was she becoming? Was it ... Was it

magic? If the folk possessed magic, surely she would know by now. Alvaro had told her magic hadn't been seen since the Maidens' existence. But he'd also left abruptly after that conversation, and that evening he'd questioned her choice in sword.

'I do not know what the truth is. And rather than telling you something that may possibly be inaccurate, I feel it is better to withhold the information until I know the truth.'

Had he known of the possibility of her possessing magic?

She grunted into the ground. Magic hadn't been seen since the Maidens' existence—*if* they even existed. Which meant she couldn't possess magic. But that begged the question: What had she done?

She could go back to Alvaro's home and read about the Maidens in the hopes she would find an explanation as to what had happened, considering she had somehow manipulated elements—and perhaps she would do that later. But she'd planned to visit the library after her training anyway to read more about the Oracle and their belief that the Maidens would return. If that belief became a reality, maybe they could explain what was happening to Ivy.

She pushed herself off the ground and brushed soil from her clothes. As she stood, her gaze landed on some watching flowers that turned away as soon as she spotted them. Flowers couldn't see, and they also couldn't move. But the rules of this world didn't replicate those in the human realm. Perhaps here, flowers had minds of their own.

Sentient flowers were the least of her worries.

A deep sigh fell from her lips, and she trudged onwards. It wasn't long until Ivy stood in the garden preceding the library, gazing at the ivory goddesses holding aloft the library's entablature, each resplendent in their own element; they had to be replicas of the Maidens. The Maidens, who had allegedly wielded elements in such a way that forged a dividing wall to hide Harukai from Earth. Except, the magic they used for that had been 'unrelated to the elements'. What other magic had they possessed?

Ivy couldn't help but reflect on her earlier display with her sword, and how it resembled the way the water and flame statues held their elements towards the roof. '... *the Maidens used their own magic, something the folk have not seen since their existence ...*'

Her tendril swirled gently between her organs.

She climbed the staircase and entered the library, finding Leyrah with a patron at the counter—a centaur with antlers and harpy wings folded against their back. Ivy lingered nearby, trying her best not to notice as some of the folk stared at her. Her mind had been too preoccupied with whatever had happened during her training session that she hadn't spared a thought for her antlers and other noticeable features. She'd avoided the Tarad, yet here she was, revealing herself as a folk amongst the folk.

Knock knock.

Her gaze snapped to the now empty counter; the centaur who had been there walked towards the exit, staring at Ivy as they passed. She ignored them and stepped towards the counter.

'Ah, hi,' she greeted. Leyrah beamed at Ivy, her eyes flicking up to her antlers that resembled her own. Ivy sighed. 'Yeah, um ... This happened.' She attempted a casual shrug that didn't match the continuous cycle of emotions circling inside her.

Leyrah kept smiling as she started scribbling on a piece of parchment, her long honey-coloured hair obscuring half her face. *Is there anything I can help you with?*

Ivy smiled, glad to not have to explain anything more. 'I hope so. I'm wondering if there are any books on the Oracle.'

Leyrah's face scrunched, but rather than writing anything, she walked around the counter and gestured for Ivy to follow. They walked to a nearby aisle with a sign that read 'Fiction' and Leyrah searched the spines at the end, pulling a large, decaying book from its home, before handing it to Ivy. The cover was a simple faded green, with silver lettering that spelt *The Oracle*.

Ivy sat at the same table she and Alvaro had been at the day before, and Leyrah brought over a bowl of fruit. 'Thank you,' Ivy said, then opened the book only to find an array of stories. This wasn't what she meant when she'd asked for a book about the Oracle. She turned around and called, 'Leyrah.' The faun clopped over. 'I was hoping for a history book,' she explained.

Leyrah laid her parchment on the table and wrote. *This is everything written about the Oracle.*

If the Oracle was as dangerous as Alvaro explained, then why wouldn't there be history books about them? *A Maiden's History* had been hidden in that secret cavern; maybe a book on the Oracle would be there, too. 'What about that room?' she asked. 'The one you showed me yesterday.'

Leyrah's face remained a stoic mask as she wrote her next note. *I don't know what you're talking about.* Then, she walked away before Ivy could say anything more.

The first story had opened with a dark beginning.

On an island impossible to find, the Oracle resides. A being of such evil they were banished from all the kingdoms, left to rot until the end of their days.

From there, Ivy had read the dreadful story of a folk stumbling upon said island, not knowing they would never return home. For the next hour or so, Ivy read story after story that were almost all copies of themselves: folk finding the Oracle and never returning home. What happened in each of those stories differed slightly, but not much. The Oracle would torture them with fake futures that lead to their demise in some form. Exactly as Alvaro had told her. However, none of them spoke of the Maidens and how they would return.

The Oracle had been mentioned in *A Maiden's History*, so why didn't they have their own history book? She closed the collection of stories and made her way over to Leyrah at the counter. The faun offered her another smile and wrote a note which was waiting for her when she arrived. *Anything else I can help you with?*

Ivy sighed, preparing to make another accusation of misinformation. However, that had worked out in her favour last time; perhaps the same would happen now. Before she spoke, she looked around the library, cautious now from Leyrah's demeanour yesterday. That harpy was nowhere to be seen.

'I want you to take me to that room,' she whispered. 'The one you showed me yesterday.'

Leyrah gulped, her eyes widening, but she didn't write.

'I really need to know about the Oracle,' she continued. 'These stories won't help me.'

Leyrah hesitated for a moment, her breathing ragged, then wrote: *Not all stories are fiction.*

Ivy released another sigh. 'Fine. I'll find that room myself.' She turned to go, but Leyrah grabbed her arm, bringing her attention back. She watched as Leyrah frantically scribbled a new message. *That book really is the only written information on the Oracle.*

'What about the room?' she asked. That tree housed an abundance of books, hidden like *A Maiden's History*. Perhaps one of those would help.

Leyrah looked around the library, and Ivy followed her gaze; the harpy was still nowhere to be seen. Once she began writing again, she tucked her hair behind her ear, revealing a red mark across her cheek.

'Leyrah.' Ivy instinctively reached across, tracing the mark with her fingers. 'What happened?' Leyrah flinched from her touch. 'Sorry, I didn't mean to ... What happened?'

Leyrah brought her hair forward, hiding her cheek once more, and ignored Ivy's question. *I can't show you that room again,* she wrote. *I should never have showed you to begin with. But I wanted to help. And I trust that the Maidens book will help you, too.*

Ivy slowly shook her head. 'All it said about the Realm Divider was that they built it and then vanished. But it did say the Oracle believes they will return. If I find the Oracle, then I can learn about the Maidens' return, and hopefully learn how to open the wall again.'

Leyrah's wide eyes and scrunched brows reminded Ivy that Leyrah had no idea why those books had been left for her. She leant over her parchment and wrote another note. *That book will not help you return home. It will help you save our people.* Her quill moved in an urgent hurry, but the words were a blur.

Ivy stared at those first words, now lost of her own. What did that mean? She'd assumed the folk were lost forever since they never returned. But even if they could be saved, why was it Ivy's job to save them? The entire Thidin Kingdom and Noa Kingdom armies—in this moment, Ivy could not for the life of her remember what they were called—would be a better fit for the role, if only there was a way for them to leave this world.

And how would *A Maiden's History* help? A better question would be: How did Leyrah know what the book was for? She'd explicitly told Ivy she didn't know why the books had been left for her. Had she lied?

Leyrah tapped her finger against the desk, pulling Ivy from her stupor. She looked to the parchment and read the rest of Leyrah's message. *Read* A Maiden's History *in its entirety, but not just the words on the page. Read the words that are not there. They will help you ~~fulfil~~ with what you need to do. Do not go searching for that room. It is hidden for a reason. The Oracle stories will tell you how to find them. Trust me.*

How could Ivy trust her? She'd lied about *A Maiden's History* at first, and it seemed she'd lied about why the books had been kept aside for her.

'Did you …' There were too many cryptic messages that Ivy couldn't decipher in this moment. But there was one question she needed to know the answer to. 'Did you lie to me? About the books? About why they were left for me?'

Leyrah nodded, tears tumbling down her face. Then, she pointed to the bottom of the parchment where a final message was written: *Burn this note.*

Twenty-Nine

After the unnerving encounter with Leyrah, Ivy spent the afternoon at Alvaro's home trying to read. She sat outside beneath the front window, bare feet buried in the grass with the Oracle short stories collection propped up on her knees.

Not all stories are fiction.

Thoughts rattled her brain, distracting from her reading. They ricocheted off the edges of her mind and created a headache. She'd wanted to ask Leyrah more about the books, demand the truth about why they had been left for her, but Leyrah had ushered her out of the library before a single word could escape her lips. Leyrah *knew* why those books had been left for Ivy.

That book will not help you return home. It will help you save our people.

Read the words that are not there. They will help you ~~fulfil~~ with what you need to do.

That scribbled out word lingered in her mind. *Fulfil.* What had Leyrah been about to say? 'Fulfil' was not a simple word people wrote accidentally. The word had *meaning*. Each stroke of the letters was purposeful, until she chose to change her sentence. 'Fulfil' meant ...

'We've waited years ...'

'I didn't think it was true ...'

Ivy was *someone* to these people. She had to save them, had something to fulfil. And whatever it was must be related to those books. Was it part of rescuing her mother? Or was it something else entirely?

Leyrah's request to burn the note only raised more questions. But with her demeanour and lies surrounding the books and that hidden room, Ivy supposed it wasn't entirely surprising. The air of this world was thick with secrets. About Ivy and her future, about whatever it was she needed to fulfil. Despite Leyrah's lies, she seemed to regret doing so. The least Ivy could do was burn the note like she requested. It was currently slipped between the cover and front page of the Oracle book; she would find a moment to throw it in the firepit at dinner.

She desperately wanted to return to the library and demand answers from Leyrah, but she wasn't sure it was a good idea to ask her any more questions. The red mark on her cheek, her cautious glances, her lying, the harpy reading upside down ... People don't read upside down. That harpy was a part of this, and it was clear Leyrah was afraid of him. Was he responsible for the red mark on her cheek? Had he tampered with the Maidens books? Or had he forced Leyrah to do that against her will? And what kind of hold did he have on her to make her lie?

Yes, it was best if Ivy stopped asking Leyrah more questions, if only to keep her safe.

Just as she tried to focus on the next story in the collection, she was assaulted with the memory of her training that morning. It was one thing after another in this damn world. Reading these stories, and Leyrah's cryptic messages, had temporarily distracted her. But now that she was alone, the scene resurfaced. Flames had coated her sword; water had splashed out of it as she struck Theon. Whether it was intentional or not—which it most certainly wasn't—she had wielded elements. Even a fool would know they had only appeared due to her emotions in that moment.

What did that make her? And was it also related to the books she now had, kept aside specifically for her? To whatever she needed to fulfil?

Ivy planned to read *A Maiden's History* properly that evening to hopefully gain more insight but had hoped the Oracle stories could distract her a bit longer. She supposed she would need to find a moment to ask Alvaro—she was certain he knew something—but there was also something else she needed to speak with him about. Which was more important? Or were both equally as important?

Thankfully, before she could think more on it, Alvaro stepped out of the tunnel framed by curving trees, and her tendril instantly made itself known. There was more to him than he would have her believe. She'd enjoyed reminiscing about her mother the previous night with him, but the way he spoke about her, and the types of memories he had, caused her thoughts to spiral into something she wasn't ready to have revealed just yet.

'Find Alvaro. He will keep you safe.'

'Oh, good evening, Miss Ivy,' Alvaro said as he clopped down the stone footpath towards the front door. 'I was not expecting you to be out here.'

'I ... I just needed some fresh air.'

'Of course. I presume you were cooped up in the library for most of the day?'

'Yeah, it uh ... It can get a bit stuffy, I guess.' Her heart beat wildly.

He smiled, then glanced to the cover of the book she read. 'Something you found today?' he asked.

'Ah, yeah.' Ivy slowly closed the book and stared at the embossed title on the peeling cover, thankful for something else to talk about. 'I was hoping there would be more on the Oracle's beliefs in here.'

'Perhaps. Just ... do not go looking for them, Miss Ivy.' Thankfully, he stepped inside before she could reply. A few seconds later he opened the window above her head and said, 'Now, I have to replant the vegetable garden. Would you like to help?'

'Ah, sure. And then we'll meditate?' she asked.

He just smiled and stepped away from the window. She took the book inside, placing it in the trolley of books she kept downstairs, then followed Alvaro. Once at the vegetable garden behind his home, they knelt by a half-empty bed of soil with only two carrots growing.

'As you can see,' Alvaro said, 'we need more carrots. Over there'—he pointed to an empty patch next to the zucchinis—'is where the cucumbers should be.'

Ivy watched as he replanted the carrot seeds, and when he was done, they moved to the empty cucumber patch where she followed his instructions on replanting them. Now was the perfect moment to ask her questions, but her tendril twisted inside her throat.

'Brilliant. Now, wait here.' Alvaro walked around to the front of the house.

While Ivy waited, she decided to practise her meditation, if only to relax her mind before speaking with Alvaro. Deep breaths—in through her nose, out through her mouth. Keeping her eyes closed, she got to her feet and stretched her arms to the sky. She wanted to wait for Alvaro before getting into the movements, but something about the cool breeze blowing past, the gentle rustling of leaves, and the lingering soil on her fingers had her beginning the movements without realising.

Although she'd only done this meditation once, her subconscious carried her through the movements, as though her soul had performed this before. Ivy raised her right leg, aligning her foot with her knee, toes pointed down. Both hands met and clasped at her centre. Wind blew between the gaps and contours of her body. Her raised leg went back, and she guided her hands forward to match the motion. Her foot and palms flexed, as though she were pushing energy, pushing nature. Her arms opened—one moving down, the other aiming above her head, her body opening to the elements.

Every thought pushing down on her shoulders lifted, vanishing into the clouds. Her body moved of its own accord, unknowingly dancing in the garden. The nearby salty sea stung her nose in a delightful way, the sound of waves against the sandy shore a familiar song.

The breeze carried Ivy across the land and over the dividing rock wall. Sundown turned to midnight sky, and she slugged through its inky depths. The beach she once called home waited for her over the rock wall, a figure on the shore amidst the thick night beckoning her down. Long dark hair fell in tight curls down her back, sapphire eyes shining bright against her dark skin.

Mum.

Suddenly, Ivy also stood on the beach, the edges of her vision clouded by shadowy, inky blackness. 'Mum,' Ivy said. Blood dripped down Dorothea's face, pouring from scars across her cheeks and eyebrows; blue and purple patches marred the skin around her eyes and cheekbones. 'Mum?'

Tears cut a path down Dorothea's cheeks. Her hand kept beckoning Ivy closer, as if she wasn't already on the beach. Ivy followed her mother's movements until she was almost touching her, but the beckoning continued. Her eyes weren't looking directly at Ivy, but rather at the left side of her face. She turned, but no one was behind her.

'Mum?' Ivy grabbed her mother's shoulders and shook. 'Mum, what's happening?'

'They search for you.' Her voice was distorted, like she was speaking underwater. 'You can't let them find you.'

'Who?'

'You can't let them take you.'

'Mum, who are you talking about?' When she didn't answer, Ivy screamed and attempted to shake her from her stupor. Her beckoning continued. 'Where are you? *Mum?*

'Miss Ivy?'

Ivy opened her eyes, her tendril suffocating her thundering heart. She knelt in the grass of Alvaro's garden, her body contorted and hunched over herself. Tears lined her face. Water rushed around her organs. Wind howled, leaves of the circling forest and Alvaro's home blowing out of control. Each breath stumbled over the next.

'Miss Ivy.' Alvaro knelt before her, matching her height. 'Look at me. Follow what I do.' He breathed deeply through his nose and exhaled through his mouth. 'Your turn.' Ivy looked around frantically at the storm that had seemingly appeared from nowhere. 'Miss Ivy.' Her gaze returned to his. 'Just breathe.' She did as he commanded—in through her nose, out through her mouth. As she breathed, the storm dissipated, the rushing waves inside her slowing to a gradual rhythm. 'Much better,' Alvaro mumbled.

'What was that?' Her voice trembled.

Alvaro stood and offered his hand, which she took, and he pulled her up. 'Are you okay, Miss Ivy?' he asked, ignoring her question.

'I don't know. I think so.' Her tendril loosened around her heart but didn't entirely let go. 'I was meditating, like you taught me, and I ... I saw something.'

'What did you see?'

'I'm not sure.' With each passing second, the image in her mind became darker, blanketed by the inky blackness. Her fingers fiddled with the sapphire gemstone on her ring. 'Mum was there, I think ... Yeah, she was. She was saying something ...'

'What was she saying?'

'I ... I don't remember. It's fading.' Ivy watched the last remnants of the image, of her mother bloodied and bruised, vanish into darkness. 'She was hurt.' Her arms were wrapped around herself now, soothing her soul. Tears continued their path down her face. 'She had blood everywhere, and bruises ... What was that?'

Alvaro's jaw clenched as he watched her tear-stricken face. 'I ... I do not know. It seems as though ...' His face scrunched in thought. 'You said she was saying something.'

Ivy nodded.

'And you are certain you do not remember what she was saying?'

She closed her eyes and reached into the remaining inky blackness, trying to pull the image back to her mind, but those details were gone. The only things she could still see were the blood and bruises.

Ivy shook her head.

'Hm. Do you know who she was speaking to?'

She nodded again and said, 'Me.'

He looked away, deep in thought, then looked back and asked, 'Was there another version of you she was speaking to? Or was she speaking directly to you, as though you were with her?'

'Uh, the second thing ... I think. It was just me.'

It was Alvaro's turn to nod. 'I do not know what you experienced, Miss Ivy. As I have told you, powers of the mind are a dangerous ability, but—'

'Powers of the mind?' Ivy interrupted, her breaths escaping with no rhythm. 'Like ... like the Oracle? Did I see the future? Is that Mum in the future?'

'Miss Ivy.' His voice was stern. He squatted until he was level with her height, resting his hands on her shoulders, before demonstrating the deep breathing again—in through the nose, out through the mouth. 'I do not believe you saw the future. If you did,

I feel Dorothea would not have been speaking directly to you, but rather to someone else who appears in the future scenario. In all honesty, I do not believe you saw anything other than a dream. Or rather, a nightmare.'

She sniffled. 'How can you be certain?'

'I am not certain. But ... but there is no point in worrying about something if we do not know what it is. Although, if it happens again, please tell me.' He stood and took a deep breath. 'Now, I think it is best if we leave it aside and get to our training. Does that sound okay to you?'

Once again, Ivy nodded, lost for words for the time being. It hadn't felt like a dream. It had felt like ... like she'd fallen through space and landed in a distorted version of what could be happening to her mother. The blood and bruises marring her mother's delicate skin would cling to her like a poltergeist. And what had her mum been saying? Something about ... searching?

Her tendril tightened its grasp on anything near its vicinity. First her element-wielding display that morning, and now this.

What was happening to her?

'Good.' Alvaro's voice broke through her thoughts. 'Follow me.' He guided Ivy to the forest, away from the house, away from the bathing pond, and away from the tunnel. Only now did she notice the supplies he had with him: a large sack that looked like a pillowcase, a bow, and a quiver of arrows. They stopped a few metres inside the forest behind some bushes and shrubs. 'I know we only started meditating yesterday, but since ...' He sighed. 'We do not know when we can go to the human realm. It could be next week, or it could be tomorrow. And for when that day comes, I would feel more comfortable knowing you can at least *hold* a weapon other than your sword,' he said with a smile.

Ivy chuckled, but she couldn't quite shake the nightmarish vision as easily as Alvaro had.

'But I will not merely show you how to use a weapon. What I will be teaching you is how to work with the elements of nature to achieve your goal. How to utilise them, control them, manipulate them in your favour.'

She wasn't sure how Alvaro managed to move past her incident, but she tried to do the same and focus. It was a strange coincidence that he wanted her to work with the elements on the same day she'd unintentionally used them.

A crunch sounded, signalling the presence of a rabbit on the other side of the brush. Alvaro raised his finger to his lips and mouthed, 'Watch.' He quietly pulled an arrow from the quiver on his back and nocked it in the bow, then pulled the string taught, aiming for the helpless creature. Ivy watched his controlled breathing, in through his nose and out through his mouth, just as he had taught her. With a near-silent *twing*, the arrow went flying.

Ivy gasped as the arrow struck true. 'Why the hell did you do that?'

Alvaro lowered the bow and turned to her; his brows furrowed. 'That is our dinner, Miss Ivy.'

Her eyes widened. '*What?* You're telling me I've been eating rabbit this whole time?'

'Why, of course you have. What else would you eat?'

'Certainly not rabbit.'

'Well, we did have fish the other night. I sometimes go fishing at the secluded beach through these trees.'

The same beach where he and her mother had met.

Ivy sighed. 'Fish is okay.'

Alvaro's lips scrunched to the side. 'We could not eat rabbit, if you would prefer.'

'No, no, it's ... it's fine.' She sighed again. 'So, what's our training?' she asked to change the subject.

'This.' Alvaro handed her the bow with an arrow and showed her how to nock it while keeping it aimed at the ground.

'What? You want me to ...' She looked to the helpless creature but quickly turned away at the sight of its unmoving form, an arrow still protruding from it. 'I don't think I can do that,' she told him.

Alvaro sighed. 'I will not force you,' he started. 'But are you not wanting to learn how to fight?'

She nodded.

'And why is that?'

'To save Mum.'

'And how do you suppose you will accomplish that feat?'

'I ...' Ivy hadn't thought that far ahead. She didn't even know where her mother was, let alone how to save her.

'Those humans are dangerous, Miss Ivy. I know you were raised as one of them, but they are a threat to our kind. You will no doubt need to fight some of them in order to save your mother.' His hand found her shoulder. 'I do not want to be harsh with you, but if you cannot slay a rabbit, how do you expect to attack a human?'

Her tendril coiled like a snake around her lungs. He was right. If her mum was being held captive by the very people who had been abducting the folk for as long as this world had existed, then the only way to save her was to fight back. That was why she'd decided to train to begin with, wasn't it?

'Okay,' she whispered.

'Okay,' he echoed. 'Now, control your breathing.' *In through her nose, out through her mouth.* 'Your goal is to secure our meal, and being grounded in nature will you help you achieve that. Focus on each of your senses.'

Ivy wriggled her toes, soil crawling between each one. Blood from the first rabbit stung her nose, causing a stray tear to escape. She parted her lips, allowing the sweetness of leaves to dance on the breeze and coat her tongue. Her gaze homed in on another rabbit in the distance, oblivious to the danger it was in as it continued chewing each grass stem, the sound finding its way to her.

'Now,' Alvaro continued, as if knowing she had done what he'd asked, 'focus your senses on the elements of nature.' Ivy did as she was told, feeling the breeze sting and prickle her skin, hearing it whistle through the leaves and brush. Each grain of soil crawled over her feet and under her toenails. It squelched as she wriggled her toes again. 'You may not find all the elements here, but do not worry. Focus on what *is* here.'

There was a beach nearby. She closed her eyes and concentrated on the familiar sounds of home; waves lightly combed a sandy shore and harshly attacked a rocky one. Air, earth, and water were all here. The only element missing was fire.

'Are you ready?'

She opened her eyes. The innocent creature sat in low-lying grass, nibbling on the same strand. Living its life. Doing nothing to harm anyone, to cause its inevitable demise. Innocent, like her mother. Memories flooded her mind.

Elias dragged Dorothea away, back towards the house, the dagger still to her throat.

Another tear escaped, sliding down her cheek and falling off the end of her chin. Her innocent mum didn't deserve this. Ivy didn't deserve it. None of the folk in Harukai deserved the torment that now plagued her. All because of …

'I will find you, Ivy.' Even his voice had changed ever-so-slightly, a deep and unnaturally calm cadence. 'Unless you find me first.'

For the briefest of moments that night, her father's mannerisms, his voice, and the way he held himself, had all changed. Could all of this be because of him?

'It's not me he needs. It's Ivy.' She choked on the last word as Elias pressed his arm further against her throat.

Her tendril tightened around her lungs, but now it was comforting—a reminder of everything she had gone through and everything she would continue to go through.

'Miss Ivy, are you ready?'

The rabbit was not her mother. Her mother would live; the confirmation soared through her bones, her pores, and every fibre of her being. She would rescue her mum. She would enact her revenge.

Ivy took a deep breath, brought herself back to the elements, to nature, and nodded.

Alvaro stood behind her and guided her arms into position until she was aiming at the rabbit. 'Release.'

THIRTY

Moonlight painted the blankets white; Ivy's skin was radiant under its ethereal glow. She could easily be mistaken for sleeping with her still form and closed eyes, but her mind was wide awake.

Yesterday, she'd grown antlers and a tail. Today, her sword had spat water at Theon while simultaneously being coated in flames. Today, she'd had a darkened, warped vision of her mother. Today, she'd shot an arrow at a rabbit (and, thankfully, missed).

Today, she'd been told she needed to save the folk of Harukai. That she had something to fulfil. Today, she'd … she'd gone through far too much in far too short a time.

Save our people … fulfil …

Blood dripped down Dorothea's face, pouring from scars across her cheeks and eyebrows; blue and purple patches marred the skin around her eyes and cheekbones.

Elias dragged Dorothea away, back towards the house, the dagger still to her throat.

Too much was happening for her to keep up. Not only had her life changed so drastically to the point she was starting to lose sight of what her life once was, but *she* had changed just as much. She didn't know who she was anymore.

What she *did* know, however, was that her mother was in trouble. And her father wasn't her father. Her father was ... *'Find Alvaro. He will keep you safe.'*

Her pet tendril curled around her internal organs. After helping Alvaro with dinner earlier that night, she'd decided to read more about the Oracle instead of *A Maiden's History*, putting off learning about her elemental display for just a little longer. Finding the Oracle would help Ivy with opening the Realm Divider, and from there, she could find and rescue her mother. But the Oracle had been banished, and the few short stories she'd read so far were just that—stories. Stories about the lead-up to the inevitable death of each folk who found the Oracle.

How long would it take to find the next answer? It could be weeks, possibly even months, until she found the Oracle, and if those stories were true, that search would only lead to her own demise. Or the corpse of the Oracle, if Alvaro's assumption about them was true.

And even if—no, *when*—Ivy found a way back to the human realm, back to her childhood home, there was still the question of *where* her mother was. Finding her could take months. For all she knew, her mother could be—

No, she couldn't think like that.

'It's not me he needs. It's Ivy.'

Her mother was in danger, and yet she'd been wasting time reading books and meditating. A spark lit inside her, fury slowly being brought to the boil.

Ivy threw herself out of bed, stepped into the spare skirt she left on the floor, and buckled her sword around her hips.

She would break that wall. She didn't care that Alvaro had been trying to do that for sixteen years with no luck. Ivy would throw herself against those rocks until they shuddered and crumbled to the sea floor. Until her frail bones shattered.

Ivy's bare feet marked the sand. Water inched its way closer to her toes, but she was just far enough back for it not to touch her. The belt that housed her sword hugged her hips, while her now all-too-familiar tendril hugged her lungs. She'd managed to sneak out undetected and planned to swim to the rock wall and try to accomplish what Alvaro had failed to do for the last sixteen years—and yet, had still chosen not to wear her swimmers and scuba gear—but as she'd prepared to dive into the ocean, she'd remembered the new part of herself and stepped back.

Since discovering her merfolk tail, Ivy hadn't submerged herself in water. When bathing, she'd merely squatted by the edge of the pond and washed herself with her hands—surprisingly, her tail hadn't revealed itself.

The burning flame of her fury still simmered, but that damn tendril had her caught in its grasp. Salty lines marred her cheeks with no sign of slowing. There was no other way for her to get to the wall, and although she knew her efforts would be futile, she had to *try* just one more time.

But she wasn't ready to face who she was.

'Argh! Stop crying!' she yelled at herself. Her hands flew to her scalp, grasping her hair, only to knock into her antlers. 'You're always crying. Just stop. Crying!' Her lungs were tangled in her tendril, causing each of her breaths to inhale and exhale in a jumbled mess. She fell to her knees, her skirt billowing and landing in the low waves that still couldn't reach her.

Her tears didn't stop, nor did they slow. If anything, they picked up their pace, thriving in her distress. 'This is who you are now! You're a ...' Could she bring herself to speak the truth out loud? Or would it remain hidden in her mind? 'You're a goddamn merfolk.'

Without thought, her fingers found her ring, and she pulled it off to hold it in front of her. Alvaro had been quite fascinated with it the previous afternoon.

'Find Alvaro. He will keep you safe.'

Why Alvaro? Out of all the folk in the kingdom, and especially since her mother was a merfolk, why would Alvaro keep her safe?

'That man is not—'

Despite not being entirely ready for the truth, she would ask Alvaro what he knew about her father when she saw him next, if only to rid the uncertain thoughts from her mind.

Her fingers trailed over the twisting twigs of the band, over the jagged edges of the gemstone. Her mother's ring. Her mother, who was in trouble. Who needed Ivy's help. She could let those worries consume her, or she could push them aside and try to *do* something.

'You're a goddamn *merfolk*,' Ivy repeated with a little more conviction. 'You have a tail. You have *gills*. You can breathe underwater.' Theoretically, she could, but she had yet to try.

Her blood simmered with that lingering fury. She was a merfolk, and yet she sat on the beach moping about her change of identity while her mother was in danger.

Ivy slipped her ring back onto her finger, rose from the sand and lapping waves, and took a few steps back. Deep breaths—in through her nose, out through her mouth. Her tendril only tightened at the idea of seeing her tail once more, but instead of letting it constrict her, she took hold of it and ripped it from her lungs. Then, she hiked up her skirt and ran into the ocean.

It took all of a few seconds once her legs were submerged for them to combine and become a swishing tail. Ivy did, however, manage to dive off the sand before it happened. But now she floundered about, attempting to kick her legs that weren't there. She'd started to get used to her antlers, but hadn't gone swimming with them yet, and their weight had her floundering even more. She broke the surface, and her arms took most of the effort to get her closer to the rocks.

She knew her gills had come out of hiding, could feel them contracting, but now wasn't the time to test whether she actually could breathe underwater. Now was the time to release all her anger and frustration and grief and sorrow about her entire life and identity falling out of her grasp in an inevitably futile attempt at breaking the rocks open.

There had been times when she was younger where she would keep her legs together and try to swim like a merfolk. She focused on those movements now, and although it helped, a tail was not the same as a pair of legs. Her skirt billowing around and getting in the way of her tail's sporadic movements also wasn't helping.

The time it took for her to reach the wall was far longer than she'd care to admit, but she finally made it and gripped the rocks for dear life. Her bandages were drenched, saltwater soaking through and seeping into her healing wounds. Ivy welcomed the pain.

Treading water wasn't as easy as it used to be with a tail she didn't know how to operate. She kept one hand on the rocks and unsheathed her sword with the other, bringing it back and smacking it against the wall.

The world shuddered. It rocked beneath the sea, an earthquake soon to be a tsunami. Waves splashed against the rocks, against the young female holding on, mimicking the waves splashing inside her. She pulled back and swung her sword at the wall again, and this time, that water inside her splashed with the ocean's waves, slamming the rocks just as it had Theon that very morning. The onslaught had Ivy pausing her movements, but not for long. She swung again. And again. Each time the blade hit the rocks through the splash of water she brought with it, a tremor rippled through the world.

Was that a good sign? She hoped so.

Again and again, she stabbed the wall, tremors shooting through the world, water cascading from the blade. Each unsuccessful blow had a tear escaping; at least her tears could leave freely, unlike her.

A muffled voice came from somewhere next to her, but she couldn't hear them over her crying, and didn't care to see who it was. She ignored them and took another swing at the rocks, more tears shedding alongside her grunts. Another shudder. She pulled her arm back, preparing for another swing, but as she brought the sword down, a hand grabbed her arm.

'Ivy.'

She pulled away, ignoring the assailant, and continued attacking the wall. Her blood boiled with fury, at both her useless attempts on the rocks and whoever felt the need to interrupt her.

The voice and hand were familiar, and they grabbed her again mid-swing. 'Ivy, stop—'

'*Let go!*' She yanked her arm away again, her sword almost slicing the folk. But now, she allowed herself a moment to see them. It was dark, but the glow of his scales along the sides of his face revealed his copper hair and blue eyes.

Ivy turned away and swung again, feeding her flaming fury as the world shook once more, only this time, that burning ember inside her coated her blade. But before she could try another swing, Theon grabbed her arm and snatched her sword in one fluid motion, the flame instantly dying once it was free from her grasp.

'Give that back!' she yelled, reaching for the sword.

Theon pulled his arm away, dismissing her demand, and ignoring the way the weapon had been flaming a moment ago. 'Ivy, this isn't going to work,' he shot at her.

'I have to try!' She stopped grasping for the sword and bobbed helplessly in the water, grabbing the rocks to hold herself up. 'My mum is in trouble, and all I've been doing is reading useless books and crying about myself. I *know* this won't work, but what's worse than trying and failing is not trying at all.' She didn't care that she cried in front of him. Everything was too much for her to handle. Her life was stained a bleak grey, and she couldn't allow that dreary colour to thrive in her wallowing any longer. 'I have to try,' she whispered.

'I know,' Theon said.

'No, you don't,' she snapped, fury rising once more. 'No one else here tries except Alvaro.' Alvaro had done this same thing yesterday and she'd told him not to do so anymore, that they would find another way. And yet here she was, going against her own words. 'If none of you want to try, fine. But don't let me give up like the rest of you.'

'We do try,' he ground out. 'Every single time those filthy humans break through, the legion are the ones who have to try and open this wall despite knowing it's not going to work, just to please someone who's lost a loved one.'

Filthy humans. Is that what he'd seen when she first arrived in Harukai? Just some filthy human? He'd probably thought she was here to abduct more folk.

Ivy didn't respond. Of course they'd tried, but she needed to try for herself, even though she knew it wouldn't work. She looked up the wall to the very top—or what could be seen of the top under the moonlight—and started climbing.

Thirty-One

The rocks were slick from salty water as waves continued to splash against the indestructible wall. Ivy's muscles strained with the effort of trying to pull herself up, made worse by the unknown weight of her tail. She'd climbed these same rocks in the human realm all her life, but she'd also had feet back then. Her tail was useless.

But she needed to keep going.

There, looming just to her left, was a jutting piece of rock large enough for her to sit on. She shuffled along the wall until she could spin herself onto the seat, her tail now swishing idly, skimming the ocean's surface. Her skirt covered most of the green scales, but the end of her tail was still easily visible, shining just like Theon's scales did.

'Ivy …' Theon whispered, awestruck, his eyes lingering on her tail.

There was nothing for her to say in response. He'd seen her

dotted scales that morning, but she supposed it might be different seeing an entire tail on someone who had once had nothing more than plain legs.

She turned away and looked up. The top of the wall was barely visible under the night sky; only the thin streak of moonlight shining between clouds revealed the looming wall. Her eyes trailed down those rocks, searching for the next one to climb to. Her tail would remain until it was dry, but she couldn't very well sit and wait. Up and to the right was the next rock. It took her longer to get to this one, but she made it and sat to catch her breath. She continued this journey, climbing further than she ever had back in the human realm, until her tail faded to reveal her legs once more.

Her feet wobbled as she tried to use them after having a tail, and she slipped multiple times, but never fell. No giving up. Her triceps tightened, but she didn't stop. No giving up.

Ivy had tried doing this after Theon brought her back to Harukai, but she'd been weak. Distraught. Tired. Wounded. Incapable of gripping rocks with wet hands and shredded palms. Now, however, those wounds were slowly healing, wrapped in soggy bandages. The climb was difficult, but easier than it had been that dreaded night.

Elias dragged Dorothea away, back towards the house, the dagger still to her throat.

That memory pushed Ivy forward. And finally, after straining her muscles and nearly slipping multiple times, she pulled herself over the lip of the wall.

She didn't know what she'd been expecting. Back home—not her true home anymore, but home nonetheless—the other side of the wall had another beach, also unpopulated. The rock wall sloped towards the shore so people could walk around it, but no one ever did. Except Ivy, on occasion.

Here, she thought maybe there would be more islands, more kingdoms. Perhaps even an abandoned beach. A small, inconspicuous part of her hoped the human realm would be waiting for her. But there was absolutely nothing on the other side of the wall other than a spanning, never-ending ocean.

The wall was fairly wide, and she took a few cautious steps across the jagged rocks before a grunt sounded.

Theon climbed up beside her and removed her shortsword from where he held it between his teeth. 'Like what you see?'

'I thought ... I thought there'd be something over there.'

'You thought your home would be there? Sand undisturbed, house as it always stood, mother waiting for you?'

Yes, she'd hoped for that. Hoped it could have been so simple. But of course, if it was, Alvaro could have gone over. The entire legion and militia could have. Perhaps, if it was that simple, there wouldn't be a war.

Theon continued, 'Do you really think it was that easy? That you could just swim home? You think we hadn't tried—'

'I'm not stupid!' Ivy snapped, whirling on him. 'Of course I didn't think it was that easy. I just ... I don't know.' Her boiling fury turned to a simmer, slowly dissipating with each breath. 'I needed to see for myself. Because if it really was that simple and I never checked ... I need to try *everything*.' She snatched her sword from his grasp and sheathed it at her side, then walked to the end of the wall.

Theon followed, and the pair stood in silence at the end. Ivy felt his eyes on her, but she didn't look at him. She stared out at the empty, undisturbed water. Although the sky was a deep, almost black shade of blue, the moon was now free of the clouds and shone across the water, revealing nothing but rolling waves. No masses of land in the distance, no fish or even merfolk appearing above the water. Nothing and no one seemed to exist beyond the wall.

Except her home. Her mum was hidden on that side, or perhaps *she* was hidden here, standing on the very thing that separated both worlds. Separated humans from folk. Separated her from her mum.

Ivy had swum through the wall to get to Harukai, like crossing a border. If that was the case, could she not just ... step over?

She reached her hand out, not knowing what to expect but hoping for something, anything. But nothing. Of course that wouldn't work. She'd walked to the other side in the human realm multiple times and had merely stepped onto another beach. But like she told Theon, she needed to try *everything*.

She pulled her hand back and asked, 'What's out there?'

'Nothing,' he answered without hesitation, his earlier frustration having vanished.

Ivy turned to him. 'What do you mean? There has to be something.'

His brows half scrunched as he assessed her. 'What do you know about the realms?'

'Ah ...' She hadn't been expecting him to ask something like that. 'You're at war. We can't get through. That's about it.'

Theon sat on the edge of the wall, his legs dangling over. Ivy joined him. 'The human and folk realms used to be one, with humans and folk living together. But one day, the humans randomly turned against us. It's believed they grew jealous of us, how we could breathe underwater or fly. That was when the abductions started.' His jaw tensed, but he continued, his voice low, 'But without the wall here, they were able to send those folk back. They would return to their families with puncture wounds, scratches, bruises. When asked what happened, all they could manage to say was "testing."'

Not only were the humans abducting the folk, but they were also abusing them. *Testing* them. Was that what was happening to her mum? Was that what was supposed to happen to Ivy and her mum when they were taken all those years ago?

After the humans caused such destruction among the folk, the Maidens took it upon themselves to erect the Dividing Rocks. She'd barely read *The History of the Divided Realms.* Perhaps if she had, she would have learnt all of this.

Ivy looked out across the ocean, across the emptiness. 'Why are you telling me this?' she asked before turning back to him.

'That's why there's nothing out there. That part of our world doesn't exist.'

Now her brows scrunched. 'But in the human realm, there's a beach on the other side of the wall.'

Theon shrugged. 'I don't know how the human realm works. But there's nothing over there. Trust me, we've looked.'

'So, it's just ...'

'Like I said: nothing.' He was so nonchalant about everything, like it didn't matter. Ivy supposed, it was a part of his history. He'd never known another way of life, had never had his own life stripped from his core and replaced with something foreign. Instead, his own identity had him living his life as the only one of his kind.

The never-ending ocean reminded Ivy of home, when she would sit on the beach and stare at the horizon, watching the sun sink below the waterline. Although there were no islands out there, there was still ocean.

'Could the Noa Kingdom live out there?' she asked, facing Theon once more.

'Hm.' He leant back on his hands. 'Theoretically, yes. But the Noa Kingdom isn't the whole ocean. There're proper buildings down there, made of stone. We'd have to rebuild.'

The rotting stone pillars in the human realm. Were those remnants of the Noa Kingdom, from when humans and folk lived in peace?

'And besides,' he continued, 'we can't just live anywhere. The ocean is mainly taken up by sea creatures. Our perimeter is protected from them, but it wouldn't be easy relocating. And I don't know ...' He sighed. 'That side of the wall is a mystery. There's meant to be another world over there, another half of our world. If this wall is destroyed, what would happen to anything built on that side?' He didn't answer his own question, and Ivy certainly didn't have an answer for him. It was a strange phenomenon, but she supposed the folk of the Noa Kingdom were right to be cautious.

She had no words for him. No words of comfort, of frustration. Just no words.

They sat in silence, and she watched as Theon stared across the water, like she had before. His scales shimmered mesmerising blues and greens. Copper hair fell in loose, almost-dried strands, and through the gaps, his eyes were dark under the night sky. His jaw was sharp enough to cut steel, and his lips … Ivy could trace their plumpness with her eyes easily enough, but they remained shadowed, just out of reach of the light from his scales.

Ivy swallowed and followed the streak of scales down his arm. Without thinking, she reached her hand up and grazed those scales with her fingertips.

Theon flinched and inhaled sharply, turning to her.

'Sorry,' she muttered. 'Your scales are really pretty.' Her hand was still on his arm, but she watched his face. Watched as his eyes flicked to her lips for a fleeting moment.

'Thanks,' he murmured.

This angle, his head tilted down to look at her, orange hair obscuring parts of his face … he was mesmerising. 'You're …' Ivy started unintentionally. The way his eyes bore into her with a desperation revealing itself in the creases sent a warm shiver down her spine. She wanted to tell him he was beautiful, that he was sculpted by whatever gods or goddesses existed. That no one in all of humanity or folklore had ever or would ever be crafted in such a way as he.

But she didn't. Ivy didn't finish her sentence, didn't say anything. Instead, she swallowed, took a deep breath, and turned away, allowing her hand to slide down his arm and rest on the rocks, lingering near his fingers. If Theon was the slightest bit curious about what she almost said, she would never know, for he didn't ask. He just followed her gaze to the dark horizon, his fingers sliding along the rocks until they grazed hers.

PART THREE

THE GIRL WHO SWAM

Ivy is the girl who swam between worlds. She has stumbled and bled and cried as each layer of her soul was peeled away and replaced with something new. And it pains me to paint her raw emotions for everyone to see. No ordinary person could accidentally swim into a hidden realm.
But Ivy did.

Thirty-Two

Calm waves climbed the sand, but Ivy was too far for them to reach her.

She sat on sand and soil at the tree line the morning after she and Theon had climbed the Realm Divider, flowers sprouting either side of her and leading to the forest beyond. Bark carved grooves into her back as she leant against a tree, the Oracle stories collection open on her lap.

Not all stories are fiction.

She'd considered bringing *A Maiden's History* to the beach instead, but since it had been stored in a room that Leyrah had explained was hidden for a reason, she'd decided it was best to keep it safe at Alvaro's place.

The story she read now was one of a sea folk who arrived on the shore of an island—not unlike any of the other stories in this book. This particular folk, however, caught the eye of the Oracle, and they soon seduced the folk. For two hundred years, the folk lived as a slave to the Oracle until they fell pregnant. Once the baby was born, the folk was made to deliver the infant to a family in the Noa Kingdom before returning to the Oracle's island, never to be seen again.

'What's this?' Ivy flinched at the sudden presence of someone else despite knowing he would arrive at any moment. Theon stood on the sand a few feet from the water's edge wringing out his hair, his bag beside him. 'A new form of training?' he asked with a smirk.

She watched each droplet fall down his chest and sneak into the crevices where his scales overlapped. Their moment on the wall last night had changed something between them—or maybe it only changed something for her—but now whatever had lingered deep beneath everything else she'd been feeling this week had finally found its way to the surface.

Ivy blinked and looked away, her eyes scanning everything in sight until finally landing on his face. He watched her, his lips still up in that pathetically beautiful smirk of his. Whether the smirk remained because of his snide comment or her awe at him, she didn't know.

She returned his smirk with one of her own and replied, 'It's called "reading". You should try it some time.'

'Hm.' He carried his bag to the tree line and dropped it next to Ivy, then knelt on one knee before her. His scaled leg grazed hers, and although her skirt covered her skin, her breath still hitched at the unexpected contact, which she tried to cover up by clearing her throat. 'What are you reading?' he asked.

'A bunch of stories about the Oracle,' she replied, returning her gaze to the book.

'Interesting choice of entertainment.'

She furrowed her brows; this certainly wasn't entertainment. But him saying that made her realise he had no idea of her reading habits this week. All he knew was that she needed to return to the human realm.

'It's not entertainment,' she told him.

'Oh.' Now his brows furrowed. 'So, why are you reading it?'

'Well ...' Did she tell him? There was no reason not to, she supposed. And after all, he might be able to offer new insight. 'I've been reading books about the Realm Divider to hopefully find a way to open the tunnel so I can get back to the human realm.' And then, she explained everything she'd read that week about the Maidens and the rock wall and the Oracle, and how she was reading this collection of stories to learn more about the belief that the Maidens would return. Ivy did, however, leave out the detail of the books being kept aside for her.

When she was done, she watched Theon process the information. He eyed her curiously, brows pulled together, head tilted, one side of his lips scrunched and pulled up. 'Hm.' He glanced to the side, seemingly searching for his next words in the empty space between them, but he never found them.

'Do you ...' She'd expected him to say something, anything. But she was slightly taken aback by his lack of speech. What could she ask him? His thoughts and beliefs on all of this were more than likely the same as everything else she'd heard and read. But she didn't know what else to say and ached to break the stale silence that lingered. So, she asked, 'Do you believe in the Maidens?' Since

Alvaro didn't believe in them, she hoped she could find someone else who did. Perhaps that could make her search for them easier.

He hummed again, glancing away once more in search of his answer. 'The Noa Kingdom's beliefs are a lot more solidified than those of the Thidin Kingdom, in the sense that we don't particularly believe in the Maidens.'

That was an unnecessarily long-winded way of saying *no*. 'So, you don't believe in them?'

'Like I said, we don't particularly—'

'Do *you* believe in them?'

He swallowed. 'I have to. I believe in everything. It's part of who I am.'

No words formed on her lips. Although her question had been answered—and in her favour, no less—she couldn't help but wonder what an incredibly unusual statement he'd made. How could someone believe in *everything*? Wouldn't certain beliefs contradict others?

But Theon believed in the Maidens. Somehow, that confirmation helped her realise they may not be entirely mythical.

When Ivy still hadn't said anything, Theon spoke once more. 'When I was given to my mother, I was left with a poem.' He opened a pocket on the right side of his belt that she hadn't noticed before, but she didn't pay attention to what he removed from it. All she could focus on were the words he'd spoken. He'd been *given* to his mother.

Her face must have given her thoughts away, because Theon chuckled. 'It's no secret she's not my biological mum.' He gazed down at a scrap of parchment in his hands and read, '"For the

Maiden to bloom once more, and for life to be reborn, the vine must shed her final leaves and pass her story through untold weaves." I've scoured poetry books and historical texts,' he continued, 'but this poem doesn't exist. Everyone I've asked has never heard of it. I don't know who wrote it, or why I have it. All I know is that my mother found it with me, so, I hold on to it. But the Oracle's belief that the Maidens will return, whether it's true or not, finally gives this poem some meaning.'

That poem must be why he believed in the Maidens when the rest of the Noa Kingdom seemed to be on the opposing side. He handed Ivy the poem, and she scanned each swirling letter.

Read the words that are not there.

The handwriting ... She held it against the book; each letter curled the same, each 't' crossed the same. 'It's the same handwriting,' she said.

'What?' Theon leaned forward, his breath intertwining with hers as he analysed the handwriting of his poem and the story. 'But this book is so old,' he whispered. 'How ...'

'Sorry,' she said without knowing why.

He shook his head, took the poem from her hand, and tucked it in his belt pocket. 'You're fine. I just ...' He sat back and stared at a flower nearby, and she allowed him the moment to process whatever this meant.

Ivy returned to the book and lightly dragged her fingers across the calligraphy, then turned the page to the next story. Just like the others she'd read, it started out mostly the same: someone finds a nameless, deserted island.

Not all stories are fiction.

Her brows furrowed. Ivy flipped back to the previous story and read the description of the island: *Sand circled the island before leading into a dark forest. The island itself sat in the middle of a vast open ocean, no other islands in sight.* She flicked through the book to a random story and read the location description: *Rolling waves brushed against the shore of a deserted island.*

How had she not realised before? She'd been too distracted by cryptic messages and unanswered questions and her shambles of a life and identity. But still, the answer was right in front of her.

There were two islands visible across the water, and she could only assume there were more spread out across Harukai. Were they inhabited or abandoned? Surely there was at least *one* deserted island in this world.

She flicked to the first story in the collection: *On an island impossible to find, the Oracle resides.* Alvaro had said the Oracle was banished, and that no one knew where they were. Maybe that was the beauty of this unknown. The answer was right under everyone's noses, too obvious to be true.

'Ivy?' Theon asked.

'Hm?' She looked up from the old parchment pages to find his attention had returned to her.

'What is it?' He must have noticed her searching through the book.

'Oh, it's ...' Alvaro had been concerned about her reading this book and had warned her not to search for the Oracle. Could she confide in Theon? Or would he run to Alvaro? She liked to believe he wouldn't, but she didn't know him well enough to risk that. She could tell Alvaro herself and see if there was a way for both of them to find the Oracle. 'It's nothing,' she finally answered.

His eyes saddened, but he quickly slipped a smirk onto his face. 'You're so bad at lying.'

Ivy closed the book and tucked it away in the bag she used to carry her clothes to the bathing pond. 'I told you: it's nothing.' She stood and watched him follow. Theon towered over her, and seeing him this close, his bare chest and shining scales mere inches away, caused something to stir inside her. Ivy wanted to touch those scales like she had her first day here, like she had last night. But she pushed that feeling aside.

'Let's train.'

Thirty-Three

After training, a sweat-soaked Ivy swerved between trees and mushrooms, her body caged with aching muscles on her way to the library. She'd chosen not to use her sword during that session, and Theon hadn't questioned. Instead, they'd gone through exercises, weights, and basic sparring techniques like they had during their first session together.

But all she could think about was the way she'd used her sword yesterday morning. How she'd wielded elements the way the Maidens had once done. The Maidens, who the Oracle believed would return. The Maidens, who Theon had strangely received a poem about when he was born.

Everything was tied to the Maidens. She already had a book about them; perhaps she should change her course, return to Alvaro's home, and scour that book for answers. But no matter what she learnt about them, it wouldn't change the fact that they didn't currently exist. The Oracle believed they would return. That was the path she needed to follow.

Fulfil …

That single word lingered in her mind, haunting her—a hidden truth just out of reach. Every fibre of her being ached with the need for answers as she charged past watching flowers and idling mushrooms. Ivy knew exactly where those answers would be hiding. Whether Leyrah could help or not, she didn't know. But rather than drag Leyrah further into the mess that was her life, Ivy hoped she could find that hidden room herself.

Through the clearing and up the staircase she went, bursting through the mahogany door, only to find the space behind the counter empty.

Ivy scanned the library, but Leyrah was nowhere to be seen. She shrugged; at least she could find her way to the back of the library without Leyrah stopping her. But just as she started to head in that direction, a familiar set of wings in her peripheral snagged her attention. There, in that same sitting area near the counter, the harpy sat. And with him, the same faun she'd seen him with the other day, who she'd assumed was just another folk.

Was it coincidence they were together again?

She caught the harpy's eye, remembering Leyrah's terrified glances in their direction and the red mark across her cheek. Fury sparked to life inside of Ivy. Those dark eyes of the harpy, partially hidden by brown curls, remained on her as she stormed towards him. She didn't know what she planned to do, what she planned to accuse him of, but it was clear he was a part of whatever game this was that somehow involved Ivy. And Leyrah didn't deserve to be thrown in the midst of it all. But before she had a chance to do anything, Leyrah stepped in front of her.

Long caramel hair framed her petite face; a small white bandage lined her cheek. 'Leyrah,' Ivy started, reaching towards the bandage. Leyrah quickly jerked back, then gestured towards the counter before striding over. Ivy followed, feeling the harpy's eyes boring into her spine.

How can I help you? Leyrah asked.

Ivy opened her mouth, not entirely knowing which of her infinite questions she would ask, but froze before any of them could be freed. Was it safe to say anything with the harpy in earshot? She didn't want to risk putting Leyrah in any more danger, especially now she had a new mark on her cheek.

'Can you please show me where the romance books are?' she finally asked.

Leyrah's brows scrunched in confusion—perhaps she'd been expecting Ivy to ask about the Maidens or Oracle once more—but she walked around the counter to show her the romance books. Ivy made to follow but noticed Leyrah's parchment and quill abandoned on the counter. She snatched the items from the desk and followed Leyrah's clopping hooves into the labyrinth of books.

It wasn't long before Leyrah was guiding Ivy into an aisle and gesturing to the shelves, but when she saw Ivy holding the parchment and quill, her brows once again scrunched together. Ivy looked around, and thankfully, they appeared to be alone for the time being. This would have to be quick.

Rather than rummaging through the overflowing filing cabinet of her mind, she asked the first thing that came to her lips. 'I want you to tell me what you meant yesterday,' Ivy whispered, shocking herself with the topic she chose—she'd expected herself to ask about the hidden room.

Leyrah shrugged, feigning confusion.

Ivy quietly grunted and continued, 'When talking about the books I've been reading, you said they would help me fulfil something, but then you crossed it out. What did you mean?'

Leyrah's eyes widened, and she quickly looked around the small space. Once she realised they were alone, she pulled a book from the shelf, then took the parchment from Ivy and placed it on the cover. Ivy moved beside Leyrah to see the parchment at a better angle and held the inkpot between them while Leyrah dipped the quill and began to write. Only the quill froze above the parchment. Leyrah's eyes focused on the blank page, and Ivy could almost see the fight in her mind about what to write. Just when she thought Leyrah would remain frozen forever, the quill began to move.

Fulfil your destiny.

Ivy's breath caught in her throat, tangling in her tendril.

I wasn't supposed to tell you, Leyrah continued. *I never thought you would be in my lifetime, but when you first stumbled into my library, I couldn't believe my eyes.* A teardrop splattered on the parchment. Ivy flicked her gaze to Leyrah and saw tears lining her eyes.

'Leyrah, why are you crying?' she asked, but Leyrah didn't pause to answer her question. Ivy returned her gaze to the parchment, yet her focus was on the words now seeping beneath her skin, unbeknownst to the ones Leyrah continued to write.

None of it made sense. *I never thought you would be in my lifetime,* as though she knew of Ivy's existence before they had met. Yet she had never expected their paths to cross. How had she known about Ivy? And why hadn't she been allowed to mention her destiny?

Suddenly, as though she'd been submerged beneath icy water, memories rushed to the surface.

Are you who I think you are?

'*Is that who I think ...*'

'*Is she ...?*'

You'll need some books ... I was told you would need these.

'*It must be true ...*'

'*We've waited years ...*'

'*She looks like ...*'

'*It's really you ...*'

Everyone in the Thidin Kingdom knew who she was. Once she'd learnt she was a folk, Ivy thought perhaps that was how they knew her, but that never explained why they'd been *expecting* her. Why they'd *prayed* to her. It never explained why the books had been put aside for her, or *who* had left them there.

Fulfil your destiny ...

That single line answered all those questions yet raised a new one.

What destiny?

The inkpot left Ivy's hand, clattering on the hardwood floor, black liquid spreading at her feet. Both her and Leyrah flinched at the sound, but neither moved. Ivy was frozen like those statues guarding the library entrance. Leyrah finished her note before shoving the folded parchment sheet in Ivy's hand. What words lay beneath each fold of the parchment? What truth waited to be unveiled?

Leyrah collected the discarded inkpot and mouthed 'Leave,' before exiting the aisle, leaving Ivy alone with nothing but words of her destiny to keep her company.

Ivy finally left the library, but only after Leyrah returned with a cloth to clean the ink—she had practically shooed Ivy from the aisle. All the strange comments from folk across the kingdom rattled in her mind. She'd managed to ask Leyrah what her destiny was, but the faun had merely pointed to the folded parchment in Ivy's hand.

Now outside, she stared across the clearing, the Maiden statues towering either side of her, terrifyingly beautiful. Her tendril softly encased her lungs, embracing them like her mother used to embrace her.

Fulfil your destiny.

That was the most potent quote, the one that gave life to all the comments made towards her. Ivy had a *destiny,* and for some reason, Leyrah hadn't meant to tell her about it.

Was the harpy the reason for Leyrah's secret-keeping? Did the rest of the kingdom know about this destiny? Had Alvaro known this entire time?

There were too many secrets and mysteries in this land. If no one here would tell her the truth, perhaps the Oracle would.

Ivy unfurled the parchment in her hand and read the rest of Leyrah's note.

There is more to you than you know. Read the books about the Maidens. Read what isn't written. Find the Oracle. Fulfil your destiny. You will return home and rescue your mother, I'm sure of it. But you will also do so much more.

New questions to plague her mind. What was this destiny she supposedly had to fulfil? What else would she learn about herself that she hadn't already discovered this week? What else would she accomplish? She needed to find the Oracle and learn how to return to the human realm. But now, there was so much more to her life than merely rescuing her mother.

Fulfil your destiny.

She walked down the stairs and made her way to the pond and waterfall. Leyrah had said she wasn't supposed to tell Ivy any of this; she could at least destroy the note. But as she stretched out her hand, preparing to drench the parchment in the waterfall, a scribble in the bottom corner caught her eye. It was so small Ivy struggled to read it; however, she still managed to form the words: *Save us.*

THIRTY-FOUR

*S*ave us.

Fulfil your destiny ...

That book will not help you return home. It will help you save our people.

Pieces of this distorted jigsaw puzzle were falling into place, the picture now almost completely formed with only a few smaller pieces missing—those indistinguishable ones that when you lose them, the picture is still easily detectable.

Ivy could mostly see what the puzzle was saying: she was destined to save the folk. But the missing pieces now begged the questions of *how* and *why*.

How was she destined to save the folk of Harukai? And *why* was she the one who was destined?

This week had been one discovery after another about herself. About her life, her identity, and now her destiny. Her past, her present, and her future. The tendril she had come to know and ...

tolerate snaked around her lungs once more. Ivy didn't want any more discoveries. Why couldn't her life be simple, like she'd been raised to believe?

A Maiden's History would help her save the folk, according to Leyrah. Ivy supposed it was time for her to start reading it in its entirety. But the Maidens no longer existed. Would finding the Oracle not be the best course of action at this time? Learn about the Maidens' return and how to open the Realm Divider. After all, she couldn't very well save the folk if she couldn't return to the human realm.

At least her new discovery on the Oracle's whereabouts would make that task slightly easier. Ivy just needed a way to travel across the ocean. Of course, she now had a permanent way of doing so; perhaps she should officially test her ability to breathe underwater.

Her tendril tightened at the thought.

As she crossed through the Tarad, making a beeline for the garden tunnel that led to Alvaro's home, she stumbled and fell onto the soft path made of soil and grass and fallen leaves. She righted herself, brushing soil from her front, and checked the vicinity for whatever could have made her fall. Voices of nearby folk increased, like people in the midst of a heated discussion. Raised voices turned to yelling, but Ivy ignored them. Her feet skirted cautiously through leaves as she searched for a protruding tree root or some other cause of her fall, but nothing was revealed. She shrugged, assuming she had merely tripped over her own two feet—and between you and me, I would not put it past her to perform such an action—and continued on her way.

Two more steps later, however, and she stumbled again, only this time the ground *shook* before she fell. Her bag carrying the Oracle book tumbled from her grasp, landing nearby. As she righted herself once more, she found folk nearby had also fallen, and she watched as they stood and ran deeper into the kingdom. Some screamed, and Ivy realised what she initially thought was the raised voices of an argument was actually that same screaming. Others didn't make a sound. Folk shoved past her, causing her to stumble *again*, only this time she didn't fall. Children were gathered in the arms of parents, seemingly unknowing of what had occurred, just like Ivy.

The ground shook again, more aggressive than before, and reminiscent of the shuddering from Ivy failing at breaking the wall last night. A centaur galloped towards her, and she jumped out of the way, right into a faun with sparkling fairy wings. They made to run, but Ivy grabbed one of their arms.

'What's happening?' she asked.

'Let me go!' the faun screamed, squirming in her grasp.

'What's happening?' Ivy repeated, louder this time and with a hint of irritation coating her tongue.

The faun struggled to break free, but their eyes soon found Ivy's face, and they stopped. Tears brimmed in their eyes. 'You ...' they whispered.

'None of that,' she snapped. Ivy was tired of learning she was something more than just ... herself. She couldn't handle that suffocating tendril encasing her any longer. She didn't want any more crypticism, couldn't handle the ... *destiny*. 'Tell me what's happening.'

'The-they're here,' the faun stuttered, watching Ivy with utter awe coating her tear-stained eyes.

'Who?' she demanded, but at this point, the question was irrelevant. There was only one reason why the folk would fear the arrival of someone.

'The humans.'

Ivy released the faun's arm, but they didn't run. Their eyes searched her, and a tear ran down their cheek, ran like the rest of the folk were running.

'You're so young,' the faun finally said, then turned and ran, jumping into the air and flying away.

Ivy watched as sparkling and feathered wings alike carried folk into the depths of the kingdom, to where Ivy had yet to find. On the ground, hooves, claws, and feet ran, thumping and clopping in the same direction, all running *away* from the beach and the rock wall.

Ivy stood motionless watching the folk dissipate, listening to their screams fade, until she was the only one remaining in the abandoned Tarad. Stalls were still opened—like ghosts of the once bustling Tarad—as though the folk who ran them didn't want to waste a single moment closing their shops. These folk ... they were utterly terrified. Terrified of what the humans had done, what they continued to do. Terrified of the race that Ivy was raised as.

The world rocked beneath her feet. Was this what she'd caused when she'd thrown herself and her sword at the rock wall just last night? Had folk stirred from their slumber, frightened for their own safety? She supposed so, for the earthquake-like vibrations shaking the ground now were the same. And she had somehow caused that shaking—the same shaking that indicated the arrival of the humans.

If she tried hard enough, perhaps she really could open the rock wall. But she *had* tried hard enough—as hard as she possibly could—yet there was no sign of the tunnel having opened. Perhaps if she kept training with Theon, she would be strong enough—

What was she thinking? The humans were *here*. No matter how frightened they made the folk, they were still here, in Harukai. And now she finally had a way back to the human realm.

Back *home*. When had Ivy stopped referring to it as such? She knew Harukai was where she'd been born, but the human realm was where she'd been raised. Except now it was just a storage unit for the memories of that night.

She turned and ran through the Tarad, boots crunching on leaves as she swerved between stalls, trees, and grassy mounds. Once she made it to the tree line with the path that led to the beach, she felt a watching gaze bore into her spine. No, not a single gaze: multiple. Goosebumps rose on her skin despite the heat of the sun. She slowly turned, uncertain of who—or what—she would find, but no one was in sight. Her eyes scanned the still empty Tarad. Only when she gave up and started to turn back to the trees did she notice them. The flowers that lived at the roots of trees and sprouted from the tops of Tarad stalls, some tiny ones even blooming on low-hanging vines. Every single one faced her. *Watched* her, as they had been ever since she stepped foot on the shore of the Thidin Kingdom.

An eerie chill blanketed her, before her tendril hugged her tightly. 'What do you want?' But of course, they didn't answer. They were only flowers, after all. 'Stop watching me!' she cried.

They didn't.

The world shook again.

Ivy turned and ran down the path to the beach. She felt the gaze of the flowers in the forest following her as she did so, but she didn't stop for them. She was so close to leaving this world, to finding her mother. Those flowers were certainly the least of her worries.

Nothing would stop her.

The beach was empty as she stumbled out of the trees; the rock wall still divided the realms. She wasn't entirely sure what she'd been expecting, but this certainly wasn't it.

Where were the humans?

Why was the wall still intact?

She ran down the sand to the water and scanned the ocean, not knowing what to search for. Another shudder, and the beach shook violently, rocking Ivy back and forth until she couldn't stand. She crashed to the water, landing on her hands and knees in the low waves with a resounding *splash*. Before her tail could make an appearance, she fumbled backwards and sat on her feet on the sand.

Leaves crunched from the forest. Objects jingled; voices muttered. Ivy turned just as a familiar faun stepped out of the trees backwards, speaking to a large group of folk carrying weapons and shields. 'Jaxath, your unit will guard the tree line. Senille, I need your unit split to either side of the beach. Rani, your unit will stand beside me at the shoreline.'

The faun turned and froze when he found Ivy kneeling near the water watching him. The rest of the folk filed onto the beach and into their positions. 'Miss Ivy,' Alvaro said. 'What are you doing here?' He strode to the shoreline to meet her, squeezing past the line of soldiers that had just formed, presumably Rani's unit.

The world had stopped shaking for the time being.

'I ... I'm waiting to go back,' she replied. Alvaro's mouth opened then closed, then opened and closed again like a puffer fish, but no words exited his lips. 'They're coming, aren't they?' she asked, although she already knew.

'Yes,' was all he said.

'When will they be here?'

His eyes turned to the Realm Divider. 'Soon.'

It was unlike Alvaro to speak with so few words, but now wasn't the time to question him. She followed his gaze and gasped. There, carved into the rock wall, was a large, gaping hole. Much, much larger than the one she'd originally swum through. Most of it was above the water line, but the bottom dipped beneath the surface.

The wall was open, but no one exited.

Water rustled a few feet ahead of her, and out of the ripples rose a copper-headed figure. Theon's body was like the side of a cliff, water cascading in a waterfall down the ridges of his scales. They coated his entire body like armour, save for his neck and face; it seemed he really could move them on a whim.

His eyes met hers and his brows scrunched. 'Ivy, what are you doing here?'

'I'm going back,' she told him.

His mouth opened, his brows still scrunched, painting his face in confusion. Then realisation struck him like a bolt of lightning. His mouth slammed shut and his jaw tensed. Ignoring her, he strode forward and met Alvaro where he stood just behind Ivy. Theon's proximity to her caused her to tense just as his jaw had. Ivy wasn't sure why he was mad; he knew she planned to go back.

'They're on their way,' Theon told Alvaro. 'It looks like only one boat is coming through, but we can see one guarding the exit, as usual.'

There was a moment of silence as Ivy watched the water turn as still as a frozen ocean. Then Alvaro sighed and said something that caught Ivy off guard. 'Let them come to shore.'

Her head swivelled back just as Theon exasperatedly said, 'What?'

As desperate as she was to return home, she'd never expected Alvaro—or anyone for that matter—to simply let the humans come to shore.

'You are certain there is only one group on their way through?' Alvaro asked. Theon only nodded his response. 'Then bring them to shore.'

From this angle, Ivy couldn't entirely see Theon's face, but she saw his right cheek tighten. 'I don't think that's a good idea—'

'Theon, you need to listen to me,' Alvaro interrupted. 'Only one group tells me they are more than likely after only one thing. One person. And while we could try and keep them from taking her, she will inevitably find her way through.' A tear ran down his cheek. 'To me, this looks like our only chance to bring her mother back.'

'Find Alvaro. He will keep you safe.'

Seeing that single tear, and everything it possibly meant, caused something to break inside her.

Theon broke the silence. 'We don't even know if she's—'

'Do not'—Alvaro stepped forward, his nose almost touching Theon's—'finish that sentence.'

Theon's face remained as tense as the anticipation for the arrival of the humans currently swirling through Ivy's bloodstream. His throat bobbed and he faced her, eyebrows still pulled taut. His face twitched and he rolled his shoulders, then took a deep breath. Without a word, he made his way back into the ocean.

Waves rushed to her knees at the same time her heart began to tear. But as Ivy watched him vanish beneath the surface, a large object on the water had her forgetting whatever her next thoughts would have been.

A boat had exited the tunnel and was heading directly towards the beach. But not just any boat; the very same one that had been abandoned near her home all her life. She'd never gotten a closer look at it before, but now she was able to see the white peeling paint, like scars marring its skin. As the boat made its way closer to shore, an all-too-familiar figure exited the centre cabin and stood at the front.

'Ah, General Alvaro,' Elias greeted, his arms splayed wide. 'What a pleasure it is to see you.'

Thirty-Five

'D ad?'

'*That man is not—*'

Ivy knew he wasn't her father, but he'd been her father all her life. Familial instincts would always take over.

Despite knowing the humans were arriving, she'd never questioned the possibility of Elias being with them. He'd taken her mother, but with all the other changes that had happened that week, she hadn't considered the fact Elias would be amongst the same group of humans that regularly abducted folk. That had abducted her and her mother.

'*I will find you, Ivy.*' Even his voice had changed ever-so-slightly, a deep and unnaturally calm cadence. '*Unless you find me first.*'

The boat continued its journey closer to shore, more people filing out of the cabin. Merfolk sprouted around the vessel, presumably the legion, with their weapons raised and waiting. With the legion in the water and the militia on land, Ivy wondered how the humans ever made it further than the beach.

Theon was among the legion, closest to the shore, his back facing her. His large fin between his shoulder blades was visible, but everything below that was underwater.

Only once the legion had all risen did Alvaro speak. 'I will do you the courtesy of allowing you to freely yet ungraciously step down from your vessel.'

'Civility, Alvaro?' Elias crooned. 'That's unlike you.'

'I assure you that you will remain unharmed.'

More questions flooded Ivy's mind. How did they know each other? Why was her father with these people? But there was only one possible answer: Elias was part of the abductions.

'Is that a promise?' her father asked with a hint of a smirk.

Without hesitation, Alvaro answered, 'You have my word you will be unharmed while you make your way to our land.'

Theon and the other soldiers at the front parted to allow the boat to anchor closer to shore. Ivy watched her father jump from the boat and land with a splash among the merfolk, while the rest of his troop remained on the boat. The sand bank must be in reach because there was no floundering to stay afloat, no swimming to shore. Just an awkward walk through the water, the Noa Kingdom's legion glaring as he passed.

Once the water was just below his knees, his eyes found Ivy and widened. He froze. Then, his face contorted and suddenly he was running to her. 'Ivy!' He fell to his knees in front of her, mirroring her position, and threw himself around her. 'Oh, Ivy, I'm so glad you're safe.' He pulled away and grasped her face in his hands, his eyes running between her freckles and scales and antlers. Tears mixed with the saltwater splattered on his cheeks. 'You ... You've changed so much.'

She didn't know what to say. She should be ecstatic to see him, to finally have a way back to her mum, but her tendril only coiled tighter than she ever thought possible. If he was here, where was Dorothea?

Elias dragged Dorothea away, back towards the house, the dagger still to her throat.

'Where's Mum?' Ivy asked.

For the briefest moment, his features fell at her question. 'Let's just get you home,' he said.

Home. So many memories in that place, all drowned by what had happened that night. That place wasn't her home anymore.

'Is she safe?'

'Come on, Ivy.' He stood, ignoring her question, and pulled her with him. 'I can keep you safe. And your mother. Let's just get you on the boat.'

He held her elbow and started pulling her into the ocean, but something didn't sit right with her.

'They will know if Ivy returns. She'll be safe with me.'

Elias dragged Dorothea away, back towards the house, the dagger still to her throat.

Ivy stopped with only her boots submerged. Her tendril was like a snake, curling and twisting around her internal organs. 'Dad, just tell me where Mum is.'

Elias released an irritated sigh and rolled his shoulders back. 'I just want to get you to safety. And then I'll tell you.'

Water lashed around her feet, splashing to her knees. Why was he avoiding the question? What was he hiding? He claimed he wanted to keep her safe, that she'd already been safe with him—but she was safe here, with Alvaro.

'Find Alvaro. He will keep you safe.'

She pulled herself free from his grasp and stepped out of the water. 'Tell me where Mum is. Tell me she's okay.'

And then, something in her father snapped. His head twisted to face her, nearly turning a complete one hundred and eighty degrees. An inky blackness glazed across his eyes. 'Why won't you just *listen to me*?' he hissed in a voice that certainly wasn't his own but sounded too familiar.

'I will find you, Ivy.' Even his voice had changed ever-so-slightly, a deep and unnaturally calm cadence. 'Unless you find me first.' Everything about him had changed that night, just as it had now.

Elias's face contorted again as his body spun to fully face her, that blackness returning to his eyes for the briefest of moments. 'Ivy,' he whispered, his voice the same one she had grown up hearing. 'Are you okay?' He took a few steps towards her, but she instinctively stepped back, further up the sand.

What was that? What was wrong with him?

'That man is not—'

Her mother's words from that fateful night replayed again. She knew the truth but had yet to ask the question. She wasn't human, and Elias was. Too many truths had been revealed in her short time in Harukai, and a small part of her had wanted to hide from this one for just a little while longer. But she couldn't hide forever.

'Ivy?' her dad asked, a tremor lining his tone.

Deep breaths—in through her nose, out through her mouth. She already knew the answer, but needed the verbal confirmation from him, and from him only. 'You're ...' She swallowed, tears beginning their journey down her cheeks. 'You're not my dad, are you?'

His eyes flicked behind her to Alvaro, confirming something else she refused to acknowledge just yet, but she kept hers locked on Elias. When his gaze found hers, his eyes were filled with tears. He swallowed, then finally answered, 'No.'

Ivy allowed that single word to seep beneath her skin, mixing with her blood and tangling with the tendril inside her. It was strangely comforting to have that confirmation despite already knowing it was the truth. Maybe now she could officially grieve the loss of him.

'I'm sorry,' Elias started, taking another step towards her. This time, she didn't step away. He grabbed her hand and whispered, 'I'm sorry, Ivy.'

Another question rose to the surface, born from the confusion surrounding his arrival in Harukai. He was with the very humans the folk were so afraid of. He knew Alvaro by name. The memory of the folk in the Tarad running to safety from the humans, from the man who raised her, draped over her mind like a weighted blanket. There was so much more to him than merely being her non-biological father. Who was he?

Before she had a chance to think any further, the question fell from her lips. 'Did you ... Did you abduct me and Mum all those years ago?'

He watched her with a deep longing she had never seen from him in her lifetime. But it was there, plain and simple. And she knew what the answer would be, with that love and sorrow spreading like an illness across his features. But she needed him to tell her. His mouth parted, but before any words could be voiced, his face contorted again, that inky blackness glazing across his eyes once more.

'Of course I did,' he growled in that voice that belonged to him but wasn't his.

Ivy flinched, pulling her hand from his and stumbling back, bumping into one of the militia's soldiers.

'Dad?' she asked through broken sobs, instinct taking over. 'What's wrong with you?'

'What's wrong with me? You really haven't figured it out yet?' Elias spat.

Hadn't figured what out?

'That man is not—'

Well, she already knew the answer to that question. What else hadn't she learnt?

His eyes. That strange blackness that kept coating them whenever his face twisted unnaturally, and the way his voice changed each time. There was certainly something wrong with him, but *what*?

He had abducted her and her mother. *He* was the one the folk were so afraid of. The man who had played the part of her own father, the man she had lived with for sixteen years, was responsible for all those abductions. How many folk had he taken from their world, their homes, their *families* while she was alive?

Ivy's heart raced; her breathing quickened. Around her, waves threw themselves against the sand. She was side-tracking; there was something about Elias she hadn't figured out, and the answer clawed against her flesh, begging to be released.

The blackness in his eyes, his contorting features, his change of voice. It wasn't a question of what was wrong with him. It was a question of—

'Who are you?'

Elias's lips peeled back in a hideous snarl that nearly reached his eyes. 'Look at you, darling, finally asking the right questions.'

The way his pet name for her sounded in this strange, distorted voice unnerved her. Ivy's father had called her that. Her *father*, not this person before her, this person who was just ... *wrong* in every way.

More tears rolled down her face. Ocean waves aggressively lapped behind Elias, climbing over each other in their desperate attempt to reach them. 'Don't call me that.'

His snarl fell, landing in a straight line covering his teeth. 'Whatever. Let's go.' Then he stepped forward, grabbed her arm, and dragged her towards the ocean. Ivy squirmed in his grasp, just as she had that dreadful night he had taken her mother away. She couldn't go in the water—her tail would appear—but more than that, she couldn't go with this *thing* that had taken on the role of her father.

Waves splashed against her flesh and crashed against her bones. They drenched her organs and drowned her tendril. 'Let me go!'

'Why?' he snapped. 'I thought you wanted to go home.'

He was right, of course. That's all she had wanted since the tunnel in the rock wall closed before her very eyes. She needed to find her mother, and he would take her to wherever she was.

But this wasn't the way to do it.

'I will find you, Ivy ... Unless you find me first.'

He would lock her away, do whatever it was he needed her for, and her mother would remain unfound and forgotten, just like the rest of the abducted folk.

'Wait,' Ivy blurted.

Elias stopped moving and turned back to her, still holding her arm. The toes of her boots were at the water's edge. Waves piled over each other behind Elias, reaching past her hip height, mimicking the waves inside her.

Why did she want him to stop? He was about to take her back to the human realm. It didn't matter that he wasn't her father, that she would be leaving Alvaro and Theon and all of Harukai behind. It didn't matter that he needed her for something. Perhaps she could still find a way to free her mum, if only she was taken to her first.

So what was the problem? Why did her tendril wrap around her lungs, holding them back against her spine?

'You still haven't told me where Mum is,' she whispered.

'Ugh, my God, Ivy. You're asking what's wrong with me, but really, *I* should be asking what's wrong with *you*!' His face was inches from hers, blocking everything else from view. The boat, the Noa Kingdom's legion sprawled throughout the ocean, and even the rock wall, were all hidden from sight. 'All you've wanted since being here is to go home to your precious mum, and that's exactly where I'm taking you. You were so desperate to return you threw sand at rocks!' Elias laughed in her face. 'I'm giving you exactly what you want: to be reunited with your hostage of a mother. With that filthy siren.' He glanced past her, a wicked smile plastered to his face, to where she assumed Alvaro still stood.

Her mother was a *siren*?

But Ivy didn't follow his gaze, didn't allow herself a moment to process her mother's race. Instead, she was stuck on one tiny fact he'd let slip.

'If she goes back,' Elias explained, *'then* they *will know.'*

'They will know if Ivy returns. She'll be safe with me.'

His contorting features, the inky blackness sliding across his eyes, his change in voice and demeanour. It was as though someone else lived inside him, like something had possessed him. Someone who knew how badly she had wanted to return to her childhood home, who knew about her tantrum on this very beach as she threw sand at a towering rock wall. Elias couldn't have known that. But whatever lived inside him did. And it needed her for something. Her mother was a hostage, and they would be reunited.

All this desperation, everything Ivy had discovered, her destiny, would all be for nothing. But she also couldn't just stay here. When would she get another chance like this? Her tears continued their treacherous path. Maybe she didn't need to go alone. If someone could go back with her, then together they may have a chance at saving her mum.

'Can ...' she sniffled. 'Can I bring Alvaro?'

His brows furrowed. 'Alvaro?' he spat. 'Why would you want to bring *him*?'

The waves inside her were vigorous in their assault, not unlike the ones behind Elias. They towered menacingly, reaching higher and higher with each crash against the sand. 'I ...' What could she say? She couldn't very well tell him her plan. But she knew if Alvaro couldn't go with her, she would fail. She would be held hostage alongside her mother, lost and soon to be forgotten. She couldn't go alone. 'Let me go,' she managed to whimper.

'What? You don't want to go home?' Just when she thought he couldn't get any closer to her, he did. Their noses practically touched as Elias said with a snarl, 'You'd rather stay here with these filthy folk?' The wind picked up, swirling now like an oncoming storm, picking the ocean up with its spinning, a replica of the waves rolling around her organs—the same waves she'd released from her sword.

Filthy folk.

An ember sparked to life inside her; there was nothing filthy about the folk. She opened her mouth, but before she could say anything—not that she knew what to say—an arm flung around Elias's chest, pulling him back. Elias reached for the arm, releasing Ivy, and she stumbled back, falling onto the sand.

Theon now stood behind Elias, one arm across his chest, the other holding a dagger to his throat. 'How does it feel?' Theon snarled, each word dripping with malice. His lips curled in a twisted smile that didn't suit his face.

'Miss Ivy.' Alvaro dropped beside her, his hands grasping her tear-stricken face, which she guessed resembled his own. His eyes agonised over her form in a way she'd only seen from her mother whenever she'd hurt herself. That look seemed to answer the question she had yet to ask him.

Elias's gurgled voice drew her back to him. Theon pressed the dagger further against his throat; a thick liquid began to pool on the silver blade.

'Stop!' Ivy shrieked.

Theon faced her, his vicious snarl dropping instantly—but not the dagger. Realisation at what he was doing spread around his eyes. Elias, on the other hand, merely laughed. A crackled cackle that was far too loud for someone with a dagger against their throat.

'You pathetic little thing,' Elias croaked. But then, his face twisted, and once more, that strange inky blackness temporarily coated his eyes. The stark colour of it drew her attention to the eerily similar colour of his blood that stained Theon's dagger. 'Ivy!'

The man who she once called her father had returned.

'Dad,' she said instinctively, choking on the word and everything it now meant.

What he said next was something she had never expected him to say. 'Don't come home.'

Those vicious waves climbed atop each other as they attempted to reach her, but she pulled her feet away for fear of her tail appearing at the most inconvenient time. 'What? Why would you say that?'

'I was wrong.' He choked on his words, tears streaking down his face. 'I thought you would be safe if you stayed with me, but that's not true anymore.'

'... She'll be safe with me.'

'Don't come back until you're ready,' he continued. 'I thought I was protecting you, but I should have been teaching you.' His neck twisted and rolled, the blade cutting into his skin, but his eyes remained the same. 'I'm sorry,' he said, his eyes flicking between her and Alvaro. Too many thoughts, too many questions. But before Ivy had a chance to think about what he was saying, he turned to Theon and said, 'That tunnel won't stay open for long. I need you to knock me out and throw me on that damn boat. Then send me away.'

Theon's cruel smile returned. 'Gladly.' Blue scales appeared out of nowhere and swam over his face, leaving his unbound hair flowing behind him. They *could* move on their own. Without hesitation, he reared his head back—

'NO!'

—and smacked his scaled forehead against Elias's.

Thirty-Six

Ivy stayed slumped in the sand with Alvaro and watched as Theon and two others from the legion carried her father's unconscious body towards the boat and hoisted him over the edge. Theon held onto the railing, yelling orders at the rest of the crew. An argument ensued, with Theon pointing to Elias lying unconscious on the boat's deck, then threatening them with the same dagger he'd held to her father's throat.

'Come, Miss Ivy.' Alvaro gently tugged her arm up as he stood, and she willingly followed his guidance. The thrashing waves had calmed to a dull ache, attempting to wash whatever sorrow lingered in Ivy's bones. That twisting, spiralling wind was now nothing more than a gentle breeze.

He wasn't her dad.

But he was. He may not be her father, but he'd raised her like his own child. Yet he was also the one who had taken her and her mother away from Harukai, from their true home, and most likely her true father.

No, Elias hadn't done that. Whatever monstrous thing living inside him was to blame for abducting her and Dorothea. But *why*? Knowing who was responsible wasn't enough. Ivy needed to know why this was done—not just to her, but to all the folk of Harukai.

The boat was making its slow escape from this realm, Theon still holding on to the edge. She assumed he would stay with them all the way to the tunnel and watch them leave. Why was she just standing on the beach, watching her father leave? She could swim to the boat now and go to the human realm. She could swim straight to the tunnel and follow the boat through.

But Elias had told her not to return until she was ready. That he should have been teaching her. What did that mean? What did she need to be ready for? What should he have been teaching her?

Fulfil your destiny.

'Miss Ivy.' Alvaro's soft voice weaved its way through her thoughts. 'How are you feeling?'

'I ...' How *did* she feel? Everything that had happened today was just the cherry on top of the existential crisis that was this week. In just eight days, she'd watched her mother be taken away with a dagger pressed to her throat, become trapped in a foreign land, learnt she wasn't human, grown pointed ears and scales and a tail and antlers and white freckles, been told she had a destiny to fulfil, and discovered her father—who wasn't actually her father—was essentially being possessed. Her tendril caressed her internal organs, but it too was weighed down by all the changes in her life. How did she feel? 'I'm tired,' she finally answered.

His lips turned up in a sad smile. 'I am just glad you are all right.'

Her eyes met his, and that question lingered on her lips, but she couldn't bring herself to ask. She needed the confirmation, but she also needed to rest, to recover, to think. It didn't matter when she asked, though; she had a feeling she knew the answer already, and although her tendril tightened at the possible truth, she still found herself hugging the faun who had taken care of her this week. The faun who had kept her safe, just as her mum had promised.

Ivy made her way back to Alvaro's home, stopping through the still empty Tarad to collect her bag that had been abandoned, just as the stalls had been.

Alvaro and the Thidin Kingdom's militia spent the afternoon assuring the folk that the humans had left. He wanted to take Ivy back to his place himself, but she insisted that as the General, he go with the militia.

She slumped her way through the garden tunnel, her feet carving deep lines in the soil. Vines hung in her way; she let them drag over her. Let them tangle and pass through her antlers. Flowers followed her; she ignored them.

The tunnel opened to the clearing and Alvaro's home, and she stood at the exit, staring at the magnificent tree. Was this her new home? She had, after all, been living here for the last week. But she'd also spent part of that week suffocating in the spare room, wallowing in a sadness that was now a drop in the ocean of her internal wounds. She couldn't go inside and continue to live this new life full of nothing more than reading and training and training and reading. Not yet.

To her right was the path to the bathing pond. To her left was the firepit. And she knew that straight ahead, behind Alvaro's home, was his garden, with vegetables and herbs and fruits. She veered off the stone path that led to the front door and walked around the tree to the garden. Standing as still as a statue, she eyed the grassy space where she'd meditated with Alvaro.

The memory of yesterday evening, when she was assaulted by that strange vision, lingered like a lost soul. Right there, in front of those vegetables, she had performed those movements, controlled her breathing, then fallen to the ground from the vision of her mother trapped on the beach that was once their home. She desperately wanted to know what it meant, but not as badly as why Elias had taken her and her mum to begin with, why the folk were under a constant threat of abduction, and why she was the lucky one spared the fate of never returning to Harukai.

There were too many things about her life now that lived in an unknown limbo, and even though no one seemed to have any answers—or rather, no one had any answers they cared to share in their entirety—Ivy knew there was one way she could learn everything.

Ivy scanned the clearing, her gaze tracing each tree along the forest's edge. Trees—everywhere in this place was just *trees*. She watched the forest she once admired through a new lens, each trunk now a bar of her unusually large prison cell. She'd spent all week trying to break free and still hadn't managed that feat.

Through those trees, directly behind Alvaro's home—which was also a dang *tree*—was the beach where Alvaro claimed he and Dorothea had first met. Ivy hadn't considered visiting that beach, as though only knowing of its existence from someone else kept it hidden from reality. But she'd heard the ocean's waves against a sandy shore when Alvaro had shown her how to hunt, so she knew it was real.

She entered the clustered forest, and to no surprise, those same flowers followed her every move, more mushrooms scattered the ground with some reaching as high as her hip, and autumn-coloured leaves graced her feet. Only now, all their vibrancy had been drained in her sombre vision.

It wasn't long until the forest opened to a small, secluded beach, just as Alvaro had described. Gentle waves lapped at the shore; blue water tipped with a white foam blanket. Ivy imagined her mother here meeting Alvaro for the first time. How had it happened? Alvaro never told her the details, and now it was something she ached to know. Had her mum spied on Alvaro from a distance, similar to how her and Theon had officially met? Alvaro had said she'd been temporarily escaping her life—perhaps she'd been lounging on the shore, basking in her freedom before Alvaro interrupted her.

Her thumb grazed her ring, a smile playing on her lips at the imaginary scene. What had her mum looked like in her merfolk form? If Ivy's scales were the colour of her eyes, would Dorothea's have been the same? Sapphires shimmering in the sun.

Wait, her mum wasn't a merfolk. Elias—or rather, the other soul living inside him—had said she was a siren. Could that be true? Alvaro would have told her if her mother was a siren, right? She figured that was a fairly large part of her own identity. Except, Ivy had scales—sirens didn't. She knew that from her mother's stories. And Alvaro had told her he'd seen those scales when she was young, so he must not have wanted to confuse her.

So, what did that make her?

Ivy kicked off her boots and left them at the tree line along with her bag, then buried her toes in the sand. Slowly, she traipsed towards those gentle waves, to the familiar song of the ocean calling to her soul. Its lullaby quietened the screaming thoughts and questions in her mind and soothed her lingering tendril.

She untied the laces of her shirt and discarded it somewhere on the sand. Next was her skirt, which she easily stepped out of as she continued to walk, and soon she was left in only her undergarments. Those, she decided, would stay.

The ocean's welcoming touch graced her toes, and as the low waves made their descent, Ivy's footsteps followed. Once the water reached her knees, she dove.

She remained beneath the comforting waves until she felt her legs become a swishing tail, then swam to the surface. Once above the water, her first instinct was to reach for her neck; gills contracted in time with each of her breaths. Treading water was still difficult, but her tail seemed to sway naturally with the current, making it slightly more manageable.

Curious to see her tail, she leant back and tried to kick it above the water, but all she did was create some bubbles. It seemed she would need to practise swimming and manoeuvring her tail, just as she still needed to practise walking with the weight of her antlers.

She could very well swim to the beach to better admire her tail, but since she was a merfolk, Ivy supposed she could easily see in saltwater. So, she ducked below the waves and opened her eyes, expecting the salt water to sting, but instead it soothed, like her eyes were made for seeing through salt water. Which, she supposed, they were.

Emerald scales sparkled in the water. Her tail was ... It was magnificent. When she'd first seen it, she never thought she could love it, but now, it was the most beautiful thing she'd ever seen. Ivy was a *merfolk*. Her tail idly swished up and down, and she noticed the end wasn't scales at all, but a fin. A wide, beautiful green fin.

Her lungs began to constrict, and on instinct, she broke through the surface. Cool, salty air filled her lungs. Weren't her gills supposed to help her breathe underwater? Maybe they were unable to work since she'd been holding her breath, but she couldn't just start breathing underwater, no matter how clear the proof was that she could.

Whether she could breathe or not didn't matter right now. All she wanted to do was admire her tail, so once again, she dropped beneath the waves.

She watched her tail swishing softly on its own, then moved her gaze to where more scales dotted her torso and arms before colliding to cover her breasts beneath her bra. The emerald scales mixed with her white freckles was mesmerising.

A flash of colour was spotted in her periphery, and she looked towards the sand bank. Somehow, the same vibrancy of the Thidin Kingdom bled into the ocean. Seaweed was stark against the water, but further down were bright flowers unlike any Ivy had ever seen.

Flowers in the ocean was something she never thought could exist. As she swam around them, they too followed, just as the ones in the Thidin Kingdom did.

Her lungs began to tighten once more, but she didn't want to go above water just yet. She was close enough to the surface where she could easily break through and breathe if she needed to. She touched her gills and felt them moving, but she still couldn't breathe. Slowly, Ivy opened her mouth and released the breath she held without inhaling any water. As she did so, water brushed over her gills, and suddenly, oxygen entered her lungs.

On instinct, she breathed, filling her lungs with more oxygen from the water that entered through her gills. Keeping her mouth open, she inhaled and exhaled, her lungs only receiving oxygen. 'Oh my God,' she said, the water causing her voice to muffle. 'I'm breathing underwater. Holy shit I'm breathing underwater.' And then, she laughed.

She flicked her tail, and her body jolted. Ivy still lacked any expertise, but she didn't care. 'I'm a merfolk!' she yelled to no one.

She flopped about, laughing and kicking her tail and *breathing*, until she decided to break through the surface once more. Fresh air filled her lungs, which was a surprisingly nice reprieve from the saltwater. A small part of the heaviness that had been weighing her down all week was lifted. She was a *merfolk*, and she now embraced the absolute hell out of that.

She'd managed to swim further away from the beach, which shocked her considering she barely knew how to swim with her tail. Ivy decided to slowly make her way back to lay on the sand and bask under the afternoon sun, but before she got too far, something to her right caught her eye.

Roughly ten or so metres away was a small rocky shore with a wooden bridge between the gaps of rocks. The bridge itself was only a few metres long, and tied to the end of it were three rowboats. She swam towards what she could only assume was a small harbour of sorts. Once she was at the bridge, she was able to hoist herself up on the edge just long enough to notice it was decorated with broken planks and mould. Clearly, it hadn't been used in some time.

Despite the fact she was swimming in the ocean with a mer-folk tail and had just discovered she could breathe underwater, this harbour and the boats brought her back to her current reality. Her mother was still stuck in the human realm, while Ivy was stuck here with no way through that rock wall. She had a destiny to fulfil, and the Oracle was the only folk who could give her the answers she needed—to her destiny and about opening the Realm Divider. Perhaps Ivy could use one of the rowboats to search for the Oracle. Of course, she could just swim, but she still needed time to get used to her tail. These rowboats, on the other hand, were here now.

She swam around to inspect the boats, expecting some rotting decay, but they seemed to be in usable condition. A puddle of water lived in the bottom of each boat, and there was a distinct line to indicate how far the water could reach, with the top half being a much lighter shade from fading in the sun. But other than that, there didn't look to be any degradation.

Ivy ran her fingers along the edge of one and was surprised to find the surface much smoother than she was expecting. Upon closer inspection, she noticed a clear film coating the boat, seemingly protecting it from any severe damage.

She dove beneath the surface and swam back to the small beach. If coincidence were a god, she would thank them, for it was they who had brought her to those boats. And it was those boats that would take her to the answers she sought.

Thirty-Seven

There was nothing stopping Ivy from leaving.

She was destined to save the folk of Harukai. While those exact words hadn't been said, she could read between the lines well enough. Ivy needed to get back to the human realm, and the only way to do that was to find the Oracle and learn about the Maidens' return. The only uncertainty was that there was a huge chance the Oracle may not be alive, and an even bigger chance that if they were, they wouldn't tell Ivy anything.

But she needed to try.

That night, she'd ached to ask Alvaro the question that had been gnawing at her all day: Who was her biological father? But he hadn't returned until much later in the evening, and by then, exhaustion had dragged her into its depths. The next morning, she'd woken up later than she usually did, and Alvaro had already left for the day—a frustrating coincidence.

A cup of tea and half-eaten bowl of fruit was left on the side table between the sitting chairs. She grabbed the cup of tea, only to find it was cold. How long had he been gone? How long had she slept?

Ivy sat in her usual seat and finished the bowl of fruit. The question clawed at her insides, begging to be answered, but she knew the answer. It was right there in the way Alvaro had marvelled at her ring, in the memories he'd shared of Dorothea, in the way he'd torn himself apart to try and bring her and her mother back from the human realm.

Tears ran down her face before she knew they'd been waiting.

Alvaro was her dad.

It was as clear as the air and water she breathed. They shared the same emerald green eyes, the same dimple in their left cheek, the same stubbornness, the same determination.

Alvaro was her dad.

She should find him. To tell him she knew the truth, or to just ask him the question so he could answer it himself. But she didn't move from her seat.

Since she'd discovered the abandoned harbour and awaiting rowboats yesterday, Ivy had been aching for the moment she could leave. Now, she didn't want to leave the safety of Alvaro's home, the safety of the Thidin Kingdom. She wanted to stay here and get Alvaro's confirmation that he was in fact her father. But her life wasn't about wants anymore. It was about needs, and she needed to find the Oracle.

Deep breaths—in through her nose, out through her mouth. She did this until all her tears were spent. And when she was done, she wiped those tears and climbed the stairs to her room.

A large leather bag lived in the bottom of the cupboard. Ivy began gathering everything she thought she needed. Starting with clothes, she packed what she had labelled her pyjamas—a large button-down shirt and a spare skirt she only wore when around Alvaro in the mornings and evenings—undergarments, a few skirts and shirts to match, and socks. Sadly, she had yet to find a pair of pants in the drawers that fit her comfortably.

Her hair comb was on the dresser and as she grabbed it, she noticed her seashells. The same ones she'd found in the human realm the day she discovered Harukai. She hadn't properly seen them in days; they'd started to blend into her surroundings, becoming a part of the room. But now they watched her—a reminder of everything she had lost, yet everything she would soon gain.

She grabbed her favourite—a pinky-white sparkling spiral shell about half the size of the palm of her hand—and put it in the bag with her hair comb. An extra blanket Ivy kept at the end of the bed was next to be packed. Her sword stood in its sheath by the bedside table and she buckled it around her hips.

Next were the books. Ivy climbed down the ladder and rummaged through the trolley from the library. Sadly, she couldn't fit all of them—and even if she could, the bag would be far too heavy for her to carry—so she chose two: *A Maiden's History* (the official copy, wrapped in the cover of the book about the Maidens myths) and the Oracle stories collection.

At the bottom of the pile was a book she didn't recognise, called *Harukai's Kingdoms*. That must be the extra book Leyrah had grabbed for her after taking her to the secret room. Perhaps the book had a map of the realm. She quickly flicked through, and luck must be on her side, because one of the first pages was a full-page map of Harukai. Ivy prepared to tear the page out, but she froze. Leyrah knew about her destiny; she must have chosen *this* book for a reason. Her fingers trailed worn pages and the edges of the aged leather-bound cover. Ivy couldn't bring herself to destroy something so delicate. So, she squished the entire book among her other items.

She took a fresh bar of soap, a clean towel, and some bandages for her still-healing hands from the kitchen cupboards, then climbed upstairs for the smaller bag she used to carry her things to the bathing pond. Her next stop was outside and to the back of the house; most fruits and vegetables were pulled from their beds and thrown into the small bag, just enough to last a few days without going rotten, before she made her way back inside. Hidden near the sitting chairs were two bows and two quivers stuffed with arrows. Ivy grabbed one of each, hooking them across her body, then rummaged through the kitchen drawers until she found scrap parchment and a quill.

Her hand hesitated above the page. Did she really need to do this? Alvaro had warned her not to look for the Oracle; that was exactly why she needed to leave in this way. But what could she possibly say to soften the blow, especially since he was more than likely her dad? Nothing, she quickly realised. And so, her hand flowed across the page.

Alvaro,

I've left to find the Oracle. I remember what you told me about them, but I can't waste any more time. You said yourself those books won't tell us anything. The Oracle is the only option from here. I'm certain they'll have the answers we need.

Thank you for taking care of me, and for keeping me safe. Thank you for making this world feel like home. Thank you for spending all these years trying to bring me and Mum back. And thank you for being you. Kind, caring, generous, and loving. I'll see you again soon.

Miss Ivy.

She wanted to mention how she knew he was her father, but on the off chance her assumption was wrong, she decided to leave it out.

Once done, Ivy placed the folded note on the side table next to his chair with 'Alvaro' scribbled on the front. She took a moment to double-check she had everything she needed—clothes, comb, soap, towel, bandages, books, blanket, food, bow, arrows, sword, favourite shell. Then, she triple-checked. When she was certain she hadn't forgotten anything, she looked around the small room, re-membering every detail—vines of light leaves swirling along the walls, colourful flowers in their potted homes blooming towards her.

During her short time in Harukai, Ivy had never given much thought to the way the flowers always seemed to face her, until yesterday when she'd sprinted towards the beach. And now, in this final moment, she wondered: Did the flowers also know who she was? If they could speak, would they say the same as the folk had? Would they pray to her, worship her? Or would they merely accept her as one of their own?

A singular flower in a pot on the bedside table faced her, their petals only half-open. She reached over and grazed their purple doors, and at the touch of her fingers, the flower bloomed, their petals opening wide.

Perhaps they already had.

She inhaled the scents of Alvaro's home: lavender, bamboo, and cedarwood. 'Goodbye,' Ivy said to the tree. To the flowers, to the leaves. To the bamboo furniture, to the teacups, and to the sitting chairs beneath the window. To the kitchen where she had cleaned Alvaro's wounds. She said goodbye to Alvaro.

With tears flowing down her cheeks, Ivy stepped outside and latched the front door behind her.

THIRTY-EIGHT

I vy stood at the edge of the forest—the beginning of the path that led to the bathing pond. It wasn't like the human realm with a tub of hot water, or a shower. But she had grown comfortable with the serenity and vulnerability the pond offered. What would her life be like now, on her journey to find the Oracle? Would there be crisp ponds on the islands she searched, or would she have to bathe in the ocean? She sighed and pushed herself across the clearing to the forest behind Alvaro's home.

Alvaro's home. But perhaps it had become her home, too.

At the tree line, Ivy looked back, memorising the picture of what had become her home in a foreign land. Just beyond the large tree she could see the trees outlining the tunnel. A picturesque walk towards an even more picturesque kingdom; her mother's stories hadn't lied. She waved to the tree and a gentle breeze blew past, causing some of the leaves to wave back.

Through the forest Ivy walked, her eyes brimming with tears.

Alvaro's home had definitely become her home, too. Alvaro had become a friend, a carer. A father. Saying goodbye was one of the most difficult things a person could do, but at least she had the chance to say goodbye—something she hadn't been able to do with her mum.

Ivy exited the forest onto the beach. The same beach where her mum and Alvaro had met. She could see the two of them now, sitting on the sand, watching the waves roll in, possibly the start of something magical. Perhaps once she found and saved her mum, her and Alvaro could share those moments once more.

Instead of swimming to the harbour—that would have been an unnecessary struggle with her luggage—she walked through the trees lining the shore until they led her to the rocks guarding the bridge.

She made her way along the rickety bridge, each plank creaking and bending beneath the weight of her and the two bags she carried. The three rowboats remained just as they had the day prior. They were all roughly the same size, but the centre one was the only one with two sturdy-looking oars tucked inside.

She dropped her bags in towards one of the ends, as far away from the small puddle as possible, then awkwardly climbed in after, holding one of the bridge posts for support. Ivy attached the oars to the pegs on either side of the boat and spent a moment figuring out how she would sit comfortably while rowing.

Gosh, was she really going to do this? Traverse the ocean in nothing but a rowboat on the off chance that a future-seeing folk would be out there and alive?

Yes, she really was going to do this. It was the only morsel of information she had that could potentially help her return to the human realm.

From here, Ivy couldn't see the beach where she'd been training with Theon. What would he be doing now? Had he wondered why she didn't show, or did he assume she needed a break after yesterday's events? After he'd held a dagger to Elias's throat before knocking him unconscious?

She wished she could have seen him one last time, said a final goodbye, but she couldn't risk him stopping her; she didn't know him well enough to know how he would react. Instead, Ivy memorised the contours of his face in her mind, and the way his copper hair framed his jawline. She memorised his scales and the way they traced his muscles so perfectly. And she memorised his smile, his cheeky smirk, his eyes. The way he had looked at her that night they sat on top of the rock wall.

She gave one last look to the forest, to wherever Alvaro was. Could Ivy do this to him? Could she do this without him? Her tendril came out to play, curling lightly around her lungs. Deep breaths—in through her nose, out through her mouth. She had no other choice.

Ivy stood and untied the rope from the post, then gently pushed the rowboat away from the bridge. The sapphire gemstone on her ring sparkled in the sun. Across the water, islands speckled in the distance waited for her.

'I'm on my way, Mum.'

Ivy's story will continue!

Acknowledgements

Am I supposed to introduce this section, or do I just jump straight in?

There are so many people in my life who have continuously supported me on this journey, from my parents who always encouraged me to follow my dreams, to friends who helped me with military terminology (which was only partially useful for this book). But there is one person in my life who has always been and always will be my absolute biggest supporter. Daniel, you pushed me to keep going through university and writing my book even when I was having multiple mental breakdowns and deciding to give up instead because you knew better than myself that this was my dream. And you were right. If it wasn't for you, I genuinely don't think this book would be published. I love you.

I have to thank the incredible book community I found online. Threads is a place I go to ramble and ask questions that I could probably find through Google if I searched hard enough. But the online book community was always there, supporting and helping in any way they could. Without them, I probably would have had an existential crisis before giving up entirely.

My wonderful editor, Chloe. When I sent you what I believed was my final manuscript but was probably more like a draft 1.5, you still believed in my story. Your love for my world, characters, words, and the story itself helped me continue at a time when I thought I couldn't. And your irrevocable love for Theon made me see him in another light and gave me the confidence in him and his place in the story that I had lost. Thank you.

To Sarah, your manuscript assessment gracefully tore my manuscript apart limb from limb so that I could reshape it into what it needed to be, and I genuinely can't thank you enough for that!

Ciara, my amazing cover designer. It was such bad timing, but despite your injury and my incessant changes, messages, and near do-overs of the cover, you absolutely delivered better than I could ever have imagined! I'm sorry for the incessant ramblings and messaging you more notes after I thought I'd told you everything, but it was all worth it. I not only have a favourite artist and the most beautiful cover I've ever seen, but I've also found one of my closest writer friends. Thank you for not giving up on me and this cover.

@mgsdesiigns deserves an absolute round of applause and standing ovation. I ordered what I thought were simple interior designs that I ended up changing time and time again, and yet you delivered each and every time to help me get the perfect interior graphics for my book. There aren't enough words to apologise for my continuous changes and to thank you for persevering.

@starturnart, your sketches are some of the most beautiful and elegant drawings I've ever seen. I don't think I could have found a better person to depict what the races in this story look like. You went absolutely above and beyond, thank you!

My cartographer, Saumya. I am absolutely in love with this map! Not only did you take the awful map I designed and turn it into a masterpiece, but you also managed to wade through my absolutely nonsense notes, provided me with three versions (greyscale and two colours), and did it all in three days! You are an absolute superhero, thank you!

My small yet mighty beta team. You guys made me realise my doubts were valid, but you also made me see things that I had never even considered, helping me see and love my story in a new way.

And my ARC readers. (As I write this I haven't actually got ARC readers yet, so this will either age very well or very poorly.) I appreciate each and every one of you for taking a chance on me and my story. Your trust in me for providing you with a world and characters you can fall in love with inspires me to keep going.

And finally, you. To think that there are actually people in this world who I have never met (and who I sadly will probably never meet) who actually want to read my story is insane, and I still don't believe it. It is your belief in me and my story that pushes me to keep going. Thank you for believing in me.

Let's charter a rowboat to the next book!

ABOUT THE AUTHOR

First, this woman gets me to write her entire book. Then, she has me write the blurb. And now she also wants me to write her god damned author bio? What am I supposed to say about her? I know nothing other than the fact that she writes books, except really, I'm writing the books (at least, the ones in this series). She's just writing the words that I'm writing. Does that make sense?

Let me tell you a little something about *me*. I'm the narrator, and I'm unfortunately unnamed at the present time—although, it's probably for the best. Not unnamed to the author, of course—she knows *everything*—but I am simply unnamed to the readers. To you. I wish I could tell you more, but that would spoil the rest of the story, and we certainly don't want that. This is also sadly not an "About the Narrator" section. Perhaps we could do that once I'm revealed.

Hey, C, did you catch that?

We should do a section about me in the later books.

So, about the author. C. M. Koch (or as I like to call her, C) spends her days transporting herself into fictional worlds so much so that if she were to get a song lyric tattooed on her it would be 'I hate it here so I will go to secret gardens in my mind' from Taylor Swift's *I hate it here (The Tortured Poets Department)*.

She spends the majority of her writing time either staring at a blank page or doing literally anything other than writing, claiming, 'At least I'm being productive!' (News flash, C, that doesn't make the procrastination any better.) But during the rare moments that words are actually flowing through her veins, it's as if her fingers can weave magical threads that craft enchanting worlds, captivating stories, and emotionally traumatised characters. Sometimes even she is mesmerised by what she creates.

C graduated from the University of the Sunshine Coast in 2023 with a Bachelor of Creative Industries, and uses that now to create characters like me that live completely rent-free in her mind (if you gave us occupations instead of emotional trauma, C, perhaps we could pay you rent).

When she isn't staring at her computer, you'll most likely find her staring at her phone or TV instead. She does, in fact, have plenty of family and friends, but instead she chooses the hermit crab life along with her partner and cat.

If you want to be witness to the life of C. M. Koch, you can follow her on Instagram and TikTok @c.m.koch_author or visit her website cmkoch.com.au